JAWS
THE REVENGE

LORRAINE GARY LANCE GUEST MARIO VAN PEEBLES

KAREN YOUNG and MICHAEL CAINE

A JOSEPH SARGENT Film

"JAWS THE REVENGE"

Written by MICHAEL de GUZMAN Music by MICHAEL SMALL

Production Designer JOHN J. LLOYD Director of Photography JOHN McPHERSON A.S.C.

Produced and Directed by JOSEPH SARGENT

DOLBY STEREO® IN SELECTED THEATRES

Soundtrack available on MCA Records and Cassettes

A UNIVERSAL Picture

JAWS
THE REVENGE

A NOVEL BY
HANK SEARLS

BASED ON A SCREENPLAY BY
MICHAEL de GUZMAN
INSPIRED BY
PETER BENCHLEY'S JAWS

Futura

A Futura Book

First published 1987 in the UK by
Futura Publications, a Division of
Macdonald & Co (Publishers) Ltd
London & Sydney

ISBN 0 7088 3691 7

Reproduced, printed and bound in Great Britain by
Hazell Watson & Viney Limited,
Member of the BPCC Group,
Aylesbury, Bucks

Futura Publications
A Division of
Macdonald & Co (Publishers) Ltd
Greater London House
Hampstead Road
London NW1 7QX
A BPCC plc Company

"The sea never changes and its works, for all the talk of men, are wrapped in mystery."

—Joseph Conrad, "Typhoon"

"In addition to eyesight that is better than we thought it was, a phenomenal sense of hearing, and the ability to sense vibrations in the water, sharks have chemical and electrical receptors that are unequaled in the animal kingdom."

—Richard Ellis, *The Book of Sharks*

PART I

Chapter 1

On an evening a week before Christmas a famished gull stood on an icy piling in Amity Harbor. For a moment, gold from the setting sun touched its sleek white breast. It pecked at its gilded feathers, as if surprised, then glimpsed the flash of cod in the depths.

Instantly it gathered itself to forage. But it sensed something it did not like beneath the surface. It cawed sharply, spread its wings, and swooped off hungry toward its nest on Amity Rock.

The light on the Rock—untended now for many years—was turning tirelessly. On the cliff below it an automatic sensor felt the evening fog gathering, and every three seconds the Amity horn began to moan.

Random impulses had lured the great white shark to warmer, shallow water from his feeding grounds off Montauk Point, as man himself was sometimes tempted to the sea.

He moved slowly through the ebony waters of Amity Bay. He was twenty-eight feet long and weighed three thousand pounds.

His flat dish-eyes were as black as the night. They were entirely without pupils but strangely knowing. Though they were as useless after dark as the eyes of any other fish, he had no need for them.

For, day or night, he was exactly attuned to his surroundings. He knew within centimeters how far it was to the rusting hood of an ancient car half buried in the mud, and where a sunken dory lay. He sensed a moray slithering from its cave a thousand yards away, and lobsters stirring in the co-op's lobster pots.

All of this he knew from receptors refined from three hundred million years of evolution. Though his kind had diminished in size—his ancestor, *Megalodon,* had jaws wide enough to swallow a modern cow—its senses had only improved.

A female fur-seal circled the Amity outer bell buoy, evaluating it as a haven. She was en route with her little one from her Arctic rookery to her winter fishing grounds off Sandy Hook.

Now, for reasons she could not understand, she was uneasy. She wanted suddenly to leave the water, but she doubted that her baby had the strength to mount the buoy. She could only demonstrate, and hope. Gauging the swell, she dived and crested on a wave. In a surge of power she heaved herself aboard, scraping belly fur on rusted rivets. She barked at her little one to follow.

The baby missed the swell, pawed with her flippers at the edge, flopped back, and tried again. Above them, the deep bell gonged.

The great white lazed below, at thirty feet. With a swish of his tail he turned sidewise, spiraling upward. His jaws opened at ten feet, and by five feet he was making a good ten knots, straight up. He took the baby whole, rose into the black night, and scissored the tail from the mother on the buoy.

He waited while she thrashed and fell from her perch, then engorged her in one piece.

With half his hunger satisfied, he glided for a while.

Because he was so heavy and because his kind had no air bladder like other fish, he would sink to the bottom if he ever stopped swimming. There he would drown when the water stopped flowing past his gills. He was doomed to a life of restless motion, like a bird with no place to alight.

Hearing a piling bumping against a channel buoy, he turned toward the lights of the harbor and swam in.

Ellen Brody, carrying a grocery bag from Fieldstone's Market, crossed the square, glancing up at the township Christmas tree.

The last of the sunlight glittered from the bedraggled angel teetering on top. Her son Sean, an Amity policeman, had put it there the previous week, rather poorly, and she was surprised that it had survived yesterday's snowstorm.

SEVEN SHOPPING DAYS TILL XMAS, flashed a sign on Lautzhauser's Men's Store.

The Christmas-tree lights flickered on, off, and on again. The same lights that had always seemed so cheerful and full of hope seemed suddenly drab and dreary. A lonely silver bell tinkled in the boughs, dangling in the sea breeze, and the foghorn groaned.

She sighed. All day long she had been filled with sadness and some nameless dread, perhaps of loneliness. This was the first Christmas she would bear without Marty. Her elder son, Michael, was in the Bahamas, and Sean and she would be alone.

Martin Brody had first placed the angel on the tree, forty feet above the ground, when Sean was a child. Marty, with his silver star glittering in sunlight and his visored cap askew, had climbed the volunteer fire company's hook and ladder. Singing "Silver Bells" at the top of his voice, he teetered wildly at the peak, pretending drunkenness. The aldermen had shaken their heads below, muttering darkly. Michael had burned with embarrassment, and she and Sean had cheered.

Almost twenty years ago. And then, each year he

had made a better show of it, until finally she grew frightened that he really would fall down.

All that before the Troubles, before the sharks. The first of the Troubles—the shark that had almost wrecked the town—had come twelve years ago, and the next, which had all but finished the job, two years after that. Sean had been barely ten. After *that* shark there had been no more climbing of the Christmas tree for Marty: His heart would not permit it, nor would she.

Now Sean wore his father's badge: number one. In his holster, when he remembered to wear it, swung Marty's battered revolver, drawn only once in his father's career, at a fellow policeman shooting seals. Sean sat daily in his father's squealing swivel chair and wrote parking tickets in the same scuffed citation book.

A dead-end job, his brother Michael said. But somebody had to do it. There were worse role models than his dad, and God knew what would become of her if he ever decided to leave.

She passed Nate Starbuck's Pharmacy, where the second of the Troubles had begun. The freshly developed photo of the great white lying on the counter, of the idiotic scuba diver leering at the camera while the monster ran him down, had started it all and lost her the only man she had ever truly loved.

It was Amity's second shark—which had died in a searing flash of voltage on the Cape North Light power line—rather than the first, which had ruined Martin's heart. Dr. MacIntosh had said, "That thing killed him, Ellen, just as if he'd torn him limb from limb."

Marty had fought the beast for the town, which didn't give a damn once the evil thing was dead. Sean's job was a sop, an insult. No one wanted it, anyway, except Sean, who would be wearing red suspenders if he thought his father had.

And they hadn't even made Sean chief.

The dread she had known all day was overpowering. Quickly she crossed the square, entered the town hall, and stepped into the police station.

Sean looked up from his desk. He had sent Polly, the clerk and dispatcher, home and was there alone. "Hi, sweetheart! What brings you here on this cold and dreary night?"

She shrugged. "I was passing." She moved closer to the radiator, swinging her hands. "The town is absolutely, positively dead. Fieldstone's is a morgue."

"Um . . ." He was eyeing the bag. They were having his fiancée, Tiffany, to dinner that night, and to decorate their tree. "What you got?"

"I'll never tell. Look, we're about to have a fallen angel in the square."

He shrugged. "I hope so. That damn thing's older than I am."

She stared at him, shocked. Didn't he *care?* She felt her eyes misting. Suddenly he was on his feet, folding her into his arms, rubbing the back of her neck.

"Mom, Mom. I'm sorry. I was thinking of something Tiffany said, and I forgot . . . That act he used to pull . . ."

She was being silly. "Sean, it's *me*, not you. I turn everything into a crying spell. I've got to get *over* it, that's all."

He stepped to his desk and drew a tissue from his drawer. "You're *going* to." He glanced at the clock on the wall. "I let Polly go home to wrap presents. Lenny won't be here until six. And I have to pick up Tiff. Seven, maybe?"

She dabbed at her nose with the tissue. She must quit sniffling every time she thought of Marty or Sean would *never* come home to dinner anymore.

The radio cackled. It was Lenny, Amity's other police officer, nominally the chief. "Sean, there's a big old piling drifting in the channel."

"Ten-four." Sean picked up the phone and dialed the Montauk Point Coast Guard. Amity owned, Ellen was sure, the last dial phones in America. He grimaced and covered the phone. "I hear a Christmas party, they'll love this." He reported the menace to navigation, listened, and sighed. "Well, as soon as you can, okay? Our fishing boats are coming in, and we're going to have fog tonight."

He hung up and shook his head. "Damn hooligan Navy. They claim they're all tied up." He moved to the window and looked out. "Probably are too. To the Montauk dock."

"You're not going?" Ellen murmured. "Let Lenny go." *Damn! Why do I do this all the time? He's a grown man!* "I mean," she finished lamely, "he's better with the boat."

"Mom," he warned, and then grinned. "Okay, if the coast guard doesn't show, I'll con Lenny into going."

She squeezed his hand and stepped back onto the street.

The mist was drifting in. The foghorn mourned from Amity Rock. The nameless dread returned.

She got into her car and drove home.

Sean pushed his chair away from the table and belched softly.

"Sean!" Ellen tried to sound outraged but couldn't: Marty had done the same thing.

Tiffany, brown eyes sparkling with wine and angel face shining, giggled. "How gross!"

God, Tiff even loved his belches! Ellen began to clear the table, a little jealous. She tried to remember if she had been so helplessly smitten when she was Tiffany's age. No, her love for Marty had dawned slowly.

Her passion for Hooper, back at the time of the first Troubles? No, for she'd taken Hooper in anger, at

Marty's bullheaded dedication to the town and to the job. Sean was just as stubborn when he wanted to be.

Now he was sitting back, being male until they cleared the dishes. He eyed the naked tree and the familiar boxes of decorations, some as old as he.

"When we finish decorating, let's open some presents!" he said suddenly.

Ellen looked at Tiff. "You won't need to *have* a child," she said softly, "you're marrying one."

"I *know.*" Tiff sighed. "No, Sean. You have to wait for Santa. And all you'll probably get will be a lump of coal."

Ellen and Tiffany finished the dishes, and the three of them began to decorate the tree.

The great white had a wide range of hearing. He could pick up sounds at half the frequency a human could and was equally attracted to a struggling fish or a banging oil drum. Fine veins filled with liquid, running from his head to his tail, sensed differences in water pressure around him. Through them he could detect the presence of a swimming seal or a drifting boat or a pelican in the waves.

His head was covered with pores that were electrical sensors, and his body with many more. Like a minesweeper, he could find targets beneath the mud: skates, stingrays, and tin cans, which he sometimes scooped up with the rest and which caused him no digestive problems at all.

The Amity foghorn blasted; the bell buoy clanged distantly. He accepted the sounds above the surface passively: They were simply there. He was listening to the log jostling the channel marker, thumping, squeaking, scratching.

The seals had taken the edge from his hunger, but the sound of man-things in the water angered him, for he owned the sea.

* * *

Ellen sat cross-legged under the Christmas tree, brushing tinsel from her hair.

The tree was not as tall as the past year's—she hadn't seen much point, with just Sean and her, in getting a big one.

And tonight the decorations, even the recent ones, had somehow lost their glitter.

Sean's sweater from Lautzhauser's Men's Store, and Tiff's lace tablecloth that had come to America from County Clare with Marty's great-grandmother, Catherine, lay wrapped on cotton snow. Ellen's presents for Mike, her older son; his wife, Carla; and her five-year-old granddaughter, Thea—all had been sent two weeks ago to the Bahamas where Mike worked as a marine biologist.

All she had to do was wait for Christmas.

She jumped when the phone rang. She was jittery tonight.

Sean got up and answered it. When he put it down, he said, "Old Larson damn near hit that log by the starboard entrance buoy." He called the coast guard. "That's what I figured," he growled into the mouthpiece. "No, I don't believe you, Chief. It's too cold for you, is all."

He yanked Marty's old Navy pea coat from the closet, angry and quick.

"What's going on?" demanded Tiffany. "Where are you going?"

"It's a log in the channel," Ellen told her. She remembered something. "You said you'd ask Lenny to do it!"

"No way." He zipped up his father's fleece-lined leather boots. "I forgot he was Joseph the Carpenter. He's rehearsing tonight for the Christmas show."

She followed him to the porch. "Please don't! Not in the fog."

"Would Dad go in the fog?"

In the orange glow of the porch light she met his

eyes. They were shadowed and very dark. She knew how he hated the water, and boats of every kind. But yes, Marty would have gone, and they both knew it. It was something he had to do.

She nodded. "I guess he would."

"Okay." He touched her lips and smiled. "Look, it's just a log!" He zipped up the jacket and shivered, smiling. "It's too cold for man or beast. Damn it, Mom, *this* winter you've got to do it."

"Fly down to see Mike?" She sighed. "Maybe, if real estate picks up next year."

"Promise?"

"I promise." She nodded, watched him go. Tiff was suddenly standing beside her, an arm around her waist.

"Come on, Ellen," she said softly. "Let's finish up the wine."

The foghorn growled and the dread returned. They turned and went inside.

Bump . . . scrape . . . bump . . . scrape . . . In Amity Harbor the restless thumping of the piling on the channel buoy had caught the attention of the great white shark. The sound drew the creature toward the buoy as a magnet draws a nail.

Its tail, shaped like a boomerang in flight and as tall as a man, swept lazily from side to side, stirring the bottom and raising great clouds of silt. A vortex like a minor whirlpool followed it on the surface.

The shark continued, turned away, drifted awhile, and turned toward the buoy again.

The Old Pavilion on Amity's waterfront—a relic of the early 1900s and long-gone tourist days—was awash in floodlights. Its sweeping veranda would act next week as a stage for the Amity Christmas Show, and parents and friends would shiver on the lawn below, wishing the thing were done.

But tonight was only rehearsal. Sean could hear the high school band for blocks. He eased his jeep through the teenage beauties preening their hair and parked as closely to the dock as he could get. He took his stocking cap off the seat, checked his six-celled flashlight, and climbed out.

He passed beneath the age-worn banner: AMITY ANNUAL CHRISTMAS PAGEANT. On the porch, Emil Tarkanian, the band instructor, led "The First Noel." Most of the assembled angels in the girls' chorus behind him would be squirming tonight in backseats of cars along country roads, but now their fresh faces shone with piety and their voices were sweet and clear.

Below, two little girls stood on a stepladder, decorating the papier-mâché hump of a camel—Justin Barlow's riding horse—with ribbons of red and green.

Amity, Amity . . . A picture-perfect town with a picture-perfect name, and beneath the surface, currents as foul as any anywhere on earth.

The elders had turned against Sean's father in the Troubles, when it suited them, and now that Martin Brody was dead, he was a hero to them all. If Sean could ever get his mother and Tiffany to leave, the town would never see him again.

He sighed, boarded the police boat, and turned the key, hoping it would not start. The ancient engine labored for a moment, then fired. While it warmed, he drew a rusty boat hook, a grappling hook crusted with salt, and some worn three-quarter-inch nylon line from the gear locker in the cockpit. Everything he needed, unfortunately, was there.

There was no excuse to quit. He took a deep breath and looked out at the harbor waters.

The fog was holding just outside the entrance. No excuse there, either.

He hated the sea, and slimy pilings, and the salt that ate at tools and ships and men.

He cast off his lines and eased away from the dock, switching on the spotlight. Over the rumble of the old Perkins diesel he heard the high school band pounding "The Little Drummer Boy" into the dirt.

He set a course for the green light on the starboard channel buoy.

The great white had heard the high-pitched squawking of the starter, and now he heard the growl of the diesel. He began to track it, closing in on it as it moved away from the wharf, which he saw with his receptors as if it had been bathed in light.

He was a scavenger as well as a predator, and the survival of his kind had depended for three hundred million years on curiosity.

His energy needs were enormous. If he was not where the action was, he starved.

Sean stared at the floating piling. The dark, water-soaked wood glistened in the spotlight. He could hear it thumping and rubbing the buoy, following the regular rhythm of the swell.

It was more than a simple log. Torn from some ocean wharf by a winter storm, it trailed its own debris: a rusted cable, a slimy hawser, the remnants of a painted sign. Faintly he made out the sun-bleached letters: DANGER.

Danger, all right, and a pain in the ass. Carefully he eased the boat alongside the creaking mess. The current was sweeping into the channel from Amity Bay. Boards nailed to the piling embraced the buoy. Sean could see the whiskered wire trailing toward the shore like the tail of a kite.

He knelt by the gunwale and leaned over the side with the line, plunging his arms up to his biceps to retrieve the line from below the thick log. He couldn't make it around its girth. All right, if he simply freed it, it would drift up the channel. Then, if it didn't stave a hole in a boat en route, he could handle it near the wharf.

He heard faint childish voices from the pavilion: "Silent night, holy night . . ."

Stretched over the side of the boat, with his ear near the water, he heard the thumping of the piling against the buoy. The sound—a soggy, lifeless rasp of wet wood on metal—made him nervous.

The freezing water filled his gloves. His fingers ached. He tugged on the two-by-fours that clasped the buoy. They let go with a shriek of rusty nails. Only the sign kept the piling snagged.

"All is calm, all is bright . . ."

The mass of wreckage suddenly shifted, as if jerked by a giant hand from the deep. The violence of it ripped the nails in the two-by-four through his canvas gloves. His hand was impaled on a spike. For an instant he was silent with horror, and then he screamed in pain.

He glimpsed an enormous shape, silhouetted against the lights of the Pavilion, and caught the glitter of ivory teeth.

"Holy infant, so tender and mild . . ."

He screamed again. He was engulfed in a sheet of freezing water. One hand went up to ward off the nightmare.

The other was caught on the sign.

Chapter 2

The great white sank to the depths. It had ingested a good part of the starboard cockpit rub rail, along with the human torso, a section of hemp, and a fire extinguisher. The latter it regurgitated, but the channel to its stomach was unhindered. Digestive juices that could sear a lobster shell began to work instantly on all the rest.

Above, a human hand and forearm thrust skyward, nailed to the danger sign, swaying in the swell. Below it, a streak of red swept toward the shore.

Across the water drifted high, clear voices: "Sleep in heavenly peace . . ."

The foghorn moaned, and at last the fog rolled in.

She sat with Tiffany sipping the dry California Chardonnay she had splurged on at Fieldstone's. The embers glowed blood-red. She fought the rising certainty that something was going very wrong.

"He's so sensitive and *gentle*." Tiffany sighed.

"Yes . . ." Her prospective daughter-in-law, sitting cross-legged on the throw rug and staring into the fire, turned and smiled at her with her great brown eyes. There was such love for Sean within them that Ellen felt her throat grow tight.

"Go on, Ellen," Tiffany murmured. "I want to hear more about him."

Ellen, fighting panic, tried to keep her voice steady.

"Well, he was such a gentle boy, it's no wonder he's a gentle man."

"I know. He loves Candy as much as he loves me."

Candy was her cocker spaniel puppy. Ellen forced a smile. "I doubt that." She got up and poked the fire. As long as they talked about him, he was here with them and everything was fine. After all, he would never leave the harbor, and even if the worn-out engine died, the tide was coming in. Besides, he had a radio on the police boat.

"Tell me another Sean story," Tiff urged her, like a kid begging for a fairy tale. Ellen cast back in memory. "Sammy the Seal," she said suddenly.

"Who was Sammy the Seal?"

A summer visitor—a fat policeman from Flushing—had shot a baby seal. Doc Lean expelled it from his animal hospital for exciting his canine patients, and the Brody garage became an intensive care unit, and Sean the seal's nine-year-old nurse.

Quite clearly, as she reminisced, Ellen saw Sammy's trusting eyes looking up at Sean, within an hour of his arrival. Sean was already his father, mentor, and advocate. They were sitting on the cold garage floor while she watched, unseen, from the laundry room.

A bowl of canned sardines, a plate of hamburger, and a bowl of milk were spread out before Sammy. The seal, who must have weighed forty pounds, was sitting on Sean's lap as he looked up at Brody.

"Daddy, he's crying all the time. Look at his eyes." Sean's eyes were moist themselves.

"He misses his mother, probably."

"And he won't eat!"

"He's had a rough day, Sean. You wouldn't eat, either."

"He won't leave the bandage on!"

"Nature knows best." Brody's nose twitched. "What the hell?"

Sean rose, red-faced. "It wasn't his fault! He just hasn't learned yet."

Brody shuddered and looked down at his son. "You are covered, my friend, with seal turd."

"He couldn't go in the *toilet!*" Sean said defiantly.

The smell was awful. Ellen saw Brody studying his son. She could not tell if he was going to yell at the seal or at Sean.

But he was merely looking for a clean place on Sean's face. He bent suddenly and kissed the tip of his nose.

"Dump your clothes at the kitchen door, streak past your mother, and take a bath. I won't breathe a word."

Sean scurried off. Ellen saw Brody fill a bucket and wash down the garage. Sammy floundered across the cement floor, drank him in with the moist brown eyes, and shook himself like a dog, spraying him with excrement. Marty shook his head and followed his son to the bath.

Like father, like son . . .

"That's a beautiful story," murmured Tiffany. She sighed. "And he hasn't changed at all."

Tiffany rose in a single youthful motion, as graceful as a dancer in *Swan Lake*. She moved to the wine bottle in its bucket by the sofa and picked it up. She started to fill Ellen's glass but froze as she looked into her face.

"Ellen! What's wrong?"

So it showed. Ellen drew in a shuddering breath and shook her head. "I don't know. Tiff, do you feel it? Is something off-kilter somehow?"

Tiffany shook her head, reached out a hand, and felt her brow. "You're as cold as ice."

Ellen began to shiver. She looked at the cuckoo clock

Brody's father had brought back from Germany after VE day. It was five minutes to ten.

When had he left? Eight-thirty? Nine? How long could it possibly take him to tug a piece of log up the Amity Channel, anyway? One hour? Two?

She heard Tiffany's voice as if from a distance. "Ellen? What is it? You're so *white!*"

Ellen blocked her wineglass with her palm. She managed a tiny smile. "The wine, I guess. Brody used to say that God invented whiskey to keep the Irish from ruling the world. Now, wine isn't whiskey, true, but I read somewhere—it was an article in the *Long Island Press,* I think, Sunday—that there's just as much alcohol in a glass of wine as if you took a shot of whiskey and poured water in it, but of course the water doesn't matter, does it? It's just the shot of whiskey that has the alcohol in it, so the water doesn't matter at all. . . ."

Tiffany, eyes as wide as saucers, stared at her.

The clock whirred; the cuckoo popped out and cawed in its raspy voice: *Cuckoo, cuckoo, cuckoo. . . .*

Ellen leapt to her feet. "Tiffany, I have to go. Something has happened to Sean!"

In a moment, bundled in her old ski jacket, she was gripping the wheel of her old Plymouth, groping through fog down Main toward the ghastly glow of the floodlights on Old Pavilion, where the rehearsal was breaking up. Tiffany, finally apprehensive, sat beside her.

Ellen jumped from her car at the Pavilion and caught up with Lenny in his flowing Joseph robes. "He's out there with that piling. And he's been out there for hours."

Lenny's fat jowls quivered in surprise. "Hours?" He grimaced. He did not like the unexpected, not at all. But he looked after the departing troupe and yelled, "Caleb, Harry, somebody! I need a boat."

"We're going with you!" Ellen insisted.

"No, you're not, Ellen." Lenny shook his head. "It's ten below freezing out there and dropping all the time."

He was adamant, and even more stubborn than she.

She could not wait in the Pavilion; it was too far from the water. So she sat with Tiffany in the Plymouth, listening to its heater growling, and the foghorn wailing, and the channel buoy tolling, while the long, long night began.

The sky lightened before Ellen's eyes. She had hardly nodded, but Tiffany had finally drifted off to sleep.

Behind her, she heard the Christmas banner flopping in the morning breeze. By the dock was the papier-mâché hump from the annual camel, soggy and probably ruined from the fog.

There was no hint of sun through the scudding clouds. She could see only a hundred yards or so up the channel, but she had rolled the window down six inches and had been listening to the grumbling of diesels as the fishermen swept the harbor all night long.

She grew numb. All at once she knew that Sean was dead. The town did not know, not yet, but the fishermen surely did. Of all men, they knew their enemy—the ocean—best. If it did not return a hostage instantly, he was doomed.

A rumbling throb, very low, grew louder. Nils Larson's boat, *Penobscot,* which had almost hit the piling late the previous night, approached out of the drifting mist. The vessel disappeared like a wraith, then reappeared in ghostly black and white and finally took on colors of orange and yellow and rusty red.

At her bow was a froth of water. To Ellen she seemed to be grinning triumphantly, as if she knew more than Ellen or the men who worked her.

Ellen opened the car door silently. Every moment that Tiffany slept was a blessing.

Slowly she moved down the dock. Yellow-slickered men on *Penobscot* were looking back to sea, down at the water, at the masthead, anywhere they could but up at her.

Under a green tarpaulin on the foredeck lay a small mound—much too small for a grown man. The men were as far from it as they could get.

Even Nils Larson, on the bridge, refused to meet her gaze. His younger son leapt ashore, took a spring line, and secured it, avoiding her eyes. She was suddenly scrambling over the rail, heading for the tarp.

Nils bellowed in Swedish from the bridge. His older son jumped forward and grabbed Ellen by the arms. His hands were like steel claws.

"No!" The boy's icy blue eyes drilled into hers but suddenly melted in tears. "No, Mrs. Brody. Yesus, no . . ."

No tears came from her, none at all, only dry-eyed shock. She was stony with it, rigid, could not think or speak.

The boy held her clumsily, and men mumbled in sympathy. Someone patted her shoulder, and she fainted, and that was all she knew.

Chapter 3

They arrived from the Bahamas at noon the next day, like tanned beings from another world.

Michael ran to the door first, letting Carla pay the taxi. He was tanned, stronger, and more taciturn than Sean, with an older brother's assurance. He had a fluid, easy way of moving that went with his way of life.

Carla was a well-known metal sculptress, tall, with tawny, sun-streaked hair, a quiet Radcliffe manner, and a wide, slow smile.

Thea was as brown as a nut, bundled like an Arctic explorer against the northern cold, in a kelly-green snowsuit, hastily borrowed from a winter tourist's child in Nassau. It clashed with her sky-blue eyes and light blond hair.

She had grown from a baby into a person since their last visit, two years ago. Today she was subdued. She had loved Sean. On the plane she had sensed Mike's sadness, and Carla's, and was the oldest five-year old today that Ellen had ever seen.

The house was full of people trying to help: Polly, the dispatcher; neighbors cooking in the kitchen. As Ellen came to the door Mike took her into his arms.

"Mom, Mom, Mom . . . I'm so awful, awful sorry."

She couldn't speak but she nodded. She had not cried at all, did not care to cry in front of others, even him. Crying was stupid. What she wanted from her one remaining son was a promise, not his tears.

"It's all right, Mike. I'm okay now—"

He squinted into her eyes. "You're not! You can't be!"

"Well, I just don't want to talk about it yet."

He looked at her closely. "We have to, you know."

"Not now."

She embraced Carla. She kneeled and unzipped Thea from her quilted green nylon cocoon. She hugged her and looked into her face. "And are you ready for Santa Claus down there, Pumpkin?"

She touched Ellen's cheek. "Will he still come?"

Her throat tightened. "Of course he will. For you."

"For *all* of us, Ellen," murmured Carla. "Wait and see."

Ellen managed a smile. "Thea, there are cookies. Polly baked them just for you." Thea remembered where the kitchen was and scampered off. "Carla? Mike? I think you need a drink."

She saw a glance pass between them, and Mike nodded. "Okay, Mom."

She walked with her son on Amity Beach. The sky was bleak and the surf was pounding. It was cold but she felt nothing.

"I knew it when he left, Mike."

His eyes burned with anger. "For a rotten piece of wood!"

"Yes." She took a deep breath and got it out. "I don't want it to happen to you."

He stared at her. "To me?"

"You're diving all day long. I want you to stop."

"Mom!" He stopped and searched her face. "You can't be serious!"

"You're damn right I'm serious. I want you out of the water."

"I'm a marine biologist! It's my job!"

"He thought it was *his* job to move that piling!"

He looked at her sadly. "And you want me to be less than him? Or Dad?"

"I just want you to *be!* Let your partner . . . what's his name?"

"Jake," he murmured. "Jake McCay."

"Let *him* do the diving. Stay in the lab or on the boat. For me?"

"Mom," he said softly, "we don't have great white sharks down there."

"You never know! That one—"

"What do you mean, *that* one?"

"It was after Sean, Mike. I know it in my bones."

He slipped his arm around her. "Mom, we're going home."

"It was, dammit. I *know* it was! And I don't want you to dive!"

He stopped and kissed her on the brow.

"I can't promise you that, Mom. Look, you have to let go and cry."

She looked into his eyes, so much like Marty's and Sean's.

"You won't let him scare you out of the water?" she asked.

"I can't."

"Then why the hell should I let him make me cry?"

The wind had shifted southeast, and everyone who had gathered in Amity's graveyard on the hill behind the church knew that this time it was bringing drizzle that would turn the snow to slush.

Ellen stood like a marble monument next to Mike, trying to send strength to Tiffany through their clasped hands.

Carla shivered on the other side of Mike. Thea, wrapped for a moon landing, clung blue-lipped to her mother's hand.

The three would return to the Bahamas the following day, and Ellen would follow in two more days, when she'd taken care of Sean's affairs.

Now, to keep herself from breaking down, she kept her eyes on the Brody headstone, squarely on Marty's name: *Martin M. Brody, b: Aug. 10, 1942 d: May 22, 1986. Beloved of Ellen, Michael, and Sean.*

The whole town was at the graveside. Next week, or the week after, the stonecutter from Amagansett would be here for Sean's inscription, long after she was gone.

A gust rattled the dried boughs of the elm above them. An eddy whipped around its mottled trunk, and a faded pink handbill for Lautzhauser's Men's Store's annual bankruptcy sale fluttered into the open grave.

No one wanted the handbill to rest through eternity with Sean, but Mike, lost in thought, did not seem to see it, and no one else wanted to climb down and get it. They were burying the only man in town who would have stepped forth and volunteered.

Reverend McCloud's cheerful voice brought no balm at all. He was a red-bearded giant, ex–high school tackle, bursting with health, and as stupid a man as Ellen had ever known. He had mouthed the same stale passages at Brody's funeral just the previous year, and it had done no good.

"A time to weep and a time to laugh . . ."

She could hear Tiffany fighting tears beside her. She was young and unused to loss. If you'd romped free in pastures all your life, the first wall you encountered seemed immense.

Tiff probably thought she would never stop weeping in the night, but that was because she had never truly wept before. Ellen had wept for Marty and knew that the tears would pass but that the ache would never leave.

"A time to mourn and a time to dance . . ."

He loved it, McCloud did. It had made his day, though at first he was aghast at what she wanted: no funeral in church, only a graveside service.

"Now, Ellen, are you sure?" he'd protested at first.

"I'm sure."

"But there's a cathartic effect in church, even if the casket's closed," McCloud said dubiously.

"The casket will be at the grave," she said, choking. "It's not *Sean* in it, anyway; there's nothing there to see. *No* one's seen him since he left me but that awful goddamn shark!"

"And *God,* Ellen," McCloud said, chiding her and ignoring her language. "We must never forget Him."

"Why not?" she demanded. "Did God remember him?"

McCloud, jolted, had recovered from the sacrilege. In his own eyes, at least, he was rising nobly to his task, exhorting everyone to remember that there was a time to live and a time to die.

All right, if he would only finish before she broke down before the town, as everyone wanted her to, so that they could talk about it until the next tragedy befell.

"A time to love and a time to hate," he shouted. "A time for war and a time for peace . . ."

She glanced at the tombstone for strength. She had made it this far without crying—she mustn't give in now. *Brody, help me, Brody. . .*

Far below in the harbor, the Amity–East Hampton ferry blasted, backing out from the dock. The drizzle began, and still McCloud went on. Was he testing his "cathartic effect" on her? Dammit, *she would not cry!*

She took refuge in memory. She was in her kitchen. She heard Sean, just nine years old, sneaking out, trying to avoid KP.

"Sean?"

The whining of the screen door stopped, telling her he was there.

"Hostess Ding Dong?" she called devilishly. There were none, but if Sean didn't help with the dishes, then who would?

He returned, so up-front himself that he was a pigeon for a fib. "Hi," he said with a smile.

She handed him a dish towel. He looked at it in shock, holding it as if it were diseased. The truth began to dawn. "We got Ding Dongs?"

"You ate them all last night, remember?"

He looked betrayed. "But you said—"

"I was thinking out loud. I didn't know there was anybody out there—nobody answered." She presented him a plate. "Don't drop it. I mean it."

He winced. "Mike says I got to finish painting the tiller or I can't crew for him in the regat—"

"*After* the dishes."

"I'll never get the boat done and he won't let me crew!"

And Sean had crewed, and the shark had come, and he'd hated the ocean ever after. It was Amity's last regatta, for no one had ever wanted their children racing to Cape North Light again, though the shark had died in an incandescent flash of power in front of everyone.

Or had it really died? Was the monster deathless? Had the first one left immortal spawn, to track them down and kill them one by one?

She pressed her temples. Along *that* track lay madness. She tried to concentrate on the tombstone, groping for Brody's calm good sense. The drizzle was casting a sheen on its rough Maine granite. Lines from Tennyson remembered from high school filled her head:

Break, break, break,
On thy cold gray stones, O Sea!
And I would that my tongue could utter
The thoughts that arise in me.

"He died," bellowed McCloud happily, "as he and his father had lived, in the service of his fellowman. And our little community is the worse for it."

She could feel the drizzle sinking in her bones. In moments he would be a part of the sodden ground. She fought another wave of despair.

O well for the fisherman's boy
That he shouts with his sister at play!
O well for the sailor lad.
That he sings in his boat on the bay!

Lenny, in full uniform, was tugging at the U.S. flag, donated jointly by the Elks and the Suffolk County Police League. It clung to one corner of the casket. Good. They could not bury the flag, so they could not bury him. Tonight would be freezing again.

Lenny jerked at the flag and jiggled; he was the clumsiest man on earth. *It should have been you, you son of a bitch. You're here and he's gone.* She wanted to tear the flag from his hand, replace it, smooth it down. She had always made Sean's bed; he claimed he slept better when she did, and she had pretended to believe him and never once rebelled.

Mike stepped forward to help him, and the flag came away. The ferry blasted one more time, rounding the buoy Sean had died to free.

And the stately ships go on
To their haven under the hill
But O for the touch of a vanished hand
And the sound of a voice that is still!

"Dust to dust," McCloud reminded them, "was not written of the soul."

She took a long, shuddering breath. The casket sank from view. She felt herself breaking down, squeezed Tiffany's hand, looked into her eyes, and spun on her heel.

"Ellen?" Lenny called. "I got to give you the flag!"

"Give it to Mike," she managed to say.

She could hear a buzz of questions behind her. The ridiculous ritual was not over; Sean was not properly bedded in his grave. But now she was at her Plymouth, parked by Mike at the head of the line of cars, behind the hearse.

Mike was suddenly beside her. "Mom, I'm coming with you. Wherever you want to go."

She could only shake her head. "Alone," she gulped. "Please, Michael?"

He stepped back as she pulled from the curb in a squeal of rubber. The windshield wipers began their screeching waltz; she could not stand the noise and turned them off.

She drove to the beach, where the first of the sharks had taken the first of his victims. For a long while she sat parked, sensing a malevolence she could not name in the gray, remorseless waves.

An awful anger burned within her. She opened the trunk and groped into the bundle of the things from Sean's locker at the station.

She drew his revolver—*their* revolver, his father's and his—from its holster and loaded it with bullets from the ancient leather belt. She kicked off her shoes in the sand.

Face twisted, head high, she marched through the drizzle into the surf. The frigid water groped for her, and she felt it not at all. Far away, she heard the bell buoy gong. The Amity foghorn answered. Across Amity Sound she could see the loom of the Cape North Light, winking in a measure she had known for half her life.

She leveled the gun at the ocean and squeezed the trigger. It kicked so hard that she almost dropped it. Her hand hurt from the jolt. In the pain of it she found pleasure. Slowly, deliberately, she fired it five more times. She drew back her hand to throw it into the sea.

No. It had been theirs, and she had so little of them left.

Gun in hand, knees trembling from the cold, she turned slowly and began to wade back toward the strand.

All the long night the great white had patrolled the beaches south of Cape North Light. At dawn, when the gray summer cottages of Napeague, Amagansett, East Hampton, and Sagaponack took shape in the drizzle, he was a hundred yards off Amity Beach.

The ampullae on his forehead detected a change in the electromagnetic fields of force through which he swam. Something metallic lay on the bottom.

For aeons his kind had investigated such electrical phenomena: skates and stingrays and even squid emitted auras of minute electrical disturbances and were his natural prey.

This time the object was man-made: a three-foot lobster pot jammed between two boulders at the twenty-fathom line. Eight big lobsters crouched inside. Their feelers waved in alarm when they sensed his presence.

In murky green darkness a hundred feet below the surface, the great white banked, stabbed at the pot, and clamped it in his jaws. He began to shake his head, worrying it from where it was wedged. He shook it loose, breaking off outcroppings of stone in a cloud of sand and murk.

The pot was a homemade latticework of heavy wire fencing. It ripped open as he shook it, and he swallowed a section of wire. As the lobsters scooted off, he lunged after them, snatching the three slowest before they could take refuge in holes in the reef.

They were not enough. He was an eating machine with enormous fuel requirements. The caloric value of the three crustaceans came nowhere near replacing the energy he had wasted in getting them.

Ravenously hungry now, he glided slowly upward.

Although his ears were so tiny as to be almost invisible, his hearing was exquisite, for he heard with his body, too, through the tiny lateral canals that laced his flanks.

Drifting slowly now, with all his senses sharpened, he heard a distant, sharp report. He quivered; anything that made noise interested him. The shot was followed by another and another, six in all. By the sixth he was swimming at full speed toward the beach.

He felt vibrations in the water. Something was sloshing ashore.

Ellen Brody slogged from the water, shivering with cold. She was wet up to her waist. She turned to look back at the sea.

The great gray breakers were building, charging in lines like white-plumed knights, hanging for a moment, then plunging into battle in the churning foam below.

She hated the surf, she hated Cape North Light, she

hated most of all the clanging bell buoy she could hear above the roar.

She sat in the open door of her car, put on one shoe, and found herself staring at the other, blankly. She took a long, shuddering sigh. She was too tired to put it on.

Then the tears came. So when the shark finally made her cry, at least she was alone.

She had not seen the great white's fin slicing through the surf.

The great white had tracked his target into water too shallow for him. Now he gave up and turned seaward again.

Before him, a half-mile sphere of water emptied of life, for he was not alone in his sensitivities: his own prey had receptors, psychic and physical, much like his.

A huge skate, gliding at ten fathoms, flapped away to sea. A giant squid on the bottom squirted like a rocket into Amity Sound: Something was above that it did not like.

A school of cod, acting with a single brain, panicked and headed for land.

The great white drifted lazily for a while. He was near waters in which he'd been conceived, sired by a male almost as big as he. His mother, enormous, gravid with young, had swept through Amity Sound like death itself, bearing him, three sisters and another brother in her right uterus, and three more young in her left. For two years he had lived in utero. He had eaten, with his remaining brother and sisters, thousands of his mother's unfertilized eggs and some thirty weaker siblings in the womb.

He had fought off his brother and sisters to survive the uterus, squirming, slashing, born to fight. Birthed live, like all sharks, at his mother's death off Cape

North Light, he had been three feet long, a murderous twenty-two-pound replica of his sire.

From that day he had been at the very apex of the oceanic food triangle, as speedy as any fish in the ocean and living death to all.

He was a cold-water animal but pelagic: a wanderer. The myth that his kind was territorial was man-made: Unlike lesser sharks, he ranged for thousands of miles.

His slender, wrist-sized brain was subject to impulse, and forces that no man knew.

Weather could change his pattern of travel, or the currents of El Niño, or the migration of his prey.

Or other, stranger forces man could never understand. . . .

On this hungry morning, impelled by a savage whim, he turned and headed south.

Chapter 4

Ellen stepped from the Eastern Airline plane into blessed warmth and light. She trailed along with fellow passengers to the Nassau airline terminal.

It was a new world. The sea breeze carried a scent of flowers: Amity would not smell blossoms for three more months. Behind her were the hues of death: black and white, gray, wintry brown. Nassau was living color, in 3-D.

If only Sean could have seen this. . . .

In a chattering mob of blacks and whites in the terminal, a tall blond man with a twinkling grin was holding up a placard: ELLEN BRODY. Their eyes met, and she thought she saw humor, compassion, and a sadness like her own.

"Welcome to Calypso's Friendly Charters, then. I'm called Hoagie Newcombe." He had a British accent, and his voice was soft and low. "Fifteenth largest airline in the Bahamas."

There were touches of gray in the hairs on his chest that she saw in the *V* of his knotted tropical shirt. He wore shorts and a Royal Navy officer's cap.

He had lazy, twinkling blue eyes that slid sidewise into hers, as if he were evaluating her. At their corners, tiny muscle movements, more felt than seen, showed his interest and somehow aroused her.

He took her carry-on bag, and they picked up her suitcase from the baggage room. "Michael wanted to come to meet you, and so did Carla, but I didn't know how much your kit would weigh." He hefted the bag. "Very reasonable, this is. You're planning to outfit yourself here?"

"I sort of left in a hurry," she said. "I'll live in a muumuu here."

They walked across the tarmac to a taxiway. A single-engine high-winged four-seater plane squatted awkwardly in the glare, at the end of a line of expensive private aircraft.

It wore faded red striping. On its fuselage in chipped green paint was printed: CALYPSO'S FRIENDLY CHARTERS. SIGHT-SEEING! SKYDIVING! OUTER ISLAND EXCURSIONS! FRIENDLY FREIGHT!

"Friendly Charters, friendly freight?" She smiled for the first time in days.

"To paraphrase Homer, 'Let me live in my house by the side of the aerodrome, and be a friend of man.' His voice trailed off and his eyes narrowed. "What the bloody hell—"

He jerked the door of the aircraft open. She squinted inside.

From the darkness shone the flattest, blackest eyes she had ever seen. Or *had* she seen them—in a dream? As her pupils adjusted, she saw a man. He was sitting in the seat behind the pilot's empty place.

He was tiny. His skin was ebony. He wore a red shirt and a dirty straw hat and hair that dangled in long red plaits. Around his neck he wore a shark-tooth necklace; his own teeth were dazzlingly white.

In his hand he clutched a gourd, like a rattle, beaded, ornate, and quite filthy. From it dangled a tiny silver bell. A pack of greasy playing cards was on the seat beside him.

She found herself trembling for no reason. The little man's eyes widened for a moment, as if in recognition.

"Madame, you are the mother of Michael?" There was anger in his voice.

She nodded, puzzled. "Michael, yes. How did you know that?"

He ignored the question. "And I think you 'ave come to escape a great grief." He smiled coldly. "That is not so easy sometimes."

"Papa Jacques, get your ass out of there!" exploded Hoagie. He grabbed the man's arm and yanked him bodily from the plane.

The little man drew himself up and glared at him, fingering his necklace. *"Mon ami,* take care!"

Hoagie grinned tightly. "Go stick pins in my doll, you little bastard. It's this lady's plane for the morning, and I'm not hauling you for free."

The man's eyes flashed. "But you mus'. You mus' fly me to Whiskey Cay, *c'est très important*. I have a patient there."

"You always have a patient," Hoagie said with a snort. "A dying grandmother? A father with four kids?"

"A little girl. She has *la fièvre*. A *baka* has enter her heart."

"Which *baka?"* Hoagie grinned.

"The barracuda god. I mus' drive him away."

"Where were you when I was married?" murmured Hoagie. He opened a luggage compartment behind the cabin and hefted in Ellen's suitcase. "Sorry, Papa Jacques. There's a real doctor on Whiskey Cay, now isn't there?"

"What does he know of the *baka?"* His eyes went blank. "And he has gone to Crooked Island."

Hoagie shot him a strange glance. "How do you know that?"

"I see him." Papa Jacques shrugged. "Your doctor is there at *la clinique,* sticking worthless pins into living dolls."

Hoagie stepped under the wing to help Ellen into the right front seat, next to his own. "The strange thing is," he murmured, "he's probably right. I flew him there last week."

He reached up and fastened her seat belt. His touch was warm and gentle. She felt herself blushing.

"Hoagie, can he do the little girl any good?"

"*I* don't think so."

"But does *she?*"

"That's for certain."

"Then, Hoagie, let him come."

"Your son doesn't like him."

"Just the same . . ."

He looked up into her face and smiled. "He's conned you, you know? But it's your airplane, Mrs. Brody. As you say."

They rattled into the sky between an Eastern jet and a Drug Enforcement Agency search plane and skimmed the turquoise waters of New Providence, heading east.

She looked down on a sea the color of polished jade, so different from Amity Sound. Beyond the last cays, she knew, lay the Atlantic, full of evil and despair.

Thank God she was here.

The great white cruised at a hundred feet, making a good eight knots. When he had left Amity, he had moved in purposeless circles, foraging far to sea, and though he had always tended southward, his route had lacked direction.

Ranging eastward, he touched the waters of the Gulf Stream. Then he turned south again, breasting the current. Though the surface above was turbulent with the mixing of warm and cold water, his dark green world below was calm and cold. This far from shore, the nearest land was under him, peaks of the Northwest Atlantic Ridge.

He swept on tirelessly, never sleeping, for to slumber was to plunge into the abyss. He had no reason to descend, for in the depths was no worthy food but giant squid, and there was easier prey at the levels where he swam.

Six hundred miles west of Cape Fear, South Carolina, he became aware of an explosive *blat . . . blat . . . blat. . . .* It came from somewhere to the east, in the direction of the Mares Deep.

His instincts told him that a sperm whale—a large bull, from the sound of it—was echolocating, to navigate or for prey.

Sperm were creatures of sunlight when they cruised, but of darkness when they dived. They found their breath where the wind swept free, and their food where the great white seldom swam, a thousand feet below the surface of the sea.

The shark had no interest in a live and active adult sperm. Great whites depended on the shock of their initial headlong rush to stun their prey. They did not like a battle afterward, and sperm whales fought savagely, to the death.

Men had called the great sperm "emperors," for their size, dignity, and violence when provoked. The rush of an angry bull whale—fifty or sixty feet long, weighing fifty tons, and fighting for his life—could crush the white. And the whale's great teeth—eight inches long—could impale the biggest shark.

But this sperm seemed different. He was sending out a hunting blast, echolocating for squid or navigating off echoes from the ridges a mile below, but the sound somehow lacked timbre. The shark sensed weakness.

The bull was sick or wounded. If so, he was fair game. Synapses were triggered in the great white's tiny brain, and he speeded the rhythm of his tail. He began the long, long quest to see where the sperm whale was.

* * *

The old sperm whale swam doggedly southward on the surface, ramming through the Gulf Stream chop. He had only one eye, his left. From the other protruded the broken half of a harpoon. It had slammed home out of nowhere, propelled by a South African pirate whaler's gun while he slumbered near an iceberg off Newfoundland a week before.

The harpoon, if it had penetrated another foot, would have destroyed the largest brain the world had ever known, seven times the size of man's.

Instead it had lodged within the eyeball, sending waves of agony through the wallowing body at every stroke of his sixteen-foot flukes. Another harpoon, unbroken, rose from his dorsal hump. This one caused no pain except when a Gulf Stream breaker slammed his back.

Knowing that he was unfit for another battle with man—whom, he suspected, homed on his hunting peal—or with his cousins, the killer whales, or even with a shark, he had held silence for most of the last two thousand miles. He would never again take a squid, he knew, and would starve if his wounds did not kill him.

But he had a destination, and he would not be deterred.

He had been an Arctic solitary for almost twenty years, driven from his harem by a younger, stronger bull. Dying, he longed for the coves of youth and to see his kind again. It was breeding season near the equator.

His ancestors had been creatures of the land. They had crawled back to the ocean before man had crept from trees. He knew that he would never mount another cow, but he longed to die in warmer waters, beached on a golden strand.

He had been traveling mostly in silence, by dead

reckoning, for days, seldom daring to echolocate on remembered peaks below.

He could see the sun by daylight. But age had dimmed the vision of the eye that he had left, so he could not navigate by moonlight or the stars.

He was sure that the Gulf Stream had swept him from the steep Bermuda Rise. He decided to risk everything for a fix on the terrain below.

Blat . . . He snorted, and listened. *Blat* . . . *blat* . . . *blat* . . .

Ping . . . *ping* . . .

The immediate echo startled him. Instantly he switched to a racheting mode, which would have sounded to man like a distant outboard motor. But to him it defined, in the pitch-black water, a perfect picture of a great white shark, rising toward him from the depths.

He flung up his flukes and dived, his back shimmering in the starlight like an island engulfed by tides.

As he sounded, trailing clouds of phosphorescence, the great white struck. It snatched off a tiny pectoral fin, a vestige of land legs, and destroyed the whale's stability. The sperm spiraled helplessly for a moment, unable to get his bearings. He felt the shark boring in on his blind side and began to flail his flukes.

But now, in a flash of searing pain, he realized that the creature was fastened to his side, burdening him. The sperm bellowed angrily, for in more agile days he might have shaken him loose and slammed out his life with one enormous swipe.

The shark hung on, but the whale would not give up. He had fought a dozen males as large as himself and won all the fights but the last. In agony, he rose to the surface and broached like a dolphin, carrying the shark with him high above the waves. At the crest of his leap he turned and fell, slamming his fifty-ton body on the writhing, tearing shark.

The blow dislodged the great white shark and stunned him. He swam away.

For a moment the sperm whale rested, rocking in waves of pain. He blew, spouting a bloody fountain fifty feet high, with a sigh that could be heard for half a mile.

The shark circled, shaking his head. The smell of blood, heavy in the water, drew him back, and he bored in on the same gushing wound.

He stayed in constant motion, thrusting and feinting and drilling in again. He squirmed and writhed whenever the whale moved, for if the whale teeth closed on his flank, they would never open, and the two would die together in the night.

Deeper and deeper the white shark probed, tearing at the wound. The old sperm weakened quickly, once the shark had gnawed to his gut. In a while, as his blood filled the water, he twitched with the passing of his life.

When he shuddered and died, he was a thousand miles from the sunlit beach he remembered, and the pod he had longed to see.

The great white feasted half the night. Lesser sharks drew near, but none dared join him.

Finally, with the old sperm one-tenth eaten, he headed south again.

Chapter 5

Hoagie Newcombe skimmed the emerald waters of Whiskey Cay, cleared a clump of palms, and eased the little plane to a coral runway hardly longer than Amity's Main Street. They landed without a bump. He taxied swiftly to a weather-beaten shack.

"Whiskey Cay International Terminal," he said, "home of Calypso's Friendly Charters." He cut the airplane's engine. As the prop ticked to a stop, Ellen peered past it to where a sparkling, tail-finned Cadillac sat waiting in the shade.

All at once Thea was racing toward the plane, her long blond hair streaming. She wore a loose blue dress, none too clean. She ran under the wing and waited, hopping up and down.

In Amity she had been a bundled waif, subdued and maturely sad. Here she was in her element, vibrant and alive. Even from here, her eyes were dazzling blue. She was barefoot.

Ellen's throat caught. Brody had missed so much, and Sean—who would have had beautiful children with Tiffany—had missed so much too.

But she had not come a thousand miles to keen like a mourner at a wake. She began to unclip her safety belt.

"Don't get out," warned Hoagie. "The local narc."

A white jeep driven by a black official in a visored cap, worn askew, rolled to a stop. The man was dressed in white shorts and wore a big gold badge. He skirted the plane, peered into nooks and crannies in the control surfaces, and finally swung open the door.

He saluted Papa Jacques, scanned the interior, nodded brusquely to Hoagie, and strolled back to his jeep.

"Okay," said Hoagie. "Now!"

She squirmed from her seat, scrambled out, and scooped Thea up.

"Santa's coming," Thea announced, "in three more days!"

Ellen looked around. "He'll never come here. There isn't any snow!"

Thea giggled. "He's got a *boat!*"

A shadow fell across them. Ellen looked up. Michael stood against the sun, looking so much like Brody that she almost choked again. He wore shorts and a scruffy baseball cap and a faded Hawaiian shirt.

He took her into his arms. "Mom, Mom, Mom . . . Is it better now?"

"Yes," she said, lying. "It is."

"Can we talk about him yet?"

"Yes," she said bitterly. "His luck was up." She swallowed. "Talk over. Okay?"

"The *bad* luck's over. 'Cause you're staying forever, with us."

"I wish I could."

Carla wore shorts and a ponytail and walked up with a long, firm stride. She squeezed Ellen's hands. She was slim and narrow-waisted, but the welder's torch and heavy iron she muscled every day had given her the palm of a carpenter and a grip like a man's. "We want you, Ellen, we truly do."

"Well, you have me for two weeks," said Ellen. "For better or for worse."

"And you've got me too," said Hoagie. "At least into town. My jeep's under anesthesia at the Old Prince George garage."

Carla glanced at him, then at Ellen. Her eyes narrowed in thought, and a grin lit up her face. "You're invited for dinner, tonight, okay? Conch chowder, peas 'n' rice."

Hoagie glanced sidewise at Ellen, in his lazy, penetrating way, as if to see if she wanted him. *I do, I do,* she thought silently, and it must have shown, for he nodded and picked up her bag. He started toward the Cadillac.

She was conscious of Papa Jacques's wide black eyes staring into hers. "Madam," he said coldly, "I mus' thank you. *Merci.*"

Michael tensed. His hostility was clear. "For what, Papa Jacques?"

The little man fingered his necklace. "She has made him bring me here."

"She didn't know any better. You charge too much, and you're not welcome on this island anymore."

"I was called here by a native, *non?*" Papa Jacques said tersely. "Can *you* say the same?"

He moved off toward the road, his gourd in one hand, his playing cards in the other.

Ellen followed Michael. The gleaming old Cadillac belonged to Romeo, a chubby, ebony Buddha with a flashing smile and a visored tour-guide cap. An ex-merchant seaman on the Cunard Line, Mike said, he spoke half a dozen languages—including classical Greek—and owned the local undertaking parlor and the island's only hearse. He swept open the rear door and helped her in.

As they started down the macadam road they passed the little Haitian. He stared at them as if he had never seen them before. His flat eyes glittered like onyx in the sun.

"What is he, really?" she asked Hoagie, shivering.

"Just another *houngan* witch doctor," he said with a grin. "Haiti's major import to the Bahamas. Papa Jacques is the worst of the lot."

"At least the others treat for free," agreed Michael from the front. "He's a *bocor:* a professional. He takes money from the poor."

"An evil mon," concurred Romeo from the wheel. "You're in danger if you cross him, Michael, lad."

"We're all in mortal danger, Romeo, with you behind the wheel."

Romeo reached across and tousled Michael's hair. But Ellen saw his eyes flash to the rearview mirror, and she caught a glint of fear.

In his smooth Nat King Cole voice, Romeo described the sights of Prince George Town through a tourist microphone as if he were a tour director.

"And on your right you have the plaza, which, if I'm not mistaken, will soon be graced by an avant-garde creation of the imminent Boston sculptor, Mrs. Carla Paxton Brody—"

"Eminent," Carla said with a sigh. *"Sculptress.* And I'm now from Whiskey Cay, not Boston. Romeo, if you're trying to sound like William Buckley, get it right."

They approached the town's sole traffic policeman, stationed at the intersection of Kingston Road and Highbourne Way. He stood on a canopied kiosk in the middle of the street, wearing whites, a pith helmet, and a gleaming gold badge. His black face shone with sweat.

A fish truck dripping with melting ice lumbered up from a side street. The Cadillac could easily have beaten it to the intersection, but the policeman held up his hand imperiously, stopping them.

"He's my brother-in-law, you see," murmured Romeo. "Thoroughly detests me." He rolled his window down. "Yah, mon. Why you stoppin' these tourists? I gwine tell your wife. You pay no heed to island economy?"

The officer's hand stayed up scornfully. Then things began to happen very fast.

A motor scooter pulled up beside them, its engine popping, with two men astride it. The man on the back was enormous. He wore a tan tropical suit and a Panama hat, mirrored sunglasses, and a flowing white mustache disguising buck teeth.

Suddenly he was leaning toward them, squinting into the rear window of the Cadillac through the tinted glass. Ellen saw his hand creeping toward his coat.

"Go, Romeo," said Hoagie tersely, then exploded into action. He yanked Thea from the jump seat and threw Carla to the floor. He flung himself on Ellen and slammed her to the seat, covering her body with his own. "Get this hunk of tin in gear and go!"

Ellen was crushed backward as the Cadillac took off. She heard the blast of a gun. A bullet slammed into the trunk. Then she was smothering, squirming under Hoagie's hard body, fighting for air.

From below window level, she glimpsed the policeman as they rocketed past. She heard his whistle shrill, then grow fainter. They rounded a corner in a shriek of smoking rubber. Held down on the seat, she glimpsed stilted wooden houses with hex signs and weather-beaten paint, palm trees and balconies and scraggly potted plants. She saw laundry flapping and TV antennas and a towering coconut palm.

By the time Hoagie let her up, she was drenched in sweat. Thea was crying. Carla was stunned. Michael was glaring at Hoagie. They were parked outside a wooden building. Above it flapped the turquoise, yellow and black flag of the Bahamas.

"Welcome to Prince George Town," rumbled Romeo. He patted the wheel of his car. "Mon, you can't beat General Motors, that's a fact."

"Hoagie," Michael murmured, his voice throaty with menace. "What do you know about this?"

"I think," admitted Hoagie coolly, "he might have been after me."

"No crap!" said Michael sourly. "I thought maybe Thea, or Carla, or me. Or Romeo. Who'd ever want to kill a solid citizen like you?"

"I said 'might have,' didn't I? For we don't really know that, do we? So let's just make our report."

"I want an answer, Hoagie!"

Hoagie shrugged. "Jealous husband? Angry father? Who can tell? You know us flying types."

"You didn't mention dope, Hoagie," said Michael very softly. "Couldn't *possibly* be dope?"

"Michael!" protested Carla.

The two men held each other's eyes. "I'll pretend," said Hoagie softly, "I didn't hear that." He opened the car door. "I'll make the report, Michael. If they need you, they can find you where? At the bottom of the sea?"

"Home with my family. Hoping nobody comes looking for *you*."

Hoagie smiled at Carla. "Rain check on that dinner, then?"

She glared at Michael and said, "We're having it tonight, and you are welcome. Still."

"I think not, luv." He turned and patted Thea on the cheek. "But you and I, we're going flying sometime very soon."

"When?" demanded Thea. "Tomorrow?"

"When the cold front passes." He smiled at Ellen. Something in her flipped. "And you, Ellen . . ."

"Yes?" She felt her cheeks grow hot.

"I don't attack women every day, and I'll have to show you that."

He was gone, running up the stairs two at a time, and she found herself lonely again.

They glided through a residential area full of beautifully landscaped homes, and down a gentle, wooded hill. Below, Ellen could see scalloped coves, piers, and anchored yachts.

"Masthead Point and Masthead Cove," said Michael proudly. "And home sweet home to us."

The house was weather-beaten, rambling, and open to the breeze. It had a mammoth porch, full of Thea's toys. Twenty yards away, where palm trees met with island pines, was Carla's studio, a guest house with a thatched roof. Ellen would stay in a bedroom attached to the studio.

A path, bordered by whitewashed rocks, led down to a ramshackle pier. At the end of it rocked an ancient sailing ketch, with her pilothouse converted to a marine laboratory. She creaked at her lines in the current through Masthead Cut, a channel that led straight to the Atlantic.

As Ellen unpacked in her bedroom off Carla's studio, she looked out the open window at the cove.

So this was where Michael's fascination with the diving had brought him, far from Amity's cold face.

It was strange. After the first shark, fear of the ocean had obsessed Brody but only aroused his older son. With the ocean banned, Michael had conquered his own fears, which were considerable, and learned to surf. Though prohibited from scuba diving, he had sneaked to classes; banned from the depths, he had plunged in, anyway, seduced by forbidden fruit.

If Brody had been a teetotaler, Michael might have been an alcoholic. Oedipus? Who knew? Well, all of this had brought him here, and a lovely place it was.

If only he did not make his living at the bottom of the sea. . . .

As soon as Ellen was unpacked, Michael dragged her down to show her the ketch. Her name was *Neptune's Folly.* She was, Michael said, a famous old Bahama cruiser, donated to their conch-study project by the Ministry of Fisheries and funded by a grant.

During the Cape North Regatta many years ago, Ellen had lost her taste for anything that sailed. The second shark had seen to that. But she was a New Englander, born to the sea. She had cruised the coast of Maine with her father as a girl, in a gaff-rigged ketch like this one, only smaller.

She understood the very boats she feared. In *Neptune's Folly* she sensed a wanderer, doomed to placid cays and still lagoons, straining at her spring lines to be free.

Michael picked at bubbled varnish on the boom. "She needs work. No funds. I'd hate to trust her past the Point."

Nestled against *Neptune's* starboard bow was a midget submarine, painted pink. A salt-streaked rubber dinghy was tied to the ketch's stern.

They entered a stately, old-fashioned pilothouse. A huge computer screen stared greenly at racks of test tubes and specimen bottles. A battered wooden icebox had a dart board on its door. A few beer posters hung on the bulkheads.

The compartment was jammed with cameras, diving tanks, face masks, and regulators.

An enormous black man was sitting at a workbench, soldering an intricate circuit with fingers that dwarfed his work. He stood up and bowed; he was Jake McCay, Mike's partner and the boss of the Fisheries' Conch Project. He spoke with the lilt of the Bahamas behind his careful words. Mike joined him at the lab bench, discussing some electronic device they were working on. Ellen moved across the cabin.

At the chart table a girl was laying out playing cards. She was absolutely beautiful. She had skin of café au lait and big brown eyes peppered with golden flecks. Her body, under an island print, was flawless. When she turned from her cards, she smiled like a reigning queen.

"I am called Louisa, Mrs. Brody," she said, holding out her hand. Her accent was faintly French. Ellen decided that she was Haitian. "So you are Ellen Brody! *Eh bien,* you look younger than your son."

Ellen grinned. "That's the nicest thing I've heard in many a day."

Louisa's eyes, searching and tender, narrowed curiously, then widened as if in fear. "Mrs. Brody? Are you quite all right?"

"Why, yes. . . ."

But suddenly she was not. A coldness started from her stomach, worked its way up to her chest, invaded her arms and legs, and she was shivering in the warm Bahamian air.

Louisa looked at her in terror, then quickly grasped her hand. She hooked their little fingers and pressed Ellen's hand to her brow.

Ellen heard her murmur something: *"Au nom Monsieur Damballah-wedo . . ."*

For a long while Louisa held her hand to her brow, and then the coldness passed, and she felt warm and deeply loved. She looked into the woman's eyes.

"What—" she began.

Louisa pressed a finger to her lips. "Shh," she whispered, nodding toward Michael and Jake. "They only laugh at me. But the cold has left your soul, *n'est-ce pas?"*

Ellen nodded, stunned. "Yes, but—"

"*Eh bien,* it may not come again." She scooped up the cards on the table.

"But how—"

Louisa shrugged. "My mother was a *mambo.*"

"*Mambo?*"

"You would say . . . a witch? *White* witch, though not so white in color—darker, much, than I." She shrugged. "She did much good in Port-au-Prince." She slipped her cards into her purse. "Me? An amateur, one would say. With Jake always laughing at me so, how can I ever know? Jake?" she called. "I feel our Cadillac is here."

"Not yet, it's way too early," the black man said, scoffing. "Romeo on time? Not even for his half-assed funerals."

In a moment Romeo appeared at the door. "Your wheels, mon, as you ordered."

Jake looked startled. He got up, moved to the chart table, and looked at Louisa.

"You want to tell me how you do that someday, girl?"

"No. Because you never believe a single thing I say."

When the two left, Michael showed her their laboratory. The equipment, though old, seemed expensive. Ellen did not understand. All for conches? "Conks," as they pronounced it.

A conch, as far as she knew, was just another shell; elaborate, pretty, but hardly worth all this.

She had to ask why. She looked into Michael's face. She had never been able to show false enthusiasm. When he or Sean had brought home an essay from English or an ashtray from shop class that she didn't understand or like, she'd told them. She was always the one who had to strip the emperor of his clothes.

She sighed and asked, "But, Michael, what does a conch *do?* I mean, to make it worth all this?"

He looked uncomfortable. "Well, some people think it's a fascinating animal."

"That's not the point. Do *you?*"

He reached into an aquarium tank and took out a live eight-inch conch. The shell was a buff-colored specimen with a pagoda-shaped tower and a lovely pink hue where it entered the interior.

"Strombus gigas," he announced. "Every bit of him is usable. Bahamians make roadbeds from his shell. The French make cameos. Hawaiians toot on it when they want to go to war. Europeans use it in porcelain." He put the shell down on the chart table and touched a finger to his lips. "Shh . . . or he won't come out. They hear everything. . . ."

He turned a dial on an instrument that looked like a radio. A deep, resonant drumming started. "That's the heartbeat of one on the bottom. This guy will hear it and come out."

After a long moment a strange creature backed from the shell, tail first, cautiously, still attached to the shell it wore. It was wrinkled and shiny, with two long tubes ending in eyes, a trunk like an elephant, a snorkel mouth, and a pointed tail. "They also come out to eat. Sometimes he eats carrion, but he makes great chowder, just the same."

She grimaced. "Not for me, he doesn't. But you don't *catch* them, do you?"

"I count them. Count 'em and tag 'em and shoot 'em on film with a strobe light to prove we did the job. Hour after hour, day after day." He shrugged. "It's a living, I guess." He switched on an enormous photographer's strobe light, in a bright yellow underwater case. It whined and squealed as it built up a charge in its condenser.

"High-tech. Look at this thing: With ths little trigger I can light up the world." He showed her a stainless-steel cylinder with a trigger on it. "Sometimes we leave a camera with a colony on the bottom, and a strobe light, and take their pictures to see what they do at night."

He pressed the trigger. She heard two beeps from somewhere deep in the hull. The strobe flashed, turning the cabin bright blue and blinding her, as if lightning had struck.

He sighed. "Their sex life stinks, but I can give you the conch population of every reef between here and New Providence: mommas, daddies, and all their little kids."

"But why?"

He looked miserable. "Because the Ministry of Fisheries thinks we're helping the economy. Because we have a grant."

He pointed to the conch on the table. It had somehow inched almost to the edge. "You ought to see them traveling on the bottom. Big ones first, then the little ones, lined up like elephants in a circus parade." He rescued the cliff-hanging conch and put it in the center of the table, on a chart. "This job can get old, you understand. Day after day, hour after hour. Conches on parade . . ."

She was sure that there was plenty of work for marine biologists in laboratories and classrooms. If only she could convince him not to dive. She tried to keep her voice steady. "It sounds . . . well, *beneath* you, Mike."

He grinned and pointed down. "It is. It's all down there."

"That isn't what I mean, and you know it."

"I love the bottom of the ocean, Mom." He prodded the creature. Startlingly it leapt from the chart table and crashed against the tank. He picked it up. "But conchs? You're right, they're a pain in the butt." He glanced at her. "I'll tell you one thing about *this* little bastard, Mom."

"Yes?"

"He may not *want* to," he said softly, his eyes steady on hers. "But to live his life, he has to come out of his shell."

On the bulkhead a clock struck four times: *Ding, ding . . . ding, ding. . . .*

She swallowed. "Meaning?"

He tossed the conch back in the tank, smiled, and squeezed her close. "Meaning it's time for chow."

Rico Lomas leaned back in the creaking old swivel chair in the office of his nightclub.

He was a slender young man with a thick neck from pumping iron, and soft brown eyes and black hair that fell in curly locks over his collar. The eyes could turn rock-hard in a moment. He knew this and used it happily when he could.

It was all a matter of presence. His grandfather had taught him that at his knee. Power, macho, *cojones* . . . you acted the part and became it.

He stared at the big man sweating before him. He tried to hide his scorn and anger behind a facade of sadness.

"You missed el Inglés? Newcombe? On Kingston Street? At the height of the sun? You are joking! *No es posible,*" he muttered. And then, in English, "There is no way!"

"Lo siento," muttered the assassin. "I regret it."

He would shortly regret it more, thought Rico. The old hit man's hair seemed to have grown whiter overnight. His snow-white mustache drooped, and his eyes were red and moist, as if he had been crying.

Lomas sighed. In this godforsaken outpost he got nothing but the dregs. Carlos Flores looked like exactly what he was: the family's oldest cocaine cowboy, unemployable for anything but murder, not bright enough for a *coquero* leader or even to use as a *traficante*.

Useless. And el Viejo—Rico's grandfather, el Gran Mafioso of Rancho San Marcos, in the lush coca regions of *los llanos*—knew it, and had sent him here.

The Old Man had a strange sense of humor, thought Rico, or was testing his grandson's guts. Well, he'd send him back or kill him here—let el Viejo chew on that.

Either way, the has-been before him was not fated to grow much older than he was.

"Jesus," he said again. "This Newcombe is my only problem between here and Great Inagua. He is trying to do on Whiskey Cay what I have done on Galleon. And you had him right between your sights. And *missed* him?"

"I am sorry, *amigo*. Just as I fired, Alejandro made the motor scooter move! It will not happen again."

Rico arose from his massive desk, which had been his grandfather's on the rancho. El Viejo had shipped it up the long Bahamian passage, probably hoping that some of his own business sense would rub off on his grandson if he used it.

It had arrived before Christmas on his father's freighter, which was carrying other cargo of considerably more value. Under seventeen tons of green bananas was thirty tons of marijuana—Santa Marta Gold. Under the marijuana lay a thousand kilos of coke, worth six million dollars once it reached the streets of Jackson Heights, New York.

Rico off-loaded the dope on Spanish Galleon Cay, which he'd virtually bought last year from Bahamian politicians. From there he shipped it, load by load, on the family's fleet of light planes to their airstrips in the

Okefenokee Swamp. But el Viejo's office furniture had stayed in Nassau.

He hated the desk: It smelled of the grass of *los llanos* and reminded him that his grandfather had started as little more than the *patrón* of a run-down cattle ranch. He wanted something shiny, modern, like the executives had in *Fortune* magazine.

But to get rid of the desk would be suicidal. Rico thought of himself as a brave man: race-car driver, sky diver, hotdogger on water skis. He had killed, to the delight of his grandfather, a National Policeman in a knife fight *mano à mano* in a cantina in San Juan de Gracia. But he would no more dare to throw out el Viejo's desk than jump without a chute.

He ground out his cigarette on the time-polished surface, wishing he had time to crush it out in the aging hit man's eyes.

Hiding his rage at the Kingston Street fiasco, he sauntered across his thick carpet to the one-way mirror overlooking his latest enterprise, the casino, grand bar, and restaurant of the Loma Bella Club.

He looked down at the restaurant. Slow night. He'd thought running the place would amuse him. He was bored because he was forbidden by his family to leave Nassau, except to go to Spanish Galleon Cay—because the U.S. Drug Enforcement Agency might grab him on any other island.

He had needed what amusement he could find, but the club was a drag.

His maître d' was making a play for one of the bunny-hopper drink girls, dressed in the Playboy Club costumes he'd inherited when he took the place over. The previous owner was an Italian mafia chieftain who had died trying to take a piece of his own action in the Bahamas.

What would he inherit from el Inglés? Nothing but

the aging Cessna, and he had plenty of those.

Peace of mind, perhaps . . .

He turned back to Carlos Flores. For the first time he noticed that beneath the white mustache the old man had buck teeth. He laughed.

"I have heard that on *los llanos* they call you the Big Rabbit."

Carlos understood little English, but he understood *that*. His neck grew stiff and his eyes turned cold. *"Sí, señor?* And who has told you that?"

Rico grinned. "They call you el Conejo Grande, I have heard."

"I asked you," Carlos muttered tersely, "who has *told* you that? Alejandro?

Alejandro was Rico's speedboat driver, valet, and bodyguard. He had been driving the Vespa when Carlos had missed.

The old man was breathing heavily. Rico hoped he would not have a heart attack: He wanted the family to kill him, as a lesson.

Rico shrugged. "Maybe Alejandro. Maybe just family gossip. El Conejo, though, it is."

"You would not dare call me that, *señor,* if you weren't your father's son. And the favorite of el Viejo, *hombre!* You would die!"

"We all die." Rico shrugged. "Some young, some old."

He pulled down the blind on the window and moved back. Suddenly he grabbed the old man, who towered over him, by the lapel.

"Why do they call you el Conejo Grande? Because you are afraid like a rabbit, old man?"

The old man glared at him but did nothing. Rico felt the thrill of power. He shoved him against the desk. "I think they call you that because you have a rabbit's guts!"

"My guts are as good as yours," growled Flores.

"No. I think you lost them. I am sending you back. Let el Viejo worry about you. I'll kill the Englishman myself."

"Not in broad daylight, *señor,*" the hit man reminded him shakily. "And that is how you say it must be done."

That was true. He wanted Hoagie Newcombe destroyed on Kingston Street in broad daylight, as a warning to the *traficantes* the Englishman was dealing with. He himself was too well known in the Bahamas to risk anything so wild.

The old man was sweating for his life. "*Señor,* you must not send me back until I kill this man." He was genuinely scared. "I owe it to el Viejo, to your family."

Rico studied him. Carlos must have failed el Viejo once before and been sent here for a last chance.

"You missed before, somewhere," he guessed suddenly. "*No es verdad*?"

"No. Never."

He was lying. As Lomas studied him an idle rumor tugged at his memory. There had been a *coquero* guard, assigned a shipment of coca paste on the Santa Clara run, who had deserted the load and fled from battle when surprised by a Leopard force of drug agents the previous July. He had even ditched his gun.

An *old* guard, it was said, who had worked for el Viejo for years. Was this the man? Yes. Of course.

"Perhaps you did not miss," he conceded. "Worse! You ran from a fight?"

"No!"

"*Sí*, I think so."

And now, if he sent him back to el Viejo, Carlos would end up rotting in the bottom of some *campesino*'s well.

Not bad leverage. If Rico gave him another shot at

the Englishman, he wouldn't dare fail, for the alternative was death.

He had a sudden inspiration. Hoagie Newcombe flew in and out of Whiskey Cay a dozen times a week. He was a hell of a pilot too. Whoever owned Calypso Charters had the only permit to drop sky divers in the Bahamas: Rico had flown with Hoagie once.

If such a pilot crashed on a routine flight, on a bright sunny day, it would not fail to excite comment among the *traficantes,* the Prince George police, and the *Nassau Daily Tribune*.

Especially if they recovered the plane and found it full of holes.

He turned back to Carlos. "Hey, *hombre?"*

"Sí?" Carlos was watching him without much hope.

"You ever shoot down an airplane?"

The old man's eyes grew suddenly alive. "No, *señor.* Not yet."

"I think you should. Why not? *Por qué no?"*

Carlos crossed the room and grabbed his hand. For a moment Rico feared that he would kiss it. But he shook it firmly and looked into his eyes.

"Indeed, *señor,"* he said, tears in his voice. *"Por qué no?"*

Ellen lay in her bed off Carla's studio. Somewhere, in Prince George Town, perhaps, a steel-drum band was playing calypso to a local song.

Out Masthead Bay, where dolphin play,
With mermaid come from U.S.A. . . .

She could hear *Neptune's Folly* worrying at her lines. Hoagie would have helped tonight. . . .

Pretty fish swimmin' 'round the freighter wreck . . .

Fishin' boat dancin' with the tarpon on deck . . .

Through the open door to Carla's studio, by the moonlight, she could see the covered iron sculpture. Carla said it was in a dormant state, like an embryo, and she didn't want anyone looking at it yet.

Conch all steamin' in the chowder pot . . .
Lobster screamin', 'cause de water hot.

Conch chowder . . . She had overcome her qualms and had some for dinner. It was delicious, fresh from the sea.

Onyx eyes staring flatly into hers . . .

She wished Brody had been there tonight.

Or Sean, his image.

Or Hoagie, with his laughing eyes . . .

Rich tourist, say mon, what the heck . . .
Gwine stay, gwine stay, on Whiskey Cay.

To stay? No, because she was not a rich tourist but a struggling dealer in other people's properties fighting to stay alive.

Michael had Carla, Carla had Michael, and both of them had Thea. But Sean was gone and she was an orphan mother.

The ocean breeze ruffled the chintz curtains.

At least, nothing could happen to any of them here. For the first time since the shark had murdered Sean, she truly slept.

Chapter 6

Michael Brody banked the tiny submersible to port, then to starboard. He peered through his face mask, hunting for a group of conch he had tagged there two weeks before. He was very uncomfortable.

The passing water tore at his mouthpiece, his wet suit clutched at his groin, and his butt itched. There was no way to scratch it short of parking the craft on the bottom, squirming out, and going at it free of the sub.

He hated the ancient submersible—and wet suits too. A year ago he'd have been diving bare-chested, bare-legged, often nude, with a double tank. The exertion kept him warm. Now, after an hour of sitting in the cockpit with the batteries doing the work, he was growing chilly despite the neoprene suit.

He was whining through crystal-clear water above a sandy bottom, forty feet below an aqua surface dimpled by the northeast trade winds.

The *Whine Bottle,* a Martak Dolphin wet-submersible he'd named for the noise its electric motor made, was only fourteen feet long and weighed only five hundred pounds. She was powered by seven twelve-volt golf-cart batteries. She had been donated to the Ministry of Fisheries by Woods Hole Institute in Massachusetts, which had bought dry-submersibles and needed her no longer. Now his fellow marine biologists, it was said, were cruising the bottom encased in Plexiglas without even getting their hair wet.

He'd begged his partner, Jake, to abandon the stupid

thing. The noise it made scared the conch, which had keen hearing, and started their ludicrous circus procession, lurching like a column of drunken elephants when he got within half a mile.

But Jake claimed that if they turned down anything from the Ministry, he'd lose their grant: "Use it or lose it, white boy. That's one thing you learn down here."

Whine Bottle was painted pink—where the paint still hung on—and had a bulbous nose and a tapered tail. Underwater she looked like a strawberry ice-cream cone on its side. Controlled by a joystick from a World War II Corsair fighter, she dove like a brick and climbed with all the enthusiasm of a carpenter's plumb held upside down.

He had learned to cruise her at precisely forty feet. Higher, she tended to rise; deeper, she wanted to dive.

She was suicidal. She had a top speed of three knots, hardly faster than he could swim. If he tried to push her faster, her batteries went dead. If he cruised her slower, she stalled like an airplane and headed in a graveyard spiral for the sand.

Someday he would leave her quietly on the bottom to perplex future underwater archaeologists and whales.

He looked at his watch. Another half hour. *Whine Bottle* had spooked every conch within a quarter of a mile.

He eased her north through a school of emerald topsail fish. A barracuda flashed by, intent on a feast. Finally, as he peered ahead, a brown shadow slowly came into focus, near a reef.

The *Leta* was a freighter, sunk by a U-boat in 1944. Despite swift currents through Masthead Cut, which continually filled and swept away sand from the gaping wounds in her hull, she had been a playground for divers for years. Then a party of four had been trapped below and drowned in '72.

Since then she had been an evil thing, placed off-limits by Government House.

Six hundred feet long, the hulk was home for a million fish. She made a reef with enough nooks and crannies to shelter anything up to a baby whale in size. If ever he got the guts or the time, he would like to explore it, though it had been stripped clean of souvenirs years ago.

"What are you doing down there?" Jake's voice came from a tinny acoustic speaker on the sub's dash. "Did you go on strike?"

Mike spoke clearly and carefully, for the water distorted voices through underwater acoustic mikes. "Not yet. But your stupid so-called submarine scared all our conch away."

"You're at that wreck! I can tell from the echo. Stop farting around and get some tagged."

Mike was getting tired of arguing with Jake, but he had to put up with it. A tight budget was a tight budget, and a Ph.D. candidate was only slave labor till graduation day.

He maneuvered the sub toward a sandy spot near the *Leta*'s hull. He turned off the battery. The *Whine Bottle* thumped to the bottom, sixty feet below the surface. He peered from the cockpit for conch. None.

Jake seemed to think the bottom was carpeted with them but claimed he had an ear problem and hardly ever dived.

Mike took his Nikon camera and strobe light, placed his hands on the top of his Plexiglas windshield, pushed, and floated up and out. He finally found a colony of pink conch and began to stalk them silently. If you didn't spook them, it was quite easy. He tagged them with markers for size and sex and shot their pictures using the strobe.

Conch divers who took them would mail the tags in

later, it was hoped. If the project could pinpoint spawning grounds and migration trends, correlated with temperature changes, they might save the great pink conch.

But results this year were spotty: No one bothered to mail in tags. No one in the Bahamas except Jake, Mike, and the Minister of Fisheries himself seemed to think the project was worth a damn.

And when the natives cleaned out the last conch, then it would be too late.

"Are you tagging them yet?" The voice was garbled.

"I'm separating the ladies from the gentlemen. Get off my back."

"Use a BPST on the biggest one you see."

The battery-powered sonic transmitter was Jake's baby: he had developed it and was very proud of it. It was the size of a small salami. You could pick up its signal through a transducer on the barge, or on *Neptune's Folly,* at almost a quarter of a mile. The BPSTs cost a hundred dollars to make, and you did not expend them lightly.

Jake recorded their heartbeats on the boat. Heartbeats, from a shell. Jake was a dreamer, a genius with a terrible temper, and as hard as the shells they tagged. He knew more about the motor systems of *Strombus gigas* than anyone on earth, but with the funding they had, his project was going to fold unless conch chowder suddenly turned out to be a cure for AIDS.

Now he wanted Mike to use their last BPST. Mike wondered whether the nearby wreck wouldn't distort the signal, but Jake knew acoustics better than he did, so he didn't question him.

He gently picked up the biggest conch. He squirted a glob of marine epoxy onto a flat spot on its shell and slapped a BPST in place. He pressed it down with his thumb and held it for five seconds. He hoped the conch, with his crazy leaping, wouldn't buck it off.

He tagged the rest of the colony with simple metal plates, which had the project's address on them. When he was through, he looked at his watch. He had ten minutes of bottom time left before he would risk the bends.

A brilliant green parrot fish flashed by. Another barracuda slithered past.

As always, he hated to leave the bottom before his time was up. Down here was a world he loved and understood. He was a part of it. For a moment he cavorted around; he was a creature of the sea, soaring and swooping through reefs and valleys, flying in a turquoise sky.

In a surge of power from his flippers, he swam off toward the wreck.

Neptune's Folly was tied to a barge permanently anchored in Masthead Bay. In her deckhouse, Jake McCay swore gently. He hunched closer to the loudspeaker, listening to the heartbeat of their latest conch: *Bop-bop . . . bop-bop . . . bop-bop . . .*

Something was wrong. He flipped a switch, displaying the signal on the screen of his old DEC computer.

He saw twin peaks rising, then two more, then a range of them marching, out of step, across the CRT. A *T* wave, a CRW, a *P*. . .

Unless this conch needed open-heart surgery, he was getting an echo he didn't want.

The heartbeat was useless. He knew instantly that he never should have made Michael waste their last transmitter so close to the wreck of the freighter.

There was nothing wrong with the BPST. The device, the pride of his heart, was doing its job. And the laws of physics were doing theirs. Water was a wonderful medium for sound: the acoustic waves from the conch's tiny transmitter were traveling beautifully, moving at four times the speed of sound in air, with nearly five times the range.

Picked up through a transducer near the keel, they told him that the conch was a large one, probably male.

If they anchored a sonobuoy near the wreck, and another near the barge, they'd be able to triangulate. Then they could track Papa Conch and his harem for months, until the battery failed. Long before that, he'd send Mike down to retrieve their BPST.

But the double signal, erratic and out of phase, told him that the signal was echoing off the freighter's hull. He couldn't read the pulse.

He pushed back from the table, thinking. Michael was his best friend—perhaps, outside of his girl, Louisa—the only one left, because his fellow islanders had ostracized him since he'd hired a white.

And maybe they were right. Whites, even Mike, must surely hate to take orders from the seed of their forebears' slaves.

Jake knew that he had hired a brilliant student but a poor employee. Mike thought the minuscule wages the project paid their deckhands—William and Clarence—were barbarous and didn't hesitate to say so.

Clarence and William, happy to be working at all, had so far only smiled. Their own solution would have been to fire Mike and split his salary, but the last thing the underfunded project needed was a shop steward.

Now he considered whether to order Mike to reclaim their device from the conch. Mike could be a stubborn man, did not suffer mistakes gladly, and hated to redo work.

Besides, he was probably getting cold on the bottom.

The death of his brother had shaken him, and he was worried about his mother. Today, of all days, was no time to push him too hard.

Maybe Papa Conch would migrate, with his harem, away from the freighter's plates?

The *bop-bop . . . bop-bop . . .* was growing fainter. He turned up the volume. It did no good at all. Perhaps the conch had moved to the other side of the freighter, where they'd never get a fix.

Still, the temptation to let it ride, in the careless island way, was almost overwhelming.

No! He hadn't fought his way to a Ph.D. from a stilted shack in the canebrake by letting things slide. Mike would have to swallow the bullet and do it all over again.

He picked up the microphone. He mouthed his words distinctly; it took months to learn to speak understandably on underwater acoustic devices, and half the time the voices came through wrong.

"Michael, mon, you're damn well not going to like this, but . . ."

He told him to remove the device. There was a long silence, and for a moment Jake feared that he had finally torn their fragile bond.

When Mike spoke, it was as if from the bottom of a distant well. His voice was garbled and indistinct, but Jake heard no anger at all.

"Okay, Jake, I think you're right."

Jake arose from the chart table. He stepped on deck, into the bright Bahama sun. He stretched, smiling. The world was good.

He'd get Michael his Ph.D. if it killed him.

When Mike got the order, he was already in the shadow of the wreck. The parrot fish had led the barracuda through a porthole high above. The big conch, under its sudden burden, had lurched across the sand, followed by its friends and family. It was heading for the *Leta*'s hull.

Quickly he spiraled downward, hearing his breath in the regulator, quieting it as much as he could, in a cloud of bubbles climbing to the shards of light above.

The tidal current in Masthead Cut was flooding, as if the whole of the South Atlantic were trying to enter the Caribbean through it. The conch leapt and bumped against the hull. Mike saw sand swirling past the freighter's mortal wound. Ordinarily the torpedo hole was hidden under sand, but today there was an opening, easily large enough for a conch, and perhaps for a full-grown man. The conch leapt toward it. A hundred dollars disappeared inside the rusting hull.

The hell with the ghosts of the merchant seamen, from the flaming days of war. The hell with the other divers, too, and the edict of Government House.

The current swept him by, but he turned and fought back. He grabbed at a jagged, rusted plate, and pulled himself inside.

All was suddenly quiet. He was in a vast gallery. Beams of turquoise light shone in from portholes high above. Dimly he saw a curving, varnished staircase leading high above. Livid schools of damselfish, clown fish, and butterfish darted everywhere. A bright blue sergeant major peered into his faceplate and flashed away in flight. A firemouth chichild with a gorgeous crimson belly nudged his arm and would not leave. He waved it aside, his attention on the conch.

The creature was leaping across the jumbled wreckage to a counter with a grille like a cashier's window. It disappeared under a jumbled mass of springs and leather that had once been a couch.

He didn't like the current outside, and the hole might close again. The salon was a fine aquarium, but he didn't want to drown here, as the others had. Time to go.

A strange and lonely thumping stopped him, as if

someone were signaling him from behind the counter.

He swam to the counter and grasped it, peering out from behind his mask. A watertight door was banging in the current. Above it was a tarnished plaque: PURSER'S OFFICE. Rusted crowbar scratches showed him that someone had tried to pry it open long ago but failed.

The latches that dogged it closed and made it watertight were still intact, but the sea and its salt had succeeded where man had not, for finally it had been a rusted hinge that had given way, and now the door hung all askew, aping the sweep of the tide.

Perhaps an unsuccessful break-in by the party of divers who had died here? But local scuba divers hired by the Ministry of Tourism had found their bodies far from here, in a forward passageway. It was said on Whiskey Cay that the first of them to die had been a woman, lost in a labyrinth of passageways forward, and that her husband had gone after her, and then another diver, and then the last.

Their lights had failed while they swam through the maze, and they had panicked and drowned when their tanks ran out.

Creak . . . thump . . . The door closed, opened, closed, opened, with just enough room for a man to inch through. Not *this* man, though. . . .

He was suddenly terrified at what might be behind the door. He glanced at his watch. At sixty feet, his time was up. He'd be lucky if he didn't get the bends; it would be fine therapy for his mother's fears of diving if he ended in a Nassau decompression tank, writhing on the floor.

As calmly as he could, he swam to the hole in the hull. The sand was building again, and as he squirmed free of the ship, the current caught him and he barely made the sub.

He climbed aboard *Neptune's Folly* and told Jake

they had lost their last transmitter in the wreck.

"Damn! What do we do now?"

"Wait until he comes out, I guess."

Jake went to get a beer.

It was ten A.M., Carla Brody was deep into her work, and everything was going wrong. The trip to Amity had delayed her, her deadline was coming fast, and the metal was fighting her.

The blue-white flame of her welder's arc shone faintly through the thick glass of her mask. The smell of ozone was heavy in her studio, and sparks jetted off like meteors.

The view through the glass never gave her any sense of the whole. She was like a blind woman examining an elephant. She cut the arc and threw back her helmet. The bead of the weld was perfectly symmetrical: not a defect. Now a new arc of steel swept outward from the trunk of her grand design.

Masterpiece or junk? She was never sure. Was Cellini? Bologna? Verrocchio? She had no idea. There were no signposts in sculpture.

What guided her was a sixth sense of too-muchness. No critic had ever attacked her for being ornate. She slapped everything on and subtracted from that, cutting and grinding, toward the end, in a shower of shooting stars. Seldom, during this final phase, did she add.

Some days she was indecisive, but usually she was unerring in her sense of what was not needed. Not today, with her rebellious iron and steel.

She glanced out toward the water. Ellen was doing the bay windows on the main house, but Carla was damned if she'd feel guilty about that.

Some on the island, white and black, attacked her sculpture, she knew, especially since she'd got the government commission to sculpt for the town's main square.

To many she was a Radcliffe princess, a goof-off, using art as her excuse to avoid the kaffeeklatsch. They thought her welding was a refuge from more tedious housewifely things.

They were wrong. It was filthy, brutal work. Her current source of steel was a wrecked Cuban fishing boat on the sun-baked southern end of the island. She had cut it there, heaved it into Mike's trailer, and hauled it home behind the jeep.

There was always grinding dust in her golden hair. Her eyes—when she looked at the arc too long—felt like sandpapered green marbles.

Her forearms had come to rival Martina Navratilova's, from the pig iron she lifted all day long, but welding was not tennis, it was work.

She *had* to sculpt, and not for art alone. Her sales in a Nassau art boutique paid half the rent. If the Fisheries Ministry didn't kick through with another grant for the Conch Project, she would end up supporting Thea, Mike, Jake, and their deckhands, Clarence and William, with the point of her welding arc.

She pulled off her gloves, tossed her leather apron on a chair, covered her work, and wandered out of the studio and back to the house. Ellen was sweeping the glass with long, furious strokes of a squeegee. She was strong, and the effort might help her find her way back to the land of the living. Still, every time she stopped, she seemed dazed.

Anyway, removing the salt spray from the windows added a fourth dimension to the view. "Ellen, if I'd known that you did windows, we'd have had you down months ago."

Wrong. Patronizing, and it brought up Sean's death somehow.

Ellen turned and smiled faintly. "You should see the dirt on mine in Amity."

Ellen's hair was tied back, and she looked better, as if she'd slept the night before. They smiled at each other, each unsure of where to take the conversation next.

"I'm so damn grateful, Ellen. I mean it."

"I'm grateful to be here. Besides, you're busy," Ellen said. "You have a deadline. I can't just baby-sit." She put down the squeegee and looked into Carla's eyes. "Carla, I'm a klutz about art. But I just *have* to ask you."

"Go ahead."

Ellen's cheeks turned pink. "Carla, what *is* it?"

"The statue?" Carla's laughter pealed across the yard. She squeezed Ellen closely. "Do you know you're the first one with the guts to ask, outside of Thea?"

"Then *what?* What is it, please?"

Carla shrugged. "It's like a baby in the womb. So far I just don't know. And the time grows nigh. I hardly get to talk to Michael anymore. There's just so much to do. And he's diving all day long."

"Does his diving bother you?" Ellen asked suddenly. "Spending so much time on the bottom?"

She shrugged. "Dishpan body? It doesn't show."

Ellen smiled faintly. "That isn't what I meant. The bends and nosebleeds and . . . what do they call it? Embolism?" She blushed. "I'm sorry. I shouldn't interfere."

"He's a big boy now, Ellen, isn't he?"

An unspoken answer, *And so was Sean*, hung in the morning air.

Carla cocked her head and studied her, lightly rubbing the forefinger of her right hand across her lips. A beautiful woman, she thought. Someday she'd like to do her in bronze: bronze, durable and strong.

And burning now, somehow, with enduring rage at something. The sea? Fate? Life?

"You're a pretty woman, Ellen Brody. And Hoagie thinks so too."

"Yes," said Ellen gravely. "Yes, I know."

Then she turned back to the windows once again.

Michael came back from his afternoon dive and tied the sub to the barge. Huge anvil-shaped clouds were gathering to the north, and he heard a roll of thunder. There was a squall brewing on the boat too. William, their tall "first mate," was staring at the deck, as if he wished he were somewhere else. Clarence, their jet-black deckhand, whose smile could tear out your heart, was glowering at the ocean.

Jake, shirtless, huge biceps gleaming with sweat, emerged from the deckhouse. "Another transmitter's gone," he said with a growl. "I haven't heard a peep from Conch Thirteen."

"Meaning?" asked Michael softly, stripping his wet suit off one arm. He kept his eyes steady on Jake's; damned if he'd let him browbeat him in front of the crew.

"Meaning the bloody BPST fell off him," Jake boomed, "and you only tagged him yesterday."

"I don't suppose his battery went dead?"

"In twenty-four hours? Not likely, now is it?"

"Maybe you need another brand of epoxy," suggested Mike, working out of his neoprene pants. "You travel cheap, you pay."

A clap of thunder sounded. Christ, it was hot and sultry, and he knew that Jake was about to explode.

"Or another brand of diver," muttered Jake, "who'll let the damn stuff set!" He picked up the underwater writing board that Mike had tossed on the compressor. "Let's see your tally, mon."

The board had rubbed against his wet suit, and the grease pencil writing had smudged. Jake shook his head. "If this is how your thesis reads, God help you at Boston U."

"If yours got by, mine ought to."

Michael instantly regretted saying it. He had to keep his temper, or else the ship, his Ph.D. program, and the whole conch project would sink without a trace. Whatever had happened topside, Clarence looked as if he were about to grab the nearest conch knife and make a run on Jake. It was a good thing the director had a build like Leonard Spinks.

"Michael, this tally sucks. Where are they all?"

"Go look yourself. I did my best."

"A blind mon could find more conch on a mountain," muttered Jake.

"Yeah, but you'd still bitch." His own temper was unraveling. He shook the water off his arms and watched William and Clarence finish securing the mini-sub. "What's the matter with you, anyway? Aren't you making it with Louisa anymore?"

"I'll handle Louisa," muttered Jake. "You take care of Carla and her blowtorch."

"What do you mean by that?"

"We're competing for the same government dollars. Do the Bahamas need more conch, or statues by a white *artiste* from Boston?"

Mike threw down his wet suit and advanced, fists clenched. "Leave my wife out of this, 'Dr.' McCay!"

Suddenly he was a yard off the deck, feet swinging helplessly. Jake lumbered with him into the deckhouse and sat him on the chart table. He raised his finger to his nose and waved it. His eyes blazed.

"Mon, don't you *never* put that 'doctor' into quotes. Ah come out the bloody jungle to get that damn degree, no white Yankee goddamn skin diver gonna 'trow it in de sea!"

Mike stared at him. Awed, he murmured, "I never heard you talk that jive before."

Jake's face relaxed minutely. He seemed ashamed. "Yah, mon? Well, you never tried to put me down before."

Mike's lips twitched. "You *rhymed,* you know?"

Jake jerked a thumb toward his heart. "All us islanders bleed in rhyme."

Mike stuck out his hand. "Sorry, Jake."

Jake struck his hand in a high-five. "My fault, old man. Bad day on *Neptune's Folly.* Ministry turned down my supplemental grant. Clarence wants a raise—"

"Needs one, you capitalistic prick. He's got four kids, and one of them is sick."

"You bloody Commie!" Jake smiled. "You know, mon, there are plenty local citizens who think I should train Clarence to dive. Too many whites on this boat taking food from black babies, spending time writing Ph.D. theses at Government House expense, drawing big salaries."

"Six hundred bucks a month? Jesus Christ!"

"I can get *six* guys out of the palm groves for that. Don't forget it when you're down there like a tourist goofing off. Want a beer?"

"Can I get down to drink it, or do I have to stay up here?"

Jake grinned, and it was like the dawn breaking. He dived into the boat's icebox and came up with two bottles of St. Pauli Girl. They clinked the necks together.

"Fair winds and following seas," said Jake.

"Merry Christmas, Jacob," murmured Mike. Rain drummed on the deckhouse, and the stupid squall had passed.

Chapter 7

On Christmas Eve the aging newscaster sat back in his three-thousand-dollar Pompanette fishing chair on the stern of his sparkling forty-foot Bertram, *Prime Time*.

He trailed a hundred dollars' worth of Ande tournament-grade one-hundred-thirty-pound test from a Murray Brothers pole that he'd bought the previous week with a Penn reel for fifteen hundred dollars. Two similar poles nodded from a rack to starboard, in case his own broke or his wife cared to take the seat beside him.

The *Prime Time*, out of Fort Lauderdale, Florida, droned through swells of molten glass. She was heading due east, under her skipper's hand, halfway between Miami and Cat Cays at the edge of the Great Bahama Bank.

The newscaster, whose face had been proved in a *Time* poll to be better known to Americans than the Vice President's, lolled in his chair. Idly he raised the tip of the pole, lowered it, raised it again. Boring.

He wondered what his wife—an unsuccessful model half his age—was doing below. Looking for more booze? Suspecting? No. She probably thought she had cleaned out the boat at the Fort Lauderdale dock. To her knowledge there was not an ounce of alcohol left aboard, except beer—which he no longer drank because it fattened his face—for the crew.

He'd pulled the bait-and-switch. He'd deliberately hidden a bottle of Chivas in a locker under the starboard bunk in the crew's quarters, and another in the radar on the bridge. She'd found and removed them both.

But those bottles had been merely bait, to give her something to chew on. It was like writing an anti-network story into the nightly news, to distract the content editor from an item he wanted more. Or, in the old days, leaving a deliberate body-count mistake for the censors in Saigon so they'd miss a story on dope use among the grunts.

He merely had been chumming the waters, and his poor damn wife had bit.

His real cache lay in the bait tank, under swarms of flashing blue-green dorados. The Chivas was in Pepsi Cola bottles. She hated the feel of squirming fish—he or his skipper always had to bait her hooks—and he'd known she'd never dip in there to look.

He tried to remember how many bottles were left. He couldn't; his mind wouldn't compute in the sun.

Last night at a wineless dinner, swinging at anchor off Elliott Key, they'd watched his holiday replacement, Charles M. Holycroft, on the tube.

The son of a bitch was after his job: there was no doubt. He'd opened, all boyish charm and naïveté, with a wide-eyed story of administration corruption. He'd wrapped, with tears in his eyes, on a blue-eyed eight-year-old bringing up abandoned siblings in a filthy Brooklyn slum.

"We'll have to watch his ratings," his wife said. "He didn't fluff a line."

"Meaning I *do?*"

She patted his hand. "Well . . ."

All right, last week he *had* blown two. And the studio was talking about too much sauce in the makeup room. Screw 'em, let 'em talk. He needed a drink. He headed aft, for the bait tank.

"Look," she'd called. "You know? You'll wipe him when you're back."

He never should have come. The minute you let up, some kid five years out of broadcast school was snapping at your heels. Not even a goddamn newsman, just an actor reading news.

Standing in the moonlight, he'd belted half a fifth and chased it with half a box of Clorets.

It was all her fault. Seeing baggy eyes where there were none and hearing a husky voice—Christ, he'd had a cold—she'd only dragged him down to dry him out.

Now he sat back in his fishing chair, well sun-blocked against ultraviolet: "Can't risk skin cancer, can we? Or even nasty little wrinkles by our mouth?" He wore glasses so dark, he could hardly see: "Eyes were a little red on the special, remember?"

He looked at the sun. It was sinking.

Mast over the yardarm: cocktail hour. She had him dead sober at cocktail hour! On his own frigging boat!

On the flying bridge he heard his crewmen opening beers. He craned his neck around and stared accusingly up at his skipper, a tanned, lanky cracker who was probably banging his wife.

There had been a day when the kid would not have dared open a beer without offering him one. Now he shrugged regretfully and turned back to the wheel.

Cowed and whipped, the both of them, by a pair of long, slim legs.

He tried to remember how many Pepsi Cola bottles remained at the bottom of the tank.

Three family-size bottles when they'd cast off from the Fort Lauderdale dock? Okay, he'd finished one the day before yesterday, before dinner, while he fished. Then another half the day before, then the half a fifth that night. A few belts before breakfast, while she slept.

A slug or two while she fixed his lunch—no, more

—he'd finished that one too. A few after-lunch drinks for luck, while he baited his hooks. Foggily he tried to add it all up. Was there only half a bottle left?

And three full days to go!

He began to shake. They'd have to pull in to Cat Cays or Nassau! He'd tell her he had to call the network, and didn't want every yachtsman in the Atlantic listening in.

And send the skipper up Bay Street on a whiskey run. He set his pole in its holder, moved to the bait tank.

He peered into the swirling water, circulated by a pump. The beautiful emerald dorados shimmered among the bubbles. He squinted through his glasses. It was dark in the tank, and he couldn't see. Suppose the last bottle was gone?

Breathing hard, he dug into the dorados. They panicked and thrashed up a foam. He began to scoop them out, frantic with fear, digging through the school to see. Soon he was shoveling with both hands, throwing them over the stern. He heard them splashing in the wake.

Oh, God—oh, God! Had he drunk it all?

Only a few fish remained. He yanked off his glasses; he had to see.

A flash of red in a corner of the tank. He sagged in relief. He plunged his arm in, up to the armpit, and pulled out the dripping bottle.

Pepsi Cola hits the spot,
Twelve full ounces, that's a lot. . . .

Thank God, thank God. . . .

The bottle was half full. He cradled it in his arms, turning his back to the cabin. He took a long, shuddering breath and looked over the stern toward the setting sun. He had seen too many sunsets, it was true, but old age and treachery triumphed over youth and virtue every time.

He lifted his bottle. "Merry Christmas, sun! And Happy goddamn New Year, and many happy returns!"

He twisted off the cap and froze, studying the wake.

The dorados were following the boat, leaping and skipping as if they missed their tank. His eyes narrowed incredulously. Something was following *them*. Out of the glittering wake a form was rising. It grew in the golden path, dark and menacing.

All at once, from the swirling foam, a huge snout rose. Majestically it climbed and became a mouth, filled with massive teeth. It became white, ghostlike, soaring higher, until it blotted out the sun, and suddenly he was in shadow. He glimpsed an eye, like an ebony plate, staring into his.

Gracefully the great white shark pirouetted, twisted, and fell into the wake, sending up thirty-foot sheets of water.

And then there was nothing.

He peered astern. Nothing at all.

The sun was sinking. The wake was calm. He found himself leaning over the transom, shivering.

He had fished for forty years, in all the oceans of the world. He had never seen a great white shark in the tropics. This one was past belief.

It had not happened. Then why was his shirt so wet? Because he had plunged his arms into the tank. Why had the dorados chased the boat? Why not? What did a bait fish know?

Then what the hell? Had he seen it or not? Where had it come from, where had it gone?

All at once he knew.

He glared at the bottle. The great white lived in there.

And lizards, probably, and dragons. Pink elephants,

too, if he kept it up, and monsters past belief.

He screwed back the top and hurled the bottle at the setting sun. It resurfaced and bobbed for a while, and soon he could not see it anymore.

He felt his wife beside him. "What happened? What was that splash?"

He turned and looked into her childish face.

"Nothing, dear, nothing at all."

The Christmas tree was fake and the ornaments were glitzy, but Ellen could feel the love in the room. Carla —taking a day off from her "torture chamber" for the first time since she'd returned from Amity—wore a Santa Claus hat with a tassel that dangled over her face. Thea was her elf, picking presents from the pile.

Thea's main present, a red tricycle from her mother and daddy, held center stage. Ellen's gift, a doll that talked and wet and probably drove a car, sat on the tricycle's seat.

Jake and Louisa were cross-legged on the floor, drinking, as Mike put it, the only decent eggnog south of Miami.

Ellen was on her second eggnog and quite relaxed. She was recounting Mike's lurid past to Thea.

"Once he locked himself in the bathroom and your grandfather had to get the ladder and climb through the window."

"I didn't do it on purpose, Thea," Mike said comfortably.

"He was old enough to know better," Ellen said mischievously. "Four, just like you."

"You know I'm almost six, Grandma," said Thea judiciously. "So you're just teasing me."

"Smart kid," said Jake. "She must have gotten it from Carla."

"Talented too." Carla smiled, brought her own head

to Thea's, and touched their brows. "You ought to see her finger painting on our brand-new clean bedroom wall."

"Mommy spanked me," Thea said proudly. "She really did! It hurt."

Carla's eyes met Ellen's. For an instant the two were communicating perfectly. Carla blushed because Ellen knew: Carla had neglected her daughter so badly for the statue this week that even a spanking felt good.

Carla's eyes misted. She swooped down, lifted Thea, and held her close. "I didn't mean to hurt you, dumpling," she murmured. "And afterward I cried."

Thea squirmed loose. "I didn't." She headed for a package, squinted at the card, and deciphered: "M-I-K-E." She picked it up and handed it to her father.

"Did you ever spank Daddy?" Thea asked Ellen as Mike opened his gift from Louisa and Jake.

"His father paddled him once or twice," she murmured.

"And Uncle Sean?"

Her mind went back. It was just before the last regatta. Sean, nine, dazzled by a yellow Ferrari, had hitched a ride with the local mafioso, a summer visitor named Moscotti. The younger son of the police chief, riding with a *hood!* She had seen him getting out. As Sean escaped to the garage, the gangster—whose own son she had welcomed, against severe parental pressure, into Sean's Cub Scout den—had warned her that children should not ride with strangers.

She had stood, face blazing, as the Ferrari roared away. Then it all came out.

"Sean!" she shrieked.

Sean appeared at the garage door, carrying the bait bucket he used to feed Sammy the Seal. He was scared. He knew that she had seen the car—and him. His face went white when he saw hers. It was probably the worst thing he had done in his life. He let out a questioning little bleat.

"Come here!" she cried. *"Now!"*

He sidled across the lawn, terrified. "I . . ."

She met him at the side of the porch. "Don't you ever, ever, *ever*—"

"I *forgot,*" he said, whining. "And *you* let Johnny Moscotti in the Cubs—"

She slapped him, hard, like a housewife in a Naples slum. He had never been slapped in his life, and he stared at her in silent shock.

"I'll tell Daddy!" he yelled suddenly. Then he whirled and went pounding to the rear of the house, heading for the mud flats bordering Amity Sound.

"Sean!" she called after him weakly. "Honey, come back!"

But he was gone.

And now, gone forever . . .

She came back to the present. "Spank Uncle Sean, Thea?" Her voice choked. She shook her head. She must not cry on Christmas morning, not in front of Thea. "Not really . . ."

Everyone was looking at her. Desperately she grabbed at a straw and pointed toward a red package under the tree. It was for Thea, from Sean, sent a month before. She knew it because she had wrapped it for him; everything he wrapped looked like a lunchbag, so he claimed.

"The red one," she whispered. "It's from him."

She ran and got it. "From Uncle Sean," she announced proudly. A silence fell, and Jake became very busy cleaning up the Christmas wrapping mess.

The present from Sean was a beach pail. On it was painted RAINBOW BRIGHT, a cheery little girl with orange hair, a star sparkling on her cheek. She was framed by a rainbow. In the bucket was a tiny shovel, a pair of little heart-shaped dark glasses—awful ones, like Elton John used to wear—a straw hat, and a pair of beach sandals.

Thea looked up excitedly. "Grandma? We can use it on the sand castle on the beach!"

"Yes, Thea," Ellen said softly, "we certainly can."

Maybe Sean would seem even closer when they did.

Chapter 8

To Ellen it seemed strange to be kneeling on the beach the day after Christmas. "We'll dig the moat so deep," she warned, "we'll have to swim to the castle."

"You're silly," Thea said.

Carla had gone to Nassau for a new cutting torch, and Ellen had Thea to herself all day long. Now she was helping Thea and Deenie build a seaside fortress. Deenie was one of Clarence's innumerable children, older than Thea and a combination baby-sitter/playmate.

Ellen was unused to the blazing winter sun. Against her granddaughter's tanned tummy, her own forearm was as white as a ghost's. The sand beneath them was as warm as it was on Amity Beach in August.

She packed a final shovel of sand into Thea's Rainbow Bright bucket.

"Silly? No. This is for real. It'll be a real castle, you'll be the princess on the conch-shell balcony, and you'll have lords and ladies bringing you your tea and Ding Dongs, and there'll be a big parade, and you'll ride in an enormous carriage the size of Romeo's Cadillac, pulled by six white mice with ribbons in their fur."

Thea and Deenie giggled, and Thea rested a sandy little hand on Ellen's shoulder. "You're *really* silly, Grandma."

The sand castle already stood as tall as Thea. There had been a long discussion on site selection. She'd warned Thea that if they built too close to the water, it would be wiped out at high tide.

Deenie had looked puzzled, as if she'd never heard of high tide, and she and Thea had insisted that they build it close to the water.

"Because this is where we found Peeper," said Thea. "The castle is his meromial. Like we had for Uncle Sean."

"Me*mor*ial," corrected Ellen, hiding the grief that his name invoked. "Who's Peeper?"

"A doctor bird," proclaimed Deenie. "He blew all de way up from *Jamaica,* las' hurricane we had."

"And we made him well, and he went home," said Thea proudly. "Me*mor*ial!"

High tide had come, and desperately they'd panicked, dug a moat, and built an outer wall, but the kids were right: The wavelets had come only a few feet up the beach, had lapped at their wall, and were receding already.

Very strange. Even the tides seemed to spare these islands, basking in precious sunlight. Everything else that the ocean touched, it destroyed.

"In Amity," she mused, "it would all be wrecked by now."

Lips pursed, Thea dug at the moat. "Is that what happened to Uncle Sean?"

"No."

"What *did?*"

She felt her body grow rigid. She had promised herself that she would not lay her fears of the ocean on the child, who was always splashing with her friends in the gentle water, seemingly unattended.

But Thea was watching her, so she had to answer somehow. "Well . . . he went out on a boat and he never came back."

Deenie nodded wisely. "My daddy, he goes out in a boat. Someday, might be, he gwine stay away."

"No." Ellen smiled. "Your daddy will always come back."

"Maybe Uncle Sean's still there!" Her granddaughter looked out at the cove. "Maybe *he'll* come back!"

"I don't think so," Ellen said, choking.

"He *could,*" insisted Thea. "He could come right in Masthead Cove."

"Papa Jacques on island now," said Deenie suddenly.

"I know," said Ellen, surprised. "We brought him here."

"You pay him, might be he do you *wete mort nan dlo,*" suggested Deenie.

"What's that?" asked Ellen uncomfortably.

"He make *bamboche*—like a dance," the child said knowingly. "Then the spirit, ma'am, he hear this, yes? And comes back from waters of the dead."

Ellen stared at her. *"What?"*

"That what Papa Jacques say," Deenie said, shrugging. "I don't know. He makin' my sister well. In Haiti he was a great doctor, ma'am."

Ellen suddenly envisioned Papa Jacques's saucer eyes, as black as night. His presence seemed very much there, and she did not like it.

She got up swiftly. "Thea, you want to come wading with me?"

Her granddaughter looked at the castle and shook her head. "I'm not finished yet."

Unhappily Ellen skirted the wavelets, moving toward the next cove. A squall line was building castles and golden spires to the west in the afternoon sun. The water was warm on her feet. She found a conch shell, vacated. Presumably the owner had gone to lunch in someone's chowder bowl.

She looked up at the house. It was quiet without the incessant hiss of Carla's cutting torch. The mysterious statue under its cover resembled nothing she had ever seen and seemed to grow taller and slimmer by the day.

She had to get back to Amity. She loved it here, but she was an extra mouth to feed. Michael would never let her pay her way, and Brody's tiny pension would hardly help if he did. Even doing windows and baby-sitting, she was just another drag.

If she went back to Amity and got the Taylor house through escrow, maybe she could return next year for a long, happier stay.

She wished she'd seen Hoagie Newcombe again. Maybe Michael had scared him off.

All at once she heard a droning from out of the west. She looked toward Nassau. Under the rolling thunderheads a little silver plane took shape, flying low.

It flashed into the scalloped crescent of the cove and bore toward the beach she was on. The throb of the propeller lessened, then quit. The cove was silent, except for the whisper of the slipstream past the wings. The plane banked and spiraled downward, obviously heading for her.

"You nut," she murmured. As the plane straightened out along the beach she saw Hoagie in the cabin, flipping her a wave.

Then the engine coughed, caught, and rose to a crescendo. A wing flailed at the sky, and he was suddenly waltzing over the lagoon. He climbed high beyond the reef, flung the plane on its back, and dived, inverted, for the water.

"Oh, God—oh, no!" she breathed. She couldn't stand it if he crashed. At the very last moment the plane pulled out and tore across the lagoon. He worked the throttle as he passed, blasting her ears with the sound.

As he flew past the children in the next cove, she could see Thea and Deenie jumping up and down, waving like excited scarecrows at the sight. He skimmed

Masthead Point and disappeared toward the airstrip, wagging his tail like a dog.

Suddenly she saw Deenie grab at Thea, as if to stop her. Thea dodged her and ran for the bush in the direction in which he had flown. She was heading for the scrub pine on Masthead Point. Concerned, Ellen hurried back. Deenie was digging sullenly at the castle moat.

"Why did she run off like that?" demanded Ellen. "Where'd she go?"

"She jes' run off," mumbled Deenie. "I don't know."

"Come on. We're going to find her." She started toward the Point, slogging through the fine, white sand as quickly as she could.

They found Thea returning from the Point, on a trail through the scraggly scrub. She was whipping with a stick at the bushes and seemed angry.

Ellen took her hand. It was hot and moist. Thea didn't look well; she was pale beneath the tan. With Deenie holding Thea's other hand, they started toward the house.

"What did you run off for?"

"He dropped something for us. Didn't you see?"

She looked down at her granddaughter. "No, I didn't. Did he *really?*" She glanced at Deenie. The girl's black eyes darted away. What was going on?

"It was white," Thea piped up. "It fell down behind the hill." Thea looked up at Deenie. "And Deenie saw it too."

"No, *ma'am!*" Deenie shook her head. "She be fibbin'. She be lyin' through her mouth."

"No, I'm not," squealed Thea. "Grandma, I *am not!*"

Ellen squeezed her hand. "I'm sure you're not. And neither's Deenie." A tropical tern, as white as a scrap of paper in the wind, flashed overhead. "Maybe you saw a bird."

"It *wasn't* a bird," protested Thea. She seemed close to tears. "I saw it, and I ran up there, and a man took it away."

"A man?"

"A black man."

Deenie glanced up at Ellen, and Ellen caught a glint of fear. Without a word the little black girl flew off down the trail toward home.

"Now, what was *that* all about?" she muttered. Thea was tugging at her hand. Her tiny palm, which had been so warm on the beach, was freezing cold.

"Grandma?" she whined suddenly. "I'm scared. Pick me up?"

Ellen picked her up and held her close. "Scared, sweetheart? Of what?"

Thea shook her head and would not answer. A clap of thunder sounded, and the rain began to fall.

Before Ellen could get her home, she'd vomited three times.

Chapter 9

Ellen left Thea's room with Michael to have a council of war. Mike was trying to be cool, but his hands were trembling.

"You never," he muttered, "know how much you need a doctor on this godforsaken island until a child gets sick."

Scared as she was, she tried to reassure him.

"You and Sean had this kind of thing all the time when you were small. A fever and—"

"She doesn't have a temperature."

"Well . . ." Ellen realized that she was smiling much too brightly, but she could not seem to stop. "That can happen too." She reminded him that he'd got sick once a year, like clockwork, around Christmas. "Sometimes you'd get delirious and say the damnedest things. Remember in the sun room? We thought that you were dying, and it wasn't anything at all."

Her mind went back to Amity, before the second shark, to a summer morning in the sun room where they ate. Brody had finally allowed Michael to take the diving class Michael had worked and skimped for all summer long. For his birthday Brody had even bought him a wet suit.

An hour before the ocean checkout for the class, Michael had become deathly sick. Now he was groaning on the wicker couch, blaming it on Sean, who had insisted on her feeding everyone a mackerel he'd caught off Town Dock the night before.

"If it was the fish," Sean wanted to know, "why aren't I sick too?"

She could feel the heat of the sun room. The bells pealed from the church, providing Brody, who had quit going, with his usual Sunday guilt.

"It was the fish, all right," Mike moaned. "It was your stupid little minnow—"

"Mike," warned Brody, "knock it off!"

Mike tried to get up, but another cramp seized him and he lay back, shivering. "Why'd Sean have to catch the frigging thing?" He groaned and glared at Ellen. "And why'd you have to cook it? For *breakfast,* for crying out loud! There wasn't even enough there to eat, just enough to poison everybody!"

Sean defended his catch. "It was a regular-sized fish. And it didn't poison me or Dad or Mom!" Sean stalked off, head held high.

She shook down the thermometer and put it into Michael's mouth. She took his pulse: eighty. He asked what time it was. Brody looked at his watch. "Nine-twenty."

Mike sat up as if galvanized. The thermometer fell from his mouth. "Nine-twenty? I got to be at Town Dock at ten! Suited up!"

Gently Brody pushed him back, and Ellen reinserted the thermometer. "You aren't going anywhere, Cousteau. Not in the ocean, anyway—with cramps, *already.*"

She took out the thermometer. Normal. High pulse but no temperature? She looked into his eyes.

He was sick, all right, but it wasn't Sean's fish or her cooking. He was scared of his first ocean dive.

He had sneaked out when his dad had left and made that dive, and afterward the terror had apparently left *him*—clamped its teeth into *her* guts—and now he earned his living at the bottom of the sea.

Was Thea sick with fear of something too?

She found that she was pacing like a tigress.

"Sit down, Mom, please," begged Michael. "I'm calling Dr. Stanford down on Crooked Island."

She sat down in a rattan chair, then got up immediately. She looked toward the dock. Clarence and William were tying up *Neptune's Folly* in the pouring rain. The boat had been forced back by the storm, thank God, or she'd be here with Thea all alone. Carla had phoned that she was trapped by the weather in Nassau; she would spend the night with her agent and his wife.

Mike was in the kitchen now, on the silly, hand-cranked phone.

But Dr. Stanford had left Crooked Island the previous night. He was somewhere off on an island they called Great Exuma, and Michael was suddenly calling Hoagie for his plane. Then the truly bad news came: Calypso Charters was grounded by the storm.

The thunder arose, the shutters chattered in the wind, and Ellen chattered, too; she couldn't seem to stop. "Michael, just because we're in the tropics doesn't mean it's something tropical. You still have flu and chicken pox, like everybody else."

"*I* didn't say it was tropical, Mom. But she's hardly been sick in her life."

"She probably caught a bug, Mike. Deenie said her sister's sick."

"Clarence's kids are *always* sick," Mike said. "Jake pays him zilch, and they don't eat right. Now, Mom, please!"

"Please what?" She blew a hair out of her face.

"Sit down. Relax." He took a breath. "Hoagie's coming over."

"I thought," she said, chiding him, "you said he'd get us shot."

"The cops say the guy must have been after somebody else. It was those tinted windows of Romeo's.

Hoagie's okay, I think. And I don't want to leave you alone."

"Where are you going?"

He hesitated and finally got it out. "Highbourne Cay. I'm borrowing the Island Commissioner's boat—"

Oh, God, it was Sean all over again. She tried to steady her voice. "Mike, it's blowing thirty knots out there and —"

"There's bound to be a doctor staying in one of the tourist hotels. So I'm going, Mom. I have to."

She braced herself, took a breath, and finally got it out. "You're right." She smiled. "Be careful?"

He kissed her and was gone.

She went back into Thea's room. The little girl was lying with her teddy bear, staring at the ceiling. Ellen felt her forehead for the tenth time in the last half hour. No fever still, but a fast, erratic pulse.

"Thea?" she whispered. The child did not move. There was more expression in the eyes of her teddy bear than in hers. Ellen turned the teddy facedown so she wouldn't have to look.

She seldom prayed, but now she did: Please God, don't take her too.

She rubbed a tiny hand for a long while, and finally the eyes closed and Thea seemed to sleep. She was easing her fingers away from the child's when she sensed someone in the room. It was Hoagie. She noticed for the first time how full his shoulders were, how trim his waist.

"If she isn't right when the weather clears," he murmured, "I'll fly her in to Nassau. So don't you fret and worry, luv, she's going to be all right."

She looked into his eyes. "Something frightened her on Masthead Point, after you flew by."

He tensed. "Frightened her? My plane?"

"No." She moved to the window and looked out at

the rain. The tropical night had slammed down like a curtain. "What did you drop, Hoagie?"

He stiffened. "Drop?"

"Thea saw you drop something."

"Oh." He hesitated. "Well, that was for you."

"For me?"

He nodded. "I had the worst dive-bombing record in the Argentine campaign."

She didn't know whether to believe him or not. "What was it?"

"A muumuu I found in a Madera Street boutique. So you wouldn't run out of clothes."

"Well, thanks. But you shouldn't have." She studied his face. "Especially since somebody took it."

He nodded. "I *saw* some blighter run out of the bush. Probably reckoned it was a *traficante* dropping dope." He shrugged. "So your muumuu's on some dusky maid in a bar on Kingston Street."

She moved back and looked down at Thea. "Hoagie, something awful's happening—it's *been* happening—and I don't know what it is. Now it's hit Thea too." She faced him. "Am I bad luck?"

"She'll be all right, Ellen. It's a thing that children do. . . ."

She glanced at him. "Do you have children?"

He was silent for a moment. "I had a daughter."

"Had?"

He only shrugged. "That's not our problem, is it? Thea is. And, no, you're not bad luck."

"I'm not sure you understand."

"Then tell me."

She told him of the sharks, and Brody's heart, and how Sean had died.

He nodded. "That *was* bad luck, but *you* aren't." He gazed away over the ocean. Thunder rumbled to the east. "Damn! If only I had deicers, I'd sneak under that stuff to Nassau and come back with some help."

"No. You mustn't take a chance."

They stood silently for a long, long while. "Luck always changes," he said finally, "at the tables and in life."

"Mine hasn't." She looked out at the water. "It's something I feel . . . a menace—since Brody helped kill the first shark. And then there was the other . . . as if we were under a curse." She shook her head. "Oh, hell! I must sound *crazy.*"

He put his arm around her shoulders and hugged them for a moment. She would have been affronted if it hadn't felt so good. "Accidents simply happen, don't they?" he murmured. "And that's life."

Ellen looked out at the water. A gust rattled the palm trees. She saw Thea's tricycle blow over on the path. Only a few short hours ago she'd thought these islands so benign!

She shivered and looked at him. "Hoagie, suppose that shark was no accident? Suppose it *came* for Sean?"

"Come off it now, Ellen. It's all chance." He told her that he had a lad in his squadron in the Falklands who attracted ground-to-air missiles as a honeysuckle bloom attracted bees.

"And he survived"—Hoagie smiled—"and lives in a lovely little cottage now in Devon-by-the-sea. Good luck, bad luck, neither one forever. I believe in luck. Now you must do the same."

Ellen could not keep the panic from her voice. "I think that shark's connected to Thea. I feel it deep inside. And I know that shark will keep coming and coming, till my family's gone and I'm completely mad."

He smiled at her. "Come on now, Ellen. Steady, right?"

"Papa Jacques," Thea said quite clearly from the bed. "Papa Jacques?"

Ellen returned in a flash to the bed. Thea's body had been rigid. Now it began to writhe. But the eyes were open again and staring. "The *baka* . . . the *baka* . . . Papa Jacques?"

Ellen took her hand. It was as rigid and cold as stone.

"Thea, darling, *look* at me."

The eyes stayed fixed, a thousand miles away. "Deenie, get Papa Jacques? The *baka* got in me. . . ."

"What's a *baka*?" she whispered to Hoagie. "Hoagie, what's she mean?"

"Bloody voodoo thing, I reckon," he muttered. "Must have heard it from the kids."

A flash of lightning lit the room, and every light in the house went dead.

"Papa Jacques, Papa Jacques, Papa Jacques," chanted Thea from the darkness. "The *baka* got in me."

Hoagie lit a cigarette lighter. In its flickering flame she saw Thea, lips distended, writhing sinuously on the mattress like a snake.

"Oh, my God, Hoagie. Oh, my God!"

He was staring at the child. "Steady, Ellen, steady. . . ."

She picked Thea up in her arms. The child was as cold as ice and still twisting.

"Hoagie! Does Louisa live on the island here with Jake?"

"Louisa? The pretty Haitian?" he asked, puzzled. "Yes, she does."

The coldness had returned to Ellen, in her stomach and in her heart, and she knew what she must do.

"Get her, Hoagie, get her here."

"But—"

"Just do it, Hoagie, dammit! Please, for me?"

He touched her cheek. "Of course I shall."

She sat with the squirming, writhing child, listening

to breakers crashing on the distant coral reef.

"Papa Jacques, Papa Jacques!"

"I know, baby," Ellen murmured softly. "I feel scared sometimes too."

"The *baka* is in me, Papa Jacques. Papa Jacques?"

"No, my darling, someone else. But she'll make the fright go away."

Carla Brody stood at the roulette wheel in the Loma Bella.

The place was jammed with natives, but very few Americans. Apparently tourism was suffering from the dollar's erratic course. She was bored, missed Mike and Thea already, and wished she'd made it back to Whiskey Cay.

When the storm had hit, trapping her in Nassau, she'd first taken refuge in the gallery on Rawson Square that showed her work. There she'd learned that they hadn't sold a piece in a week, hers or anyone else's. When the place had grown too depressing, she'd grabbed a cab through the pouring rain to her agent's home on Prospect Heights.

Her agent, Roger, was a white-haired, erudite Englishman. His wife had insisted on taking her here for dinner. The food was terrible, the music awful, the bunny-hop waitresses a tacky assault on women's rights. But she was a houseguest, her hosts were having fun, and she suffered in silence.

"Oh, bad luck, Roger," said the agent's wife, a big-busted Bahamian woman with chocolate skin and light gray eyes. "Try the double zero, there's a good lad."

He did, lips pursed, and lost. Reluctantly Carla placed a dollar on black, won, and let it ride, won again, then shifted the lot to red and won again. She had promised herself that she would not lose over five dollars, and that if she won, she'd pocket her winnings after three bets. She quit.

Her agent smiled at her. "I wish I had your willpower."

"It isn't willpower. That cutting head I bought today cost thirty bucks."

A dark young man with long, curly hair, wearing a linen sport shirt open at the neck, a gold Rolex, and a U.S. double-eagle around his neck, had been standing next to her. Before him stood a pile of blue chips, a hundred dollars each and six inches high.

Now he spoke. "Mrs. Brody? Carla?"

There was a faint Latino flavor to his words.

"Yes," she answered coolly. "Have we met?"

"I am your admirer." The young man smiled. "I have seen one of your sculptures in the place on Rawson Square. To me it is an angel with golden wings. I like it."

"It's whatever one sees it to be, I hope."

"Anyway, *es hermosisimo, señora.*"

"Muchas gracias," she responded automatically.

Praise was nice, even if it came from someone who lived in a town that erected a fifteen-foot pink flamingo in front of its principal government house.

He bowed. "As beautiful as the sculptress herself."

Was he trying to pick her up or what? Okay, she was used to that. "My husband likes them too."

"Your husband is the gentleman who wires conch for sound." The Latin nodded. "I have heard of that project and support it."

He toyed with his chips, glanced quickly at the croupier, and placed a stack on number nine. The croupier spun the wheel with a flourish. As she watched, transfixed, the ball bounced wildly. When it stopped, it dropped in nine.

Good God . . . She tried to calculate. There were five

chips on the number. At thirty-five to one, he had just won . . . what? Seventeen thousand dollars? More than that!

Impassively he dragged the stack back. Across the table her agent's wife's eyes bulged. "W-well placed, old man," her agent said, stuttering. "Damn well placed."

The Latin shrugged. "*Señor,* it makes no difference. I have won it from myself." He pressed a hundred-dollar chip into Carla's hand. "Mrs. Brody, bet this for me. Put it on red or black."

She did not like the man but did not want to embarrass her agent, so she placed the chip on black. She won. "Now leave it there," he said. She won again.

He scooped it up, tipped the dealer with a hundred, and slid her half the chips. "No," she protested stiffly. "I'm sorry, I can't take that."

"Take one, then, for a deposit on your angel with golden wings."

She faced him. "Are you serious?"

"I do not joke about art, *señora*. Or many other things."

She regarded the blue chip thoughtfully. Perhaps she had use for it.

For she'd sensed a bond between Ellen and Hoagie Newcombe. Her mother-in-law needed a night away from her sorrows and her fears, and Hoagie was said to gamble.

The hundred dollars was a windfall. Why not give it to Ellen and let her spend it here?

The storm rocked the Brody house and made the candles flicker.

Ellen watched Thea and Louisa. The shadows in the living room, where they had brought the child, were alive with menace. The little girl squirmed on the big rattan sofa, hands rigidly at her sides. She would slither up and down the pillows until they had to put her back for fear she'd fall, and soon she would be doing it again.

Hoagie was standing at the window, searching for a break in the weather. Occasionally he would glance at Louisa and Ellen. Louisa was soaked with rain. She had brought her cards and a gourd—*mon asson,* she called it. The candles at the head and foot of the couch gave the scene a funereal air.

Louisa touched the child's forehead tenderly, chanting:

My house feels the spray, Oh Toutou Bilango!
Macaya, I feel the spray.
Three leaves, three points.
Oh, house, Oh, house, Oh . . .
My house feels the spray.
Toutou Bilango . . .

She looked up. To Ellen she murmured, "We tie down now the *baka,* the *loa,* I think it is a snake. . . ."

She had torn a stick from the brush outside, wet and soggy with rain. She ripped a piece from her red cotton skirt with fingers that were strong and sure. She wrapped it around the stick.

She had found fishing line on *Neptune's Folly.* Now, incredibly, she jerked it in two with the strength of a powerful man. Her face was impassive, her gold-flecked eyes a million miles away. When she moved around the room, she floated like a ghost. In the distance, Ellen thought, there was music—ethereal, discordant. She heard the sound of a choir singing, although there was no choir within a hundred miles.

Louisa's beauty dissolved from view, and she saw dark waters flecked with fire. Somewhere down there lurked a menace, circling, but as long as Louisa's voice went on, it would not hazard near.

"We wrap the *loa* . . . we make a cross . . ."

Slowly Ellen returned. Louisa beckoned to Hoagie, who moved over as if drugged. She thrust the fishing line into his hands. Slowly, dazedly, he stretched it out at arm's length.

The other piece she gave to Ellen. As if Louisa had told her to, Ellen found herself stretching it, too, into a vertical position. Without a word Hoagie and she mated the strings in the center.

In the middle of the cross of string, Louisa held the stick. Neither Ellen nor Hoagie seemed to need instructions. They found themselves wrapping up the *loa*—the stick—with the line, until the red cloth was gone and there was only string.

Thea muttered, "The *baka* . . . the *baka* is in me." But now, she stayed motionless, bound in space and time. "The *baka* . . . the *baka* . . ."

Swiftly Louisa rose. Carrying the tied, wrapped stick, she floated to the door. And then she was running through the rain exultantly, the stick held high. Ellen found herself with Hoagie, watching from the porch.

She screamed something in Creole and hurled the stick to sea. They saw it arc in a flash of lightning, and as it struck the ebony water, they heard Thea shriek inside.

Ellen whirled and ran in. She froze.

Thea was sitting on the sofa. As Ellen stared, she yawned, got up, and strode into her room.

Incredulously Ellen followed. The little girl had crawled into her bed, beneath the covers. Now she was tucking her teddy in beside her.

"Thea?" murmured Ellen. "Thea, baby?"

"Will you read me a story?" Thea yawned. "Will you, Grandma Ellen?"

"Oh, darling." Ellen sobbed. "My darling . . ."

But by the time she bent to kiss her, Thea was asleep.

They sat in the kitchen drinking beer. The rain was stopping, the drumming on the rooftop had ceased, and a pale moon was peeking from the scudding clouds outside.

Ellen had been into the child's bedroom half a dozen times. "She's sleeping like an angel."

Louisa nodded. "She is very, very tired. Give her chicken for breakfast when she wakes."

"Chicken?" Hoagie smiled.

"Yes, *pourquoi pas non?*"

"Seems odd, is all."

"Oui." She shrugged. "My mama would have sacrificed a chicken in the living room. Michael and Carla are lucky I am not a real *mambo*, like her."

"You seemed to do the trick," Hoagie grinned.

"It is not a trick. It is a religion. It has bad and it has good."

"And you believe in it?"

She shrugged. "Sometimes yes, sometimes no. I am a Catholic, and the Church does not approve. But one cannot deny what happens. If there was an evil *loa* in *l'enfant*, then it is gone."

"Well, there was," said Ellen positively. "We all know that."

"The question is," murmured Louisa, "who put it there?"

"She hears those things from Deenie," Ellen said. "Thea's an impressionable child."

"Deenie did not put it there," mused Louisa. "Why would she? And she cannot know enough." Louisa spread out her cards. "I feel a hatred."

She began to play with them, trading one for another,

straightening them, shuffling them again. "Papa Jacques hates Michael."

"Mike tried to run him off the island last month," said Hoagie. "For charging Clarence fees."

"I feel this hatred very close. . . ."

She looked into Ellen's eyes and got suddenly up from the table. She opened the screen door slowly and gasped. "There he is," she whispered.

Ellen joined her at the door. In the moonlight, by the water, stood a man. When her eyes adjusted to the darkness, she saw that it was Papa Jacques. Slowly, the man turned. He drifted up the pathway between the painted rocks, his gourd rattling in his hand with every step.

Hoagie was behind them. He brushed through and yelled, "Hey, you!"

Papa Jacques ignored him and nodded to Louisa. *"Bonsoir, ma'mselle."*

"What are you doing here?" Louisa piped up. She sounded scared.

"I ask the same of you. I think one has tried *marrer* here, an *arrêter*. One has tied up a *loa*, a *baka?"*

Louisa swallowed. *"Oui."*

Papa Jacques's voice seemed to deepen. "A *baka* that mounted a little child? And the child, I think she cried for me? Who taught you? And when did you take to the *asson?"*

Louisa sounded scared. "My mother was a *mambo*. The *baka* is tied and gone."

"Papa Jacques," Hoagie said with a growl, "get your bloody ass out of here or I'll kick it into town!"

Louisa gasped. "Papa Jacques, he does not mean that."

"Mais oui, he does. And I shall not forget." The onyx eyes seemed to grow in the moonlight. To Louisa the *houngan* said, "Your mother taught you poorly. If a *loa* is evil, a *baka,* and you tie it, you must bury it as well."

"Oui, monsieur?" asked Louisa faintly.

"For suppose he is not a snake or a lizard but an eel who lives at sea?" His eyes swung to Ellen. "Or a shark, madam? A shark, like mine?"

A pair of headlights swept the yard, and Michael was out of the jeep. A portly old man in a Hawaiian shirt followed him, carrying a black bag. Mike strode toward the door. "What is this?" he rumbled, grabbing Papa Jacques's arm. "What are you doing here?"

"I came because your daughter had need of me. And she still does, *monsieur.*"

"You robbing, phony bastard, lay off Clarence and his kids! Get off this goddam island or I'll throw you off myself." He grabbed the *asson* and hurled it toward the water, as far as he could.

There was a moment of shocked silence. Ellen could hear Louisa murmuring beside her. *"Non, non, non, non, non . . ."*

Papa Jacques stared at Michael for a moment, looked at Ellen, swung on his heel, and disappeared into the moon shadow of the trees on Masthead Point.

Ellen watched him, and the cold returned to her stomach. She did not see him pick up his *asson,* but when she saw him next, it was in his hand, rattling as he walked.

She thought she could hear it long after he disappeared into darkness on the road to Prince George Town.

PART II

Chapter 1

Michael Brody sat at the computer in the pilothouse of *Neptune's Folly,* angrily watching the heartbeat of a six-pound mollusk resting on the bottom somewhere ten fathoms below. *He* should be down there diving, not Jake.

The boat was tied to the diving barge they kept permanently anchored above Hurricane Reef. The pink wet-submersible creaked alongside the barge, complaining gently at the swell.

Jake, for reasons unknown to Mike, was on the bottom in place of him, wearing a *triple* block of tanks, which he'd probably need, since he hadn't dived in a year. The less you dived, the more uncomfortable you were on the bottom. Apprehension generated adrenaline, and adrenaline used up air. Startled by every barracuda that passed, afraid you'd stick your hand into a moray's sacred hole, bothered even by the raucous sound of your own regulator, Jake would doubtless have to surface in less than half an hour.

A waste when Jake hated to dive, had the "bad ear" he used as an excuse, and couldn't cover half the area that Mike could himself.

And was too big to fit in the cockpit of the *Whine Bottle,* which was idle while he dived.

An enigma, like most of the morning's doings. Clarence had not reported for work, and William was moody too.

He studied the trace on the screen, trying to distinguish *T* and CRW waves on the pattern. So who cared? He'd rather be on the bottom.

Last month Jake somehow had hooked up the big DEC computer to the acoustic receiver, saving the expense of a separate monitor. He was a genius, Jake was, and was wasted on the bottom; he should be sitting here.

The trace of the conch—a green series of mountain peaks marching across the screen—grew higher. A rise in amplitude meant that the animal was moving, or excited by something below. Maybe it heard Jake thrashing around among its brothers and sisters, tagging shells.

What a way to earn a living, sitting at a monitor at the end of the earth, watching the heartbeat of a life-form with all the glamour of a garden snail.

The project was in trouble. The financial crisis in the U.S. had cut off tourist income. The Bahamian Senate in Nassau had sliced Ministry of Fisheries funds; the Ministry of Fisheries had cut the conch study grant.

He reflected bitterly that someone in the Bahamian Senate was getting rich. If the Bay Street Boys in Nassau would allot them a thousandth of the income they were getting for letting *narcotraficantes* use Galleon Cay, he and Jake could tag every conch in the Bahamas three times over.

What would become of Jake and himself when the project collapsed, he did not know. His thesis was barely started. He could not survive without the job. And unless he got the Ph.D., he saw no hope of ever supporting Carla, Thea, and the little boy they'd someday like to have.

A squawk came from his acoustic receiver. He could barely recognize a human voice. Jake had never mastered the underwater microphone and always sounded as if he were chewing on his mouth piece.

He picked up his mike. "Jake," he said, enunciating carefully and mouthing every word. "You're three-by-one in the deckhouse. I cannot read you . . . I cannot read . . . open your mouth when you speak! Do you copy? Do you copy?"

"Copy . . . yes, I copy. . . ." The voice was garbled and sounded as if he were speaking from the bottom of a GI can. "Conch on the march down here. Tagging every one . . . tagging every one I can. . . ."

He sounded harried. Good. Mike did not know why the conch were on the move, but whatever had spooked them was providing his partner with proof that the tagging was not as simple as he thought.

Strange, though, that they were on the move so early in the day. He watched the trace on the computer screen. The rate and amplitude were increasing.

He glanced at his tally sheet. C-14, the conch that had hidden in the hull of the *Leta,* had emerged from the wreck that morning, apparently bored with shipboard life. Wherever he was, from the trace of his heartbeat on the screen, he was a very excited gentleman, indeed.

Michael wondered why.

Jake McCay labored along the bottom, in water as clear as air, trailing a stream of bubbles like rising pearls.

He hated diving. He had been a diver as a child, using primitive wooden goggles inherited from his father, and for all he knew, his father's father, swimming out on a broken tourist surfboard, skin-diving for conch.

He had had good lungs and a powerful heart. Some of the conch money his mother had banked in Barclay's Prince George Branch had been set aside for his education.

Without diving, he never would have studied in Boston and never have got his degree. But somewhere in his youth, plummeting downward with a coral rock for ballast, he had broken an eardrum, and though it had healed, he never forgot the piercing pain he had endured.

He hated scuba tanks. As a boy, he'd scorned the tourists he saw using them—out of jealousy, perhaps.

He tugged at his straps now. They were digging into his bare shoulders. He wore no wet suit. He never got cold, and his suit was too small for him, anyway, since Louisa's cooking had put all the weight on him.

The conch were on the move, he was miserable, and there was a sharp pain in his ear.

Okay, Louisa, he thought, *I'm doing it, but if I bust that eardrum again, it's on your Haitian soul.*

That morning she had awakened moody, eyes dull with a strange, dark fear. She served him his breakfast in bed. She must want something. At first she would only hint at what had happened at Mike's the night before.

"Come on, Louisa," he said with a grin. "So you *are* a genuine white witch. I won't laugh."

"Well, when I got there, Thea *was* sick, and I did a *marrer*. An *arrêter*."

He'd sipped his coffee. "Whatever the hell is that?"

"You're laughing." Her lips were stubbornly set.

"No, I'm not." He studied her. Incredible. She was sharp enough to deal blackjack in a place that probably shot you if you lost, and she still believed in voodoo. "It just drives me bloody up the wall that you believe that crap."

"Whatever I did last night, it worked."

"So does St. Joseph's aspirin."

Her gold-flecked eyes turned ice-cold. *"Tu es idiot."*

"What?"

"You're supposed to be a genius"—she glared—

"and you don't know. . ." She groped for the words. "You don't know squattley-doo!"

"Diddly-squat," he said with a sigh.

She sat for a while, thinking, her fine brow creased in lines. "Is Michael diving today?"

He nodded. "Every single day he dives. Until our funds run out."

"Does he *have* to?"

"Well, woman, do you have to deal blackjack at the Loma Bella Club?"

"Yes. But I think Mike is in danger from Papa Jacques."

"I think *you're* in danger from Rico Lomas."

She removed the tray she'd put on his chest and set it on the bedside table. He stared at her. It was time for both of them to leave for work.

Instead she crawled back in beside him.

"Jake?"

He could feel the warmth of her heating up his blood. God, he was going to be late. . . .

Her voice was low and throaty and very clear. "Don't make him dive today."

"Hey, woman! What is this?"

"I have a bad feeling. He could get the bends. Or . . . what? Embolism? Papa Jacques *est très fort*, a very powerful man."

"Bullshit! And Mike won't stand for *not* diving. He likes to, and we have to tag the conch."

"But you're the boss now, aren't you?"

"Yeah, but—"

Suddenly she was nibbling at his ear, the bad one, her soft breath sending shivers from his toes to the tip of his hair. "Please, Jake? He will not dive?"

Oh, Christ . . . all right, he'd dive himself.

So he had dived, telling Mike that he wanted to see for himself how the tags were sticking to the shells. And now here he was at ten fathoms, and the ear was hurting bad.

He noticed suddenly that there was a direction to the march of the conch below. He glanced at his wrist compass. All the conch were moving south. He counted them: twelve. He made a note in grease pencil on the plastic writing pad strapped to his left forearm.

He was uncomfortable. He himself was moving north, against the current through Masthead Cut, so that he would have an easier swim returning to the barge. Suddenly, far in the distance, he saw a pale shape materializing through the crystal water, as if from some primal dream.

It was a great white shark.

At first he could not believe it. He had dived these waters from the age of ten. He had seen hundreds of sand sharks and makos and blues. Once he had spotted a tiger shark, without even feeling fear. But never in his life had he seen a great white. And this far south?

A part of him wanted to flee in terror. But the literature said no: thrashing, violent movement and speed were deadly.

He froze his motion and glided to the sand. There was no reef to shelter him, and the nearest wreck was the *Leta*, a good half mile away. He lay on the bottom, praying that his bubbles would not give him away. In his regulator, his breath sounded like a locomotive pulling from a station. He tried to quiet the sound but could not.

The shark was by far the biggest he had ever seen. Head-on, it reminded him of a jetliner taxiing to an airline terminal. It was weaving now, coming toward him, shaking his head from side to side. His mind raced through the lore of sharks. Weaving and indecision were the first hints of attack.

His thoughts became jumbled. What the hell was it

doing in water so warm? Some product of el Niño or currents no man knew?

He tensed. The great white was lazing closer, gathering speed. It had seen him.

Louisa, why did you get me into this? And all for a white man too!

He tensed and quietly drew the diving knife from the holster on his calf. Now the beast was rushing toward him. *Oh, God in heaven, save this mon's soul!*

He closed his eyes and waited. He felt a shadow passing, and a swirl of water that almost turned him upside down. He had the sense of a long, tapered tail flailing by, inches from his head.

He lay for a long, long moment in the sand. Then he hazarded a look.

Like a jet that had swooped on an infantryman, the shark was climbing in the direction of the barge. He hazarded a cry into the microphone: "Shark . . . great white!"

Then, slowly, with a minimum of motion, he followed his bubbles toward the blessed light above.

Mike heard the strangled call from below. It sounded like, "Shark . . . great white!"

Angrily he rose from the chart table. Jake's twisted sense of humor was no mystery: It came with the high IQ. Despite his size and strength, he was like one of the nerds you met in college—engineers, chemists; yes, marine biologists—who were always making the wrong joke at the wrong time.

To lie about great white sharks to a man who had just lost his brother to one wasn't funny, and Jake should know better. Shaking his head, he moved into the bright sunlight. The voice had sounded fairly close, so Jake must be coming up.

William was leaning on the rail, staring moodily at

the water. What was on his mind, Mike didn't know. "I think Jake's coming back," Mike said, expecting William to move toward the diving platform on the stern.

William spat into the water. "Don't feel right out here today."

"That's because the wrong guy's diving, William. Don't know why he is."

William shrugged. "Clarence say you throw *asson* away."

"Asson?" Mike smiled. "What's that?"

"Papa Jacques's *asson*. His magic gourd."

"That rattle? You're damn right I did. He screwed up little Deenie's head, and she screwed up my kid's!"

"Clarence say he make lil' Cissy well."

Cissy was Clarence's youngest girl. "Good," said Mike. "How much did it cost him?"

"Papa Jacques, he don't take money. Takes forty dollars, Bahamian, grinds it up with *pois congo,* puts it on Cissy's head."

"I'll *bet* he ground it up." Forty dollars was about what Clarence earned in a week. "Anyway, I told Papa Jacques to leave Whiskey Cay a month ago. I find him around my place again, he's history."

"Yah, mon, but he don't go. He is still here." William nodded moodily. "Some people say Papa Jacques don' like you, *you* gwine be history, man."

They heard a shout from astern.

"Jake's up," said Mike. "Let's go."

William sauntered aft and stepped to the diving platform. Mike followed him, to help him lift Jake's tanks. Jake was treading water. He had ripped the mouthpiece from his mouth, and he tossed his face mask aboard.

"Man," he babbled, thrashing toward the platform. "Get me out! There's a great white shark down there!"

Mike moved to help him and froze, transfixed.

A shape rushed from the depths, rose ponderously

over the stern of the barge, and rolled slowly to its side. He caught a glimpse of rows of gleaming ivory teeth.

He threw up a hand and recoiled, crashing against the air compressor. In a shower of spray he cowered there, while the massive snout crashed down on the afterdeck. The great jaws closed. There was the sound of rending metal, and three feet of one-inch stainless railing and a stanchion tore loose from the gunwale.

The shark sank back into the water, rolled, flicked a tail as tall as Mike, and disappeared in a swirl of foam.

For an instant Mike lay in shock. Then he forced himself astern. He and William yanked Jake from the water.

"You see that?" jabbered William. "You see that mother's mouf?" He grabbed Mike's shoulders and stared at him. "Why he don't take me or Jake, mon? Why he pass and go for you?"

Mike swallowed. His mouth was dry, and he felt half sick. "Maybe," he muttered, "he doesn't like dark meat."

Jake was shivering in the hot Bahama sun. Sweat was mixing with the water rolling down his ebony skin. He flipped his diving knife toward the barge's deckhouse. It stuck, quivering in the wood.

"You just got your job back, white boy. I'll never dive again."

Ellen sat at lunch with Carla on the porch, sipping her wine and gazing at the blue chip, on which was stamped, "Loma Bella: Nassau." On it was a bunny's face with a gold halo around its ears.

"A *hundred dollars?"* She gasped. "Carla, I just can't! Let's get Thea some decent clothes!"

"She doesn't need decent clothes, Ellen. Not playing with native youngsters in the boondocks on Whiskey Cay." She smiled at her mother-in-law. "No, I wasn't going to take it, and then I figured, what the hell? Let Ellen take old Hoagie on a date."

"Well," Ellen said, bristling, "he isn't all that old."

Their eyes met, and both burst into laughter. "Of course he isn't, Ellen. That's the point! Where are you going to find another crazy guy like him?"

"Crazy?" She toyed with her glass. "He's more than he seems, Carla. There's sadness in there somewhere. And last night . . . he didn't believe in any of it—I guess I don't, either, today—but he was there, and warm, and he cared."

Thea rocketed past them on her tricycle, circled on the wide wooden porch, and parked at the table. She looked up at her mother with her candid eyes of blue. Ellen touched her cheek. Cool, and as smooth as silk. Thea, at least, had no memory of the previous night, or the horror she must have known.

No one in this house was talking things out: Carla was too busy, and Mike was always gone, at the bottom of the sea.

"Where's Deenie, Thea?" asked Carla. "Did you ask her over to play?"

Ellen frowned at her, sending messages. If Deenie was going to brainwash Thea, even innocently, Thea had better get another playmate.

But she need not have worried.

"I asked her," Thea said with a nod. "She's not allowed."

Carla stiffened. "What?"

"Her daddy says she can't play with me." Her eyes began to fill with tears.

Carla hugged her and looked straight into her face. "But why?"

" 'Cause Daddy salted Papa Jacques." Thea squirmed away, heading for the water.

Ellen's brow wrinkled. "Salted?"

"Insulted, probably," Carla said, translating.

"Well, Ellen, he really did insult him. Damn, it's all my fault. I wish I'd never seen that awful little man."

"Maybe she's wrong about Clarence," Carla suggested. "Maybe Deenie's mad because Thea made her lie. About the package Thea says Hoagie dropped."

"Why *did* she lie?" wondered Ellen.

"Dope."

"Dope?"

Carla stood up and moved to the railing, looking out at the approaching boat.

"These kids are *taught* not to see things, Ellen." When she turned back, Ellen saw a shadow of fear in her eyes. "At least if it drops from an airplane. Or . . ."

"Or what?"

"Or they and their parents are liable to wake up dead."

While William secured the dock lines, Mike and Jake conferred in the deckhouse, each with a bottle of St. Pauli Girl.

It had been a long, silent trip back from the barge. Both recognized instantly what the great white shark would do to the tourist trade. People came to the Bahamas to scuba-dive, to snorkel, to swim safely in water as clear as air.

"You going to make the report or me?" asked Mike.

Jake raised his hand. "Just cool it, man. Relax. What's this report you're talking about?"

Mike looked into his eyes. They were veiled and distant. Keeping his own voice steady, he said, "We *have* to report it, Jake. You know that. You call Government House. I'll call the *Nassau Daily Tribune*—"

Jake shook his head. "Not before the annual Junkanoo. Tourists come down here to snorkel, mon, and look at the pretty fish. No *Nassau Tribune*, no *Guard-*

ian, no wives—we got to warn William about that. No girlfriends. No Louisa, no Carla, not even Clarence. No mamas, which ought to make *you* feel good; she's had enough sharks for a while."

Mike stared at him. Oh, God, not again. . . . He took a deep breath. "Let me tell you a story, Jake."

"Look, it's quitting time."

"I'll tell you, anyway. My dad was police chief of Amity—"

"You told me that," Jake said with a sigh. "And he helped kill a couple of sharks up there . . . great whites?"

"And died from it." Mike took a long, cool draft from his bottle. It tasted good. His mouth was still dry, and his hands had not quit shaking. "My mother thinks the *second* shark killed him. Well, wrecked his heart, same thing. But you know what really killed him?"

"Mike, it's late—" Jake started for the deckhouse door.

"Stay where you are!"

Jake sat down again. "Okay. What killed your dad?"

"The first one."

"Why's that?" Jake raised the bottle to his lips and studied him with cautious eyes.

"The first shark *broke* his heart. The second one only stopped it."

"And how did the first one break his heart?"

"It killed a girl. And he figured it out. And he wanted to close the beaches. And the town council wouldn't let him. So he told the local paper, but they wouldn't print it."

"I can see why not. But here they might."

"Town council, mayor, realtors . . . they pressured him. Somebody even killed our cat. So finally he gave up. And then . . ." His throat tightened. He swallowed. "And then the shark killed a boy, and a little old man, and *then* they printed it, all right, and you know who they blamed?" Eyes blazing, he stepped closer. "My dad!"

"Take it easy, friend."

Mike felt tears filling his eyes. "And, Jake, because he hadn't closed those beaches, he was never the same again."

Jake put down his beer. He sighed. "Let me tell *you* a story." He jerked his thumb toward Prince George Town. "You know what feeds us jungle bunnies? We got a choice: tourists or cocaine. These were desert islands once; they might damn well be again." He jerked a finger toward Prince George Town. "Romeo? Louisa? Take away their tourists, this whole damn chain of islands will be working loadin' dope!"

"When that shark hits its first tourist—"

"That shark's a tourist himself. He's a cold-water animal. In a week he'll be twenty miles at sea, heading back for the North Atlantic. He'll be gone, mon, and there's no *reason* anybody's got to know."

"*I* know," Mike said softly. "And you think I'm going to let Thea take her evening swim tonight?"

Jake studied him, downed his beer, and sat for a moment drumming his fingers.

"You want me to call Government House?" he mused. "That's not a bad idea. Suppose we could tell them we knew where that shark was hanging out, all the time he's here?"

"Sure," said Mike. "You tag him, man. I'll watch."

"We don't *tag* him, Mike." He got up, pulled a dart from the dart board on the icebox door, and stepped back to the line painted on the cabin floor. Lips pursed, he took aim. "We *stick* him. With a harpoon and a BPST. And the Ministry of Tourism pays the tab."

Mike gazed at him. "Holy jumping Jesus Christ! You mean it?"

He let the dart fly. It quivered in the board, a half inch from dead center.

"Mike," he said, "if you got the guts to get that transmitter back, we're going to bell the cat."

Ellen sat on the porch of the main house, brushing Thea's hair in long, sweeping strokes. Through the window of the studio across the yard she could see her daughter-in-law studying her sculpture, which remained tantalizingly out of sight from her angle.

It seemed a soaring work under its cover, and it had taken all of Ellen's willpower not to lift the jib that shrouded it and peek.

But Carla was dead serious when she said she wanted no one to see it until the unveiling. She was approaching her deadline now: the Annual Junkanoo and the presentation in the town plaza were only three days away, and she seemed frantic.

Finally, shaking her head as if dissatisfied, Carla moved out of sight. In a moment she reappeared on the porch of the studio, crossed the yard, and said, "How about a swim?"

Ellen hesitated. She didn't really want to go. "I . . ."

"Yes!" cried Thea. "We'll go swimming, Mommy."

Ellen went into her bedroom off the studio and stripped. She glanced through the open door to the studio, hoping that for once Carla had forgotten to cover it. She had not.

She caught a glimpse of her body in the mirror. She stood sidewise, looking for tummy fat. No—if anything, she'd grow skinny before she grew fat. She guessed that she was lucky: trim belly, breasts that still were firm, broad shoulders, narrow waist.

Hooper had lusted after her breasts—and her legs. Brody had cherished them. She felt a wave of longing for her husband.

She climbed into her swimming suit and started down the path to the main house. Thea, holding her hand, said, "The sand castle got all uggy in the rain, and we're going to build it again, okay?"

"I'd rather do that than swim," said Ellen. Mike was approaching from the dock. He looked tired and drawn: Sean's death had hit him harder than he'd admitted, she decided, and they had to have a talk.

Mike picked up Thea and swung her. "Let's . . ." He hesitated for a moment. "I'm taking everybody to the Golden Shell for conch burgers. Last one to the jeep has to put up the top when it rains."

"I can't go like this," Ellen said, glancing down at her swimsuit. "I'll change."

"You're beautiful," Mike said. He grabbed Thea and lifted her to his shoulders, put one arm around Ellen and another around Carla, and swept them toward the jeep.

"My God," said Carla, "you're kidnapping us! What is this?"

"I'm a terrorist at heart. No, I'm just hungry."

Ellen shot him a sidelong glance.

She knew him to his core. He very, very seldom lied, but she was certain that he was lying to them now.

Chapter 2

It was a clear, cool day, and wavelets from the steady north wind dappled Masthead Bay. They chopped against the wooden hull of the shabby diving barge.

Mike swung from the broken railing that the shark had carried away and jumped into the Avon dinghy bumping alongside.

Jake and William handed him down the three surplus U.S. Navy sonobuoys, foreign aid to the Bahamian Ministry of Fishing. They used them to triangulate the seasonal march of the conch from shallow to deeper water.

The sonobuoys were bright yellow; long, slender cylinders built to be dropped from aircraft when a sub was lurking below. They floated erect and half submerged, dangling a microphone below.

The mikes could pick up the sound of Jake's BPSTs at a range of half a mile. When they charted each buoy's position, they could tell by comparing their signals where an underwater heartbeat was originating and which way a conch—or a great white shark—was moving.

Mike whipped the snarling Evinrude into life. Standing at the tiller in his wet suit, he set a course toward Masthead Point, taking spray over the bulbous rubber bow. He took a compass bearing with a hand-held pelorus on Masthead Light, and a second on the Prince George Channel buoy. Distantly he could see the end of

Spanish Galleon Cay. He took a bearing on that, too, and marked them on the chart.

He picked up the first sonobuoy. Into its microphone he said, "*Neptune's Folly* from *Neptune's Dolly!* How do you read me, Jake?"

"Five by five, partner. Let her rip."

He tossed over a rusty dinghy anchor and played out its line to the bottom. He tested to see if it would hold and secured the sonobuoy to the line.

He tossed in the sonobuoy. It bobbed, nodding, in the waves. Ten feet down, through crystal-clear water, he could see the microphone dangling.

If some conch diver didn't steal the rig to sell it back to the Ministry, sonobuoy number one was set. He did the same thing with sonobuoys numbers two and three, anchoring one of them off Prince George Inlet, and the other near Hog Bottom Cut. Now they could hear the great white shark as it exited Masthead Sound.

All they had to do now was get a BPST aboard the great white shark, and assuming that the damn thing had a heart that beat, they could track him all day long.

If he hadn't left for cooler water sometime during the night.

Jake McCay sat at his workbench in the *Neptune's Folly* deckhouse. His grindstone screamed, and sparks cascaded from the harpoon point.

He had gotten the ancient whaling harpoon from the Inn of the Happy Whale, a tourist trap on Kingston Street downtown. Unwilling to risk refusal, he had borrowed it at three A.M. by jimmying open the window over the ladies' room and snaking his enormous shoulders through the hole.

He had never been a thief save by necessity, when as a child he had had to steal to eat. He felt badly about the harpoon—Louisa would kill him if she knew.

But, after all, if the shark was not tagged and its presence had to be revealed before the festival, the Happy Whale, like every other enterprise on Whiskey Cay, would turn its belly up and sink in bankruptcy tomorrow, sure as hell.

He had been sharpening the point of the harpoon and its rusty tines for half an hour. The old Bedford whalers had demanded rugged stuff; the iron was of a quality one never saw today. It took an edge like a straight razor, and a point like a cactus plant. Unless the shark was wearing armor plate, the transmitter would stick.

He ran his finger along the newly sharpened barbs. They were razor-sharp and cut him. He cursed and flicked his fingers; blood splattered on the deck.

Blood . . . Louisa had told him to be careful: "I dreamed of blood last night."

She was working in Nassau for the weekend, and he would not see her until Monday, but she had seemed discomfited and worried, didn't seem to want to go. She had pondered her cards late last night. "Jake, there's something you're keeping from me. What is it?"

"That's enough of that mumbo-jumbo crap. Come here."

Now he blotted at the blood on his finger. Mike appeared in the doorway, his wet suit gleaming with spray.

"Sonobuoys are planted, Skipper."

"Good." Jake turned from the workbench. "Now all we need's one of those BPSTs we got crawling around the bottom on your conch." He sighed. "So you want to take a dive?"

"*Want* to?" Mike moved to the porthole, looked out, and thought for a moment. He turned back, and his face was grim. "Not exactly, but I will."

* * *

Ellen had taken to bringing Carla coffee as she worked in the mornings. There was something fascinating about her dedication to the object she was sculpting, whatever it was, and in her daughter-in-law's total concentration on the task. She knocked on the door and waited.

The loud, low hiss of the torch inside stopped. In a moment Carla called, "Come in." The statue was covered. Carla had flipped back her welding mask and drawn off her leather gloves. Now she shed her leather apron.

"There. That's it until after lunch." She faced Ellen. "Okay, have you done it?"

Ellen blushed. She knew what was coming. "Asked Hoagie to Nassau?"

"You know damn well what I mean."

She shook her head. "What you have to understand is that . . . well, it's a different generation. We didn't ask men for dates."

"You're throwing away a hundred bucks. Those chips don't grow on trees."

"No," she said to Carla. "I guess they don't."

Ellen moved to the window and looked out at the bay. She could see *Neptune's Folly* tied to the diving barge, a good five miles away.

If Mike would only quit diving . . .

She turned back. "Hoagie's nice. I just wish I knew more about him."

"I do," said Carla suddenly. "More than I did yesterday, anyway. Philippa told me something."

Philippa was William's wife, and she came to pick up the laundry twice a week.

Ellen's heart beat faster. She hated gossip, but she couldn't help herself. "What did Philippa say?"

"Well, she used to work in Nassau for his wife."

"*Ex*-wife?" Ellen asked faintly.

Carla smiled and squeezed her hand. "*Ex*-wife, right."

Thank God for that. . . .

"And?"

"She was beautiful. A British aristocrat but a social renegade. Old Bay Street family. Loaded. Hoagie was in the RAF, never there. They had a daughter, about sixteen."

So far, so good. "Go on."

"The daughter was neglected. . . ."

Their eyes met. Carla flushed. "Look, I know I'm neglecting Thea, and you, too—"

"Carla, you have no choice. I'm a working woman too."

Carla smiled. "Thanks, Ellen, but it's getting to Mike. Anyway, Hoagie's daughter just ran free. Pretty girl. She was all over Nassau, in the clubs. Hoagie heard about it and finally resigned his commission to come home and straighten things out. But she disappeared before he got here."

"Oh, no!" That was why she had seen the sadness in his eyes. "Where'd she go?"

"Nobody knows. The police just sort of shrugged."

"But that's so *sad*."

Carla nodded. "Hoagie blamed the wife. The wife blamed Hoagie and took off for the Mediterranean. With her minister, no less! Hoagie came apart. He drank too much, gambled away what he had, and then he started flying for this charter outfit."

"And now Mike thinks he's in drugs? That's ridiculous!"

Carla joined her at the window. "Ellen?"

"Yes?"

"Philippa thinks he is too."

She couldn't believe it, wouldn't. "And you, Carla?" she asked heatedly. "Do *you* think so too?"

Carla grinned. "Do you think I'd give you a hundred bucks to take a *traficante* on a date?"

Ellen took the chip from her pocket and regarded it. On the front was a stupid bunny face, on the back a cottontail. She flipped it and it rose, whirling in the sunlight streaming through the window.

"Heads, yes—tails, no." She clapped it on her wrist and looked. She saw the bunny face.

"Heads," she announced.

"The gods," said Carla, "have spoken. Go with them."

Mike cruised the *Whine Bottle* along an endless plain of snow-white sand, occasionally banking away from Masthead Reef, riotous with clown fish and guppies. He was en route to Masthead Cut.

In a secret meeting at the Ministry of Tourism, they had been chartered to tag the shark and follow it, at least until after the Whiskey Cay Junkanoo on Tuesday. First they needed their transmitter back from the conch that had kidnapped it.

Jake's voice growled from the speaker on the sub's panel: "Steady as you go, man. The conch are congregated near the wreck."

Now that the sonobuoys were set out and charted, Jake could triangulate and send him the locations of the conch from the pilothouse. They had done it many times before. It saved the submersible's batteries, because when you knew where the conch held their meetings, you didn't have to search.

When he recovered the BPST and they tagged the shark with it, they'd be able to follow him as if he were a conch.

He saw the ghostly tan mass of the *Leta* wreck taking

form before him. *"Neptune's Folly,"* he called, "I'm a hundred feet south of the wreck now. Estimated current through the cut is maybe a knot and a half. Crabbing into it . . . I'm going to park this coffin and bail out."

He checked to see that his loot bag, in which he'd stow the transmitter, was clipped to his weight belt. He reached for the panel and twisted the submarine's rheostat—which acted as his throttle—a quarter turn counterclockwise. The whine of his propeller dropped an octave.

He pulled the mask from his face and let it fill, to clear it of fog. He replaced it, full of water, on his eyes and exhaled into it through his nose, expelling the water through the side of the mask. With his faceplate window washed and wiped, the wreck seemed closer.

He had glided almost to a landing when he noticed that the conch were moving, heading for the torpedo hole. Perhaps they'd heard him and were taking cover. *From him, or something else?*

He was suddenly uncomfortable. Three feet above the sand, he hovered. He looked to port and starboard but saw nothing. He was reluctant to ground the sub, hesitant, for the first time, to leave the hated cockpit.

Abruptly the sound of the motor stopped and the *Whine Bottle* jerked aloft like an airplane in an air current. His stomach dropped away. His head banged backward, bouncing off the padded headrest.

He half rose from his seat, twisting backward. An enormous black pupil, as flat as a pan, stared at him from six feet away. A huge, curved tooth was spiraling toward the bottom, and the shark's own blood was swirling in the water.

The shark had attacked from the starboard quarter. It had crunched the tiny submarine's stern, propeller and all, in its enormous jaws.

The submarine was hurtling toward the freighter. It

crashed against the hull again and again and again. He heard the rending of metal, a hideous screech of teeth grinding the sub's fiberglass hull and aluminum ribs.

She listed violently, first to starboard, then to port. Her bow swept upward, almost tossing him from his seat. In an instant he was hurled down again, crashing against the panel. His face mask filled with water, his regulator smashed his lips, and his tank valve slammed him in the back of his neck.

This, then, was it. *Good-bye, Carla, Thea, Mom . . .*

All at once he found himself pitched free of the cockpit and spiraling toward the sand. In an instant he was squirming toward the wreck, face mask still filled, vision blurred, regulator full of water, which he had no time to clear.

He heard the submarine settle to the sand. The monster had abandoned it—for him.

Fighting the current, he swam with all his might toward the blurred green-brown outline of the wreck.

He groped along the hull plates. He felt jagged metal with his gloved hands and jerked himself closer. It was the torpedo hole, half uncovered in the current. He squirmed halfway through and stuck, his double-tank bank jamming against the half-inch, war-torn steel.

He felt the swirl of a mighty body past his legs and drew them up to his chest, cowering like a fetus, moaning in fear.

The shark gathered himself for another charge. Half in, half out, Mike struggled to enter the hole. He couldn't, because of the tanks.

He took a deep breath, spat out his regulator mouthpiece, and worked free of his backpack. He snaked in and dragged his tanks in after him.

His lungs were searing, and his heart felt as if it would burst. He fumbled for his mouthpiece, found it. He jammed it into his teeth. It was full of sand.

With his chest in paroxysm and his lungs heaving for air, he somehow cleared the regulator and felt the blessed air pour in.

For a long while he lay inside the hole, unable to move. He could hear the shark crashing against the metal plates. He finally cleared his mask. Sand was swirling past the hole, stirred by the current or the shark.

The hole was uncovering, as it did twice daily, in the ebb and flow of the tide. If it was too small now for the great white shark, it would not be for very long.

Slowly Mike swam away from the hole through clouds of brilliant butterfish and darting, flitting guppies. He saw the conch, in a circle on the sand-strewn salon deck, the one wearing the BPST in the center. He regarded the hundred-dollar bait for which he'd sacrificed his life.

Savagely he ripped it off and stuffed it into his netted bag. At least, if they ever found his body, they'd know he had not failed.

Then he swam through the silent green vastness of the salon to the creaking door in the purser's office beyond. He pried it open and squirmed inside.

For a moment he floated, looking around. Light from a single port flickered from above. He sensed that there was something awful in the corner. When he saw it, he recoiled, and the mouthpiece fell from his lips.

On a rusted, tattered swivel chair sat a skeleton. It grinned at him, the remnant of a shirt moving in the current.

One of its hands was still intact, resting on a knee bone. The fingers, picked clean by fish, were dangling. In the current, the forefinger seemed to beckon.

His bubbles were rising, homing on an air pocket trapped above. He rose with them, removed his mask, and sniffed it. He almost retched.

The air had been there, like the skeleton, for over forty years. He jammed his mask back on and dived.

He swam to the creaking door and peered out. Across the vast salon, through the flitting parrot fish, he could see that the current was sweeping the hole wider. He could hear a crashing somewhere. The shark had not left.

Like the pocket of air above his head, he was thoroughly, eternally trapped.

Chapter 3

Ellen lay dozing on her bed. She had fallen into the Bahamian habit of taking a nap after lunch. It was quiet off Carla's studio, and the soft breeze from Masthead Bay carried a scent of palm.

Through the door she had been watching the wind ruffle the sail that covered the statue. She wondered why Carla was so secretive about it: Mike claimed that she had never been so before.

The veiled shape was a puzzle. A tall, shrouded woman blessing the earth? Or Father Time with his scythe? Death?

She dozed. Through deep, ebony waters she saw a gleaming eye. It was wide, flat, unblinking, and grew larger as she watched. It was Papa Jacques's, she realized, and it had her in its power.

Helplessly she tried to swim away. But her arms and legs were paralyzed, and she could not swim a stroke. The eye grew closer, not Papa Jacques's at all: It was a shark wearing a shark necklace, a gourd in its gleaming teeth.

And it was not heading for her but for Mike, who was down below, peering along the bottom, as if he had lost something. He was looking for Thea!

Mike! she shouted. *Michael!*

But no sound came out; her throat was paralyzed too.

She awoke thrashing, bathed in sweat. She had kicked aside the bedclothes—now she'd have to make the bed. Quickly she moved to the window.

The *Neptune's Folly* had been tied to the diving barge all morning long, but now it had cast off its lines and was heading for Masthead Cut.

Or through it? Out to sea? For some reason the idea frightened her.

Ridiculous. They were probably only anchoring over the wreck that Mike had mentioned, a haven for homeless conch.

She washed up from her nap and went to call Hoagie at the airstrip. Everyone wanted her out of her shell, and they were right. If she was going to have nightmares during her siestas, it was time that she woke up.

Jake stood on deck at the helm. He took a quick bearing on Masthead Point, another on Prince George Town, and dropped *Neptune's* old CQR anchor as closely to the wreck site as he dared; he didn't want to foul his hook in the superstructure itself.

He stepped back into the cluttered deckhouse. For the fifth time in the last ten minutes he picked up the mike and called, "*Neptune's Folly* to *Whine Bottle!* Where are you, Mike? Get back to the sub or come up!"

Not a word from below. Damn! He'd been devising a bracket at his workbench when he'd become aware that the *Whine Bottle*'s growl, which you could hear quite clearly on the deckhouse speaker, had quit. Maybe her battery had gone dead. A problem; there was no way to get her back to the surface without installing the spare batteries underwater, and the spares, which they kept in the sail locker, first had to be recharged.

He and William lugged four of them up, started their one-lunger generator, and put them on charge. He started broadcasting for Mike every few minutes. Even if he was away from the sub, he should hear Jake paging him.

No answer. There was nothing to do but wait, or dive himself and see what was going on.

He'd sworn after his last dive that he'd never go down again. He doubted if he could get William to try, either, after the previous day's shark attack.

Well, it was 1:55 P.M. He gave himself five minutes. When the ship's clock on the deckhouse struck four bells, he'd hit the water.

Slowly and reluctantly he gathered his mask and flippers and began to saddle up his tanks.

The breeze through the cut was a cool one, but he was sweating like a pig.

Chapter 4

Mike crouched ten fathoms below the surface in the purser's office, by the door. He breathed as slowly as he could, to husband the air in his tanks. He pushed the door open a few inches. He winced as it squawked, and he held it against the current.

Across the grand entrance salon he sensed motion. The current had washed the torpedo hole free, and the shark was nosing in. There was a sudden scraping, like a boot sole being dragged across a granite rock, and a light gray shape filled the hole.

All at once the shark was in the wreck. The enormous salon and the oaken spiral staircase seemed suddenly half its size. The flashing, golden butterfly fish were instantly gone. An emerald parrot fish flicked by, heading topside. The shark and Mike were the only living beings where thousands had swum a few short moments past.

The shark cruised fore and aft, rising to the top of the spiral staircase, then drifting slowly down. Mike tried to hush his breathing in the regulator, above all to still the squeaking of the door.

His mind went back to Amity long ago, to his first ocean dive in the cherished diving class. He had overcome his stomach cramps and sneaked out of the house.

They were suited up, en route to sea on their instructor's boat *Aqua Queen*—Larry Vaughan, the mayor's son; Andy Nichols, scared to death and as fat as a sausage in his wet suit; all the rest, his classmates and his friends.

Their instructor, Tom Andrews, a bearded, potbellied god who had dived everywhere on earth, was lecturing from the helm, and the subject was man-eaters.

He scoffed at all sharks and men's myths about them. "You hear everything: Don't wear anything bright, never wear anything white; shark chaser *attracts* sharks, shark chaser *repels* sharks; swim toward them, swim away from them; bang them on the nose, don't antagonize them; don't thrash around, make noise, *don't* make noise; make lots of bubbles, bubbles confuse them; don't dive at dusk, don't dive. Forget it all. You'll probably never *see* a shark in your whole poor miserable lives."

They prepared for the final chant they'd sung around the old town pool so many times before. "Okay, men," Tom bellowed, "you all paired up? All hands ready?" He lifted his hands like a choirmaster. "So what do we do going down?"

"Breathe," everyone chorused. "In and out."

"And what do we do coming *up?*"

"Breathe out, out, out!"

"And what's the fastest we ever rise?"

"As slow as our slowest bubble!"

"And what do we get if we surface too fast?"

"The bends, bends, bends!" And then, "Geronimo!" And they'd all jumped in.

He wished he had Tom with him now, but Tom had been a victim of the second shark, while Mike's father had waited above.

Was it all going to happen again?

It was harder breathing now. He was running out of air. The shark nosed closer. The door squeaked.

They said they were attracted to any kind of noise. . . .

Afraid of bubbles?

He thought of Carla with her golden, sun-streaked hair; of Thea with her shining eyes; of his mother, already in the darkest depths of grief.

He began to work his shoulders free of his tank straps. The shark sensed motion and swung toward the door, huge body immobile, slender tail quivering in the current through the wreck.

Mike took a deep breath, exhaled, took another one, exhaled, then another, trying to hyperventilate and charge his blood. It would be a long time, if he survived, to his next breath of air.

Quickly he turned off his tanks. He unscrewed his regulator from the tank block, pointed the nozzle toward the shark beyond the door, and crashed through. He twisted the tank valve open, and a thousand pounds of air pressure poured out of the nipples' holes.

There were bubbles everywhere. He could not see, and neither could the shark. Like a curtain of rising pearls, the air rushed to the top of the chamber. The shark disappeared behind it, and Mike felt the swish of the mighty tail as it fled across the room.

He sidled around it, facing it as it cowered, pointing the tanks at it, and finally, when he was past, using the pressure like a jet to speed him toward the hole.

His lungs were searing when he got there. He laid the tanks inside the hole, gushing bubbles, to form a barrier before it. He left the cloud of them and slithered out.

His chest was heaving; his whole body cried for the blessed light above.

"And what do we do coming *up?*"

"Breathe out, out, out!"

"And what's the fastest we ever rise?"

"As slow as our slowest bubble!"

"And what do we get if we surface too fast?"

"The bends, bends, bends!"

Slowly, fighting the instinct for light and air and life, he kept pace with an errant bubble as it struggled toward the sunlight above.

When he reached the surface, he was almost unconscious, but the lessons of Tom Andrews, years ago, had saved his life.

Ten yards from where he surfaced was *Neptune's Folly*. "Shark!" he croaked.

There was a mighty splash, and in a moment he felt Jake's arm around his shoulders, holding up his head.

Jake dragged him onto the diving platform, then quickly over the stern.

He lay by the compressor, in the golden sunlight, breathing God's own air.

Then Jake's black face was above him, blocking out the sun.

"You forget our submarine, white boy?"

"Rear-ended," he said with a gasp. "Other driver's fault."

"Totaled?"

"Totaled." He felt weakly in his loot bag, came up with the acoustic marker. "Hey, is this what you wanted, Othello?"

Jake nodded. "It'll do."

In the Loma Bella Club, Rico Lomas studied the reservation list at his headwaiter's stand.

He liked to know who his guests would be. He was dependent on the Bay Street Boys—Nassau's financial and political community—for much of his security in the islands, and he always sent a long-stemmed rose to the table of any politician's wife.

The reservation list was spare enough. The jungle bunnies who crowded the place every evening couldn't afford the dinner prices, although they seemed to lose a fortune at the tables.

One name caught his eye: "Seven P.M., Newcombe." A party of two.

Strange, for Newcombe hadn't crossed the threshold since he'd lost twelve grand a year ago in an eight-hour session at the baccarat table.

Trying to recoup was what had turned him into a minor-grade *narcotraficante*. Now he was turning Whiskey Cay into another Galleon and stepping on Rico's Gucci-leather toes.

Well, if that was the reason he was setting up for dope, that one bad night at baccarat would cost the Englishman his life.

Too bad. El Inglés was a good pilot. He could have used him for deliveries. He *had* used Calypso Charters before, hired Hoagie to drop him at five thousand feet over Galleon Cay, in shorts and soccer shoes, hanging from a fast-falling Strato Cloud chute. He'd descended like a god, in the yellow, black, and red of San Juan de Gracia's provincial flag.

He'd landed dead-center on the football field, in time for the final quarter of a game between his *traficantes* and the locals. He'd kicked the winning goal and known that he would live in Bahamian legend forevermore.

Thoughtfully he wandered up to his office. He sat in the ancient swivel chair behind his grandfather's massive desk. He hated it worse than ever. When he finally sold the club, perhaps it could get lost.

He scratched a match on its cigarette-scarred surface. From a solid gold cigarette case he drew a brown-papered *bruto*, a cheap coca-paste street joint. He had started to smoke them long ago to impress weak-stomached subordinates. Over the years he had grown to love them.

He leaned back and thought. The Whiskey Cay airstrip was unlighted and closed at seven P.M. If Newcombe was flying in tonight for dinner in Nassau, he couldn't fly back to Whiskey Cay until tomorrow.

Rico owned two Cigarette speedboats, identical to those of the U.S. Drug Enforcement Agency Blue Thunder Patrol; they were capable of sixty knots.

He pressed his intercom button. "Alejandro?"

"Si, señor?" answered his bodyguard and valet from the basement cocaine-cutting room.

He sucked in the raw, hard coca smoke and suddenly ruled the world.

"Get the black boat ready for tomorrow. And get el Conejo Grande to my office! *Ahora mismo!* Now!"

Alejandro and el Conejo Grande together hardly made a single brain, and he had better get them ready, for tomorrow was the day.

Mike balanced himself on the fifteen-foot bowstrip, which jutted like a javelin from the bow of *Neptune's Folly.*

He was barefoot—the better to keep his balance on the tapered spar. With one hand he clung to the head-stay, a nine-sixteenths-inch stainless-steel cable from the tip of the bowsprit to the peak of the fifty-foot mast. In the other hand he balanced the old whaler's harpoon.

He had been there twenty minutes and had another ten to go before he would be relieved by Jake. William, muttering about a bad-luck boat, flatly refused to do anything but kibitz from the safety of the forward hatch, muttering dire predictions like a black Greek chorus of doom.

Mike's leg muscles flexed like a skier's as he balanced in the swell. The afternoon wind was rising. The current through Masthead Cut had shifted and was on its way out, meeting the Atlantic breakers of the Outside Passage in a maelstrom at the entrance to Masthead Sound.

He peered through the chop, straight down. Visibility

had decreased; he could no longer see the bottom or the wreck. He wondered if the shifting sand had trapped the shark inside the ship with the skeleton.

It had been an expensive morning. A thousand dollars in tanks, regulators, backpacks, and diving weights lay within the wreck beside the hole, and the *Whine Bottle,* as old as she was, was worth at least ten thousand bucks.

He shuddered. It could have been worse. He wasn't going to dive for anything until they found the shark.

"So long, Secretariat," called Jake, heaving a haunch of meat over the starboard bow. It spiraled into the depths.

"Where do you find horse meat?" Mike demanded, almost afraid to ask. Jake admitted he had stolen the harpoon from a restaurant and seemed capable of horse thievery if pushed.

"We eat the stuff where I come from," said Jake. Mike did not know if he was kidding or not. "You don't think Carla's buying *beef* at the Kingston Butcher Shop?"

Mike peered into the water, following the bloody trail. He thought he saw a light-colored shape but lost it in the glitter of the afternoon sun on the waves.

He hefted the harpoon in his hand. It was heavy with the weight of the BPST near its head, bound tightly to the haft with stainless-steel wire. The transducer head of the device, a rounded dome, was placed so that if the point of the harpoon penetrated the shark to a depth of one full foot, it would rest against its skin; presumably it would pick up the heartbeat of a shark if it could work on the feeble pulse of a conch at sixty feet.

Jake had tested it by pressing it against his own wrist, while Mike, at the computer, turned up the volume and the gain. It thumped beautifully over the speaker, sixty times a minute—they could hear it from bow to stern—and left a fine trace of marching mountain peaks on the screen.

The last thing Jake had done to the harpoon was to saw its shaft six inches above the transmitter, but only halfway through, so that it would break off at impact, leaving the point and BPST embedded safely in the flesh.

Now Mike shifted uncomfortably on the bowsprit. He felt exposed and had the sense that something, somewhere, was watching him. "Bad-luck boat," William had said. . . .

"William," said Jake in exasperation, "get your black ass out of that hatch and help me."

Reluctantly William climbed the rest of the way out of the hatch and stood irresolutely on deck.

"Clarence say be careful," he muttered. "He say Papa Jacques put a *wanga* on this boat. Look, mon, what has hoppen to the little submarine!"

"What the hell's a *wanga?*" asked Mike, scanning the water.

"Evil charm," explained Jake, heaving a cut of shoulder off the bow with a splash. "That's Papa Jacques's whole pitch. You play along with his voodoo cure, or you step on a thorn and die."

"*Everybody* says you shouldn't have t'rew his *asson* on the ground, Mike," said William moodily. "Everybody in Prince George Town!"

"*I'll* throw his bloody *asson* on the ground," Jake said with a growl, "if I ever see him near."

All at once Mike saw something rushing from the depths, a great white shape rising like a reef out of the sea. He recoiled on the bowsprit, slipped, and clutched the headstay, flailing helplessly with his harpoon for balance.

As if in slow motion, the monster rose. Blood from the horse meat streamed from the side of his jaws: He must have been feasting somewhere near the keel, from the time they started to chum.

Mike teetered, clinging to the headstay, naked and exposed, staring into the big flat eye. He was paralyzed with fear. He knew with absolute certainty that the creature wanted him.

The huge jaws opened. He saw row upon row of jagged teeth. Half a horse leg dropped from his mouth, and he rose toward the bowsprit stay.

"Hit the son of a bitch!" screamed Jake.

Hanging from the headstay, Mike drew back his arm and took aim. "For you, Sean," he grunted, and flung the iron with all the strength he had.

The harpoon sank into the shimmering, shining flank, buried itself up to the transmitter, and quivered.

The shark did not even flinch. Off-balance from the throw, Mike tottered on the bowsprit, managed to cling to the headstay, and pirouetted around it.

He was helpless, suspended over the water. He drew back his free arm, felt a sandpaper snout brush his hand, and heard a snap like a giant steel trap.

He caught one last glimpse of the eye and saw a cold, cold promise that someday they'd meet again.

The shark crashed back into the water in a sheet of stinging foam. The shaft of the harpoon broke off, leaving its point and the transmitter well embedded in his flesh. With a whisk of his enormous, tapered tail, he was gone.

From the pilothouse they heard a sudden steady drumbeat: *Boom . . . boom . . . boom . . .*

Mike staggered back along the bowsprit like a drunken tightrope walker and clung to the main mast, shaking.

The eye, the eye, and the promise behind it . . .

It was the shark that had hit his brother—he knew it in his soul.

He was shaking from head to toe.

Someone thrust a beer into his hand. He looked up. Jake was beaming at him.

"Man, you got him *tagged!*"

"Jake," he murmured, "I must be crazy, but . . ."

"What?"

"I saw his eye."

"Yeah?" murmured Jake. "So what, mon?"

"That shark has *me* tagged too."

Chapter 5

Ellen sat across the table from Hoagie in a swirl of reggae music at the Loma Bella Club in Nassau.

The food had been terrible—and terribly expensive. She felt badly, for she knew that Hoagie would never let her pick up the check, and if he did, the hundred-dollar blue chip Carla had given her would not even come close.

The bar was crowded with islanders, black and white, and the casino, beyond, was jammed. Hoagie introduced her to a Goombay Smash, a drink with an umbrella in it, and she was pleasantly high.

She had told him about herself but knew practically nothing of him. Whenever the conversation touched on his life, he shied away.

She couldn't stand it. She liked him too much. As always, she was forthright. If something bothered her, she simply had to know.

"What do you really want to do, Hoagie? Buy an airplane? Build an airline?"

"I *have* an airplane. I have a perfectly good 1941 Stearman open-cockpit two-seater biplane sitting in Calypso's hangar on Whiskey Cay. She's called the *Yellow Peril*." He glanced at her. "She's stressed for aerobatics, and her rear seat is simply waiting for the proper ballast."

She grinned. "And the proper ballast is what? 38–28–38? With flaming red hair, or brunette?"

His lazy eyes slid sidewise. They crinkled beautifully

when he smiled. He played with his cigarettes. "Your own measurements would do quite well. And your hair would be quite lovely, peeking from an old leather helmet, which I would supply. You'd look rather smashing in goggles."

She felt herself blushing. She gazed at her drink, swirling it. "And you'd do *what* to this poor girl? Loops, rolls . . . what is it? Immelmanns?"

"One could do that, I suppose. Or . . ."

"Or what?"

"One might take off and head south, quite straight and level. To Cat Island and Great Exuma, then Crooked Island, Great Inagua. Then across the Windward passage, avoiding Cuba like the plague."

She found herself hanging on his words. She saw white-sand beaches, emerald coves, palm trees heaving in the breeze.

His voice dropped. "And finally one might alight at Montego Bay, Jamaica, where I have a little cottage that looks down on the old harbor."

She sighed. "I suppose one might, if one had the freedom." She studied his face. "Hoagie, what do you *really* do?"

His warm eyes dropped. "I fly freight, sky divers, tourists—"

"I know, I've read your airplane." She took a deep breath. "But, Hoagie, do you fly dope?"

"Dopes," he said softly, watching someone approaching, "like this one here." He did not rise, but he smiled, and the smile came through badly. "Rico! *Amigo mío*. How *have* you been?"

A flashily dressed young man looked down on them. He was overscented with after-shave. He spoke with a Latin accent. "Wing Commander Newcombe! Lone Eagle of Whiskey Cay! I welcome you, *amigo*."

"You should, old chap," said Hoagie, "after last time."

"And the lady is?"

"A very dear friend, Rico."

To Ellen the name rang a bell. Carla had mentioned him. She dug the blue chip from her purse. "You gave this to my daughter-in-law last night. So we're back."

He grinned, and the grin was as frosty as her glass. "Don't let Señor Newcombe get it. His luck, except in women, is very, very bad."

Hoagie's eyes flashed, and he watched him as he crossed the room. "That man," he murmured softly, "is a blot on the human race."

"Why do you bother to speak to him?"

"Sky diver," he said with a shrug. "Every time his macho needs a polishing, it's two hundred more in the boss's till." He nodded toward the gaming room. "Shall we see if you can make him pay for dinner, then? I'll teach you all the twenty-one I know."

He paid the bill in cash, and they wandered to the casino.

Rico Lomas spoke in the fast *llanos* Spanish that even Mexicans had trouble following. He sat at a table near the bar with el Conejo Grande and Alejandro, his boat driver.

Alejandro was a dark-eyed, ambitious, young *campesino* from San Juan de Gracia, hardly yet a man, who had killed three Leopards—Special Anti-narcotics Unit agents—from the capital when they'd discovered his mother's little coca crop drying in the *llanos* sun.

Rico could see Newcombe and the woman at the twenty-one table, capably in the hands of Louisa, his fastest dealer. They were within earshot. It pleased him to be plotting Newcombe's death within hearing distance of the man; it would please his grandfather, el Viejo, too, if the old man knew.

He drew a map of Whiskey Cay on a napkin with a pen of solid gold. Carefully he sketched in the airstrip and a tiny, man-made, dredged indentation named Salt Hole, where the island traders had tied up on ancient days to take on salt.

"You will tie to the stone quay here," he said. "As he turns the plane thus, on his final leg, his eyes will be on the airstrip, for it is very small and tricky to get in. At full power, Alejandro, you will round the point . . . like this. . . ."

He drew the traffic pattern that he knew Newcombe would fly. "He is not like some of our flying mules, he was a carrier pilot in the RAF, and his final approach will be very short." Casually he added, "I know this. I have flown with him and jumped from his little plane."

"Sí, señor," said Alejandro, eyes shining in admiration. "I remember. *Ay!*"

Rico shrugged modestly. El Conejo Grande said nothing. He was pulling at his white mustache, scowling at the napkin, apparently already overwhelmed by the complexity of the plan.

"Es difícil?" Rico exploded, exasperated. "It's too complicated for you, Conejo?"

"Of course not," el Conejo answered with a growl. His eyes flashed ominously. *"Señor,* I have told you before, my name is Carlos."

"Well, if you screw it up this time, your name is not Carlos but mud!"

The big man had no idea what he was talking about. Rico sighed and continued his briefing. He could hear his victims laughing while they lost their money to his dealer. This amused him.

When he was through, he dismissed el Conejo, to

have a few words with Alejandro: a contingency plan, they called it in the military. Just in case el Conejo failed again. . . .

Ellen and Hoagie were the only people at Louisa's twenty-one table. The rest of the crowd was gathered around the roulette wheel or shooting craps.

"Hit me," muttered Ellen. She was beginning to get the idea of the game: You tried to get as close to twenty-one as you could, without going over.

She had changed her hundred-dollar chip into three-dollar ones, for the Bahamians had a three-dollar bill and chips to match. Louisa dealt a card faceup. Now Ellen had a ten and a seven: seventeen. She saw that Louisa had an ace.

"Hit me again," said Ellen.

"No," advised Hoagie. "Stand pat. She has an ace."

Louisa sneaked a glance at Rico's table.

"He is right, *mon chéri,*" she whispered quickly. "You'll go out."

"I won't," Ellen insisted, "I mean it." She grinned. "I feel it deep inside."

"You feel wrong, luv." Hoagie chuckled as Louisa put another card down. "You should always trust the pros."

She looked at the card. The five of diamonds. They were right, she was out. She checked her pocketbook. Hoagie had refused to play: Louisa seemed glad that he had, as if he were an alcoholic turning down a drink.

Ellen had reduced her assets to four dollars. She hesitated. Well, why not? She could hardly bring Carla four dollars back out of a hundred—better to return empty-handed. She bet it and lost it. Louisa seemed genuinely sad.

"I don't care," said Ellen. It was fun to play with a

cardsharp. She had tried to play twenty-one with Sean once, and they couldn't remember the rules.

Her heart lurched. The loss she had carried from before Christmas had somehow slipped away this evening, and now—as if she had forgotten a heavy grocery bag in her car and only just noticed it—it was back. Sean was gone, and there would be no more card games, or warm summer evenings on the porch, or movies with him, ever. . . .

Louisa was looking at her strangely. Ignoring Hoagie, she murmured, "You have forgotten for a while your sorrow, *n'est-ce pas?*"

Ellen nodded. "You are truly fey."

Louisa tossed her head at her boss, retreating toward the stairway. "Now that he is gone, the hell with it. You have lost quite enough, and I am sorry. If I let you win, he would fire me, or worse." She began to shuffle her cards. "Fey? I know that word. *Oui,* I feel things, yes . . ." A slim black man in a garish shirt wanted to play; she shook her head. "This table is closed."

When he left, she spread the cards. "Some see colors no one sees, some hear sounds that others do not hear. I *feel.*" She looked up. "The child is well, I hope?"

Ellen nodded. "Yes."

"*Eh bien.*" She peered at her cards. "'Oagie? You do not fly back tonight?"

He shook his head. "Airstrip closes at dusk, you know. We're staying with Carla's agent." He grinned. "I couldn't talk her into a room in a local hotel."

"No," said Ellen, disgusted with herself for blushing. "That you couldn't."

"Why don't you take the New Providence–Whiskey Cay boat?" Louisa asked. She seemed somehow to be pleading. "*I* take the boat each night."

"Why would we take the boat?" Hoagie smiled. "I

have to get the old crate home, can't leave it here in Nassau."

Louisa looked into Ellen's eyes. "The cards," she murmured, "say *take the boat*."

Ellen felt a chill but answered, "I'm with him."

The *houngan* had not a proper *tonelle*, which some would call a church.

But he did have Clarence's house, a two-room shack not far from Masthead Point. And he had a choir, and its leader, a *houngenikon* woman, dressed in white with a red bandanna, whom he had cured of headaches many years before.

By the bed in which Clarence's children ordinarily slept, she and Papa Jacques had laid rows of rum, whiskey, and vermouth bottles, all full, alternating with cloth-covered bundles and white porcelain pots. In them lived the *loas* and the spirits of the dead. A hen, tethered by a foot, cackled, pecked, and fouled the splintered floor.

Papa Jacques's *société* had gathered, some from Whiskey Cay and others by fishing boat from nearby islets. There were thirty sweating people jammed into the rickety little room.

Papa Jacques stepped outside in the moonlight. He shook his *asson* at the moon, rattled the gourd, and tinkled the tiny silver bell hanging from it.

He moved back inside and surveyed his congregation. It was a *société* less versed in *vaudou* ways than his followers in Haiti, but just as devout.

He took a deep breath, set the rhythm with the gourd. It was not like his *tonelle* in Port-au-Prince, but he had what he needed: the congregation, the spirits, and the *wanga*.

His *houngenikon* caught the rhythm of the gourd. In her high, clear voice she began the chant:

Maître Agwe, where are you?
Don't you see I'm on the reef?
I've a rudder in my hand. . . .

Papa Jacques began the dance in a wild *martinique*, and within minutes the congregation was in a frenzy: empty-eyed women in bandannas making wild, impossible leaps across the floor; stiff-faced puppet men in straw hats, staggering but never falling; steel drums singing, tubas wailing, and all the while the *houngan*'s *asson* keeping time.

When the dance was at its peak, he hung the *wanga* from the cabin's center post.

It was one of Michael Brody's shirts, stolen by a devotee from his washerwoman's line that day.

The *houngan* fingered his shark's-tooth necklace, sent his mind beneath the sea, and went into a trance himself.

Mike Brody was trapped, drowning. The great white had nosed through the creaking door of the wreck, was filling the doorway; Mike cowered behind the skeleton of the purser, out of air. Bubbles rose between them, but the great white ignored them and came onward, and there was blood in the water. . . .

He sat up with a start. Carla lay beside him, breathing deeply. He heard a distant chant. He listened curiously. It lacked the rhythm of the steel-drum calypso you often heard when the breezes blew along the beach from Prince George Town, or the primitive *goombay* beat you heard at the Junkanoo masquerades. It had a gloomier voice to it, and a richer, jungle swing.

Curious, he got up and moved to the open window. He was wearing only boxer shorts, but the night was balmy and the moon was bright. The sound seemed to him to be coming from Masthead Point.

He was thirsty. Sometimes, if he couldn't sleep, a glass of milk helped. He moved quietly to the kitchen, careful not to awaken Carla. She had been working too hard, and he had too. They had hardly spoken a word to each other since his mother had arrived, and they hadn't made love in a week.

He should tell her of the shark. Now that it was tagged, it posed no danger. As long as it cruised Masthead Sound, he and Jake would tail it.

They had decided to study it if it stayed long enough, and if the conch project failed.

How many marine biologists had studied the heartbeat of *Carcharodon carcharias* in the wild? He wasn't wedded to conch; a thesis was a thesis and a degree was a degree.

There was a paper to be written about great whites, maybe more papers than one.

He stepped out to the porch. The music seemed to be rising in intensity. Curious, he put down the milk and wandered down the steps.

He felt oddly light-headed, as if he were still in the dream. The sea breeze ruffled his shorts as he moved along the path. When scrub and branches whipped his legs, he hardly felt it. He was barefoot, but even when he stepped on rocks and shells, it didn't seem to hurt.

He shook his head. Weird . . . that Clarence could afford to throw a party when he hadn't worked for days. Invited or not, he found that he wanted to go.

He seemed to be floating above the path, as if he had lost his will. All at once he became aware that he was being followed. He turned and saw no one, but he felt it in his soul.

He stepped aside and waited in the brush.

Thea glided along the path, eyes as vacant as the moon. She was walking in her sleep, he knew, for her hands were extended before her, as if someone were pulling her along.

Her face was impassive, utterly blank. So she was going to the party too. . . .

"Mike! Mike!" he heard Carla calling faintly, from his house. "Where are you? Thea! *Where are you?*"

He came to his senses by the side of the trail. What the hell was he doing *here?*

Thea, with her spiritless eyes, did not see him until he took her into his arms.

"Thea, Thea, baby doll," he muttered, holding her close. The palm trees rustled above them. From that point the chanting stopped.

She looked at him in wonder, as her empty eyes took life.

"Daddy, why'd you bring me here? At *night?*"

High on a hill above Nassau, Ellen Brody stood at the French window in the guest room of Carla's agent's pink-stucco mansion. It overlooked the lights of the harbor. She took off the pearl necklace—cultured, an anniversary present from Brody years ago—and sighed.

Roger, Carla's agent, had settled Hoagie in the library, on a cot. Hoagie had bowed and said good night, a humorous gleam in his eye. She wondered now if he had been serious when he proposed the hotel room or was just trying to get a smile from her.

Perhaps he had better be careful what he proposed; she hadn't slept with a man since Brody died, and that was a year ago.

She could hear him making a telephone call now, from the library. His voice was muffled. She retreated from the window, took down her hair, and was about to undress when she looked out the window and saw Hoagie heading through the garden for the great iron gate.

A walk in the moonlight? Perhaps. And maybe she should join him. She was about to turn away from the window when she saw him open the iron-grille gate. He stepped outside, lit a cigarette, and leaned there, obviously waiting for someone.

Not a walk in the moonlight, then. A late date with some woman?

Curiosity was her greatest fault. Brody had said she should have been a detective. She simply had to know.

She moved quietly through the enormous living room. She could hear her host and hostess upstairs, probably discussing Hoagie and her, and she wondered if they had changed the sleeping arrangements.

Well, certainly not tonight . . .

She found that he had left the door ajar. So he intended to return. Suppose he did, and found her following him?

Then she'd simply tell him she'd got curious. The heck with it.

She slipped down the garden path, smelling bougainvillea in the fresh Bahamian air. A pair of headlights was winding up the street, painting the stucco walls orange.

She stopped in the moon shadow of an ancient elm. The car drew to a halt, engine running. She saw Hoagie take a packet from his jacket and hand it to the man. She caught the silhouette of the driver counting money inside. The driver handed out another packet, the size of the pocketbook in her room. Hoagie put it on the hood of the car, inspected it, nodded, and began to wrap it again.

She whirled and hurried back to the house. Her heart

was beating, and breaking too. In this place and in this time, it could only be dope.

Oh, Brody, she cried silently. *Why ever did you leave me here alone?*

She went to bed, tossed and turned, and finally she slept.

Chapter 6

The long black speedboat rested in the shade of the concrete quay on the seaward side of Whiskey Cay. Carlos Flores—el Conejo Grande—checked the gold imitation Rolex on his wrist.

The Rolex was the badge of the coquero. No *traficante* would be seen without one, but there was a certain pecking order, too: If he bought a real one, which was well within his means, the family of el Viejo would consider it an affront.

It was almost eight-thirty. He and Alejandro had left Nassau before sunrise and pounded across the chop to Whiskey Cay as dawn broke to the east.

It had been a miserable trip, at almost sixty knots, into a blinding sun. Carlos hated Cigarette speedboats: Their jockeys never drove them at anything less than full throttle, and if you tried to sit, it cracked your back, and if you stood, clinging to the grab rail, then your feet gave out.

Carlos had fallen arches. He had decided, while soaking them one night, that they had collapsed from standing guard over members of el Viejo's family, who were always sitting down.

At least the boat had made it on schedule, before el Inglés had landed. Carlos had hardly slept the night before, in fear of Alejandro's being late to the dock, or engine trouble, or being stopped by a Bahamian narcotics patrol vessel before he got here.

For it was a matter of life and death, as much for him as for Newcombe. No excuse would suffice this time.

He was convinced his boss would rather see *him* dead than his victim.

Madre de Díos, what curse had fallen on him that el Viejo would sentence him to this godforsaken island and his ill-begotten grandson, at his age?

It was true he'd deserted a shipment and abandoned a weapon, but one so old and wise as el Viejo should be *simpático* to the miseries of the aging: flat feet, failing eyesight, a memory that slipped, a certain lack of zeal.

Nothing must slip this morning, or he would get no older.

"I hear something," muttered Alejandro.

El Conejo Grande's pulse began to pound. "What? What is it?"

Alejandro held up his hand, cocking his head. *"Un avion.* Single-engine, I think."

He heard nothing. "A little Cessna? Can you tell?"

Alejandro had spent much of his adult life listening for Blue Thunder speedboats on the water and U.S. Drug Enforcement Agency planes in the air. Like most *traficantes,* he claimed that he could identify any aircraft flown by man by the sound of its engine alone.

"Sí, a 182, I think, Conejo."

That name again! *"No es Conejo!* I am *Carlos!"*

The young man grinned. Yawning, he strolled to the wheel and turned his switch. *"Lo siento.* I forgot." The engine whined and caught.

Carlos dug into the side locker. Under a pair of Rico's skis, in a canvas fishing-rod cover, was his M14. He jerked the weapon from the cover, fumbling with the zipper.

Rico had suggested an Uzi. But an Uzi was for children on *los llanos* to hunt narcotics agents with. The ancient M14 was a weapon for a man. It weighed fifteen pounds and carried twenty rounds of .308 ammunition in the clip.

In his excitement he dropped the magazine.

"Careful, old man." Alejandro chuckled, tossing off his lines. The engine chortled happily. "Don't shoot off your foot. Or mine."

He still could see no airplane. He was peering into the western sky when Alejandro rounded the corner of the little basin and slammed the throttle on.

He found himself on his back in the bilges, weapon pointed at the sky. He could hear the peals of laughter from Alejandro in the bow.

He got up slowly. Nothing was broken. Slapping in the ammo clip, Carlos glared at the driver's back. He'd like to shoot him, and their youthful *patrón* too. But perhaps he'd better concentrate on Newcombe.

Now, at least, he could see the plane.

Ellen gazed sadly down through the windshield at the scalloped shore of Masthead Sound. The tiny engine droned on, making her sleepy.

She could see the diving barge in the distance, and *Neptune's Folly* underway, drawing a spreading emerald wake across the turquoise lagoon.

Michael's house, in its separate cove, and the others closer to town, baked whitely in the morning sun. The cays were a series of picture postcards laid end to end.

She glanced at Hoagie. He suddenly seemed intent on the *Folly* and what it was doing. He looked at her swiftly, then looked away.

"What is it?" she asked.

"Nothing, Ellen. Nothing at all."

A strange and reticent man. She had not spoken to Hoagie about his visitor the previous night. She had no idea what was in the packet and imagined the worst: cocaine. She hoped it was not in the plane; she imagined that if it was, it was in the scruffy, oversize briefcase in which he carried his charts and weather data.

She imagined herself in the Prince George jail, with Michael raising hell. This was awful. Suppose he was carrying it?

"Hoagie?" she began, "there's something I have to ask."

Hoagie glanced at her. He was wearing his usual flying uniform: khaki shorts with a million pockets; a tropical shirt tied in front; his battered RAF cap, worn cocked.

He looked as if he were flying a World War II mission on the old Burma Road.

"Yes?" he asked guardedly.

She could not go on. "Nothing."

"What's wrong?" he asked quietly. "Things not right for you?"

She was a poor liar but she tried. "Things are fine." She stretched. "It's such a beautiful morning, I was just sitting here, enjoying it."

"Want to fly? I'll bet by now you could get this bucket on the strip, all by yourself."

The day before, on the way to Nassau, he had given her a lesson, condensed but very thorough. She'd liked it and ended up waltzing through the sky like a veteran. He'd pronounced her a natural pilot, Amelia Earhart reborn. He probably said that to all his lady passengers, with his quiet English charm.

"I don't think so, Hoagie. I'd rather sit and watch."

He throttled back. They were descending toward the airstrip. "Shoulder harness, seat belt locked?"

"Okay," she said, checking.

"Fuel selector, both," he chanted, his hands darting among the controls. "Eighteen inches, high rpm."

He was paralleling the tiny airstrip, intent on his landing. She gazed at him, to the left. A sleek black speedboat was tugging a rooster-tail of spray around Masthead Point, leaving a curved, graceful wake on the choppy water outside the cut.

"Mixture, rich," droned Hoagie in a clipped British monotone. She felt utterly secure in his tanned, steady hands.

"Carburetor heat, on. Autopilot, off. Air conditioner, off."

He tossed up a wing in a steep, steep bank. "Flaps, coming down . . . ten degrees, fifteen . . ."

She heard the wing flaps grinding, and the nose of the plane went down. All at once she had complete vision: the whitecapped Atlantic below them, a sandy beach, then the airstrip, white official jeep, ramshackle terminal beyond. The black speedboat had stopped and was lying dead in the water, between them and the end of the runway, just off the beach.

She saw two men aboard, and one of them seemed to be pointing at them. Perhaps fishing?

All at once Hoagie muttered, "What the bloody hell?"

He flipped up the flaps, and all hell broke loose. He was suddenly yawing, weaving to the left, slamming her against her safety straps, then lurching to the right. She heard the engine roar with power, and they were diving for the water, as if he were going to ram the boat. At the last instant he pulled up in a crazy wingover.

All at once there was a brutal jolt above her, as if they had hit something.

"Damn!" Hoagie said with a growl, fighting the controls. There was another jolt, and another, and then they were climbing, fishtailing, lurching, writhing through the sky.

The smell of gasoline was everywhere, and suddenly it was pouring down her neck, inundating her.

"Petrol tank, in the wing," grunted Hoagie. He grabbed his microphone. *"Nassau Center, Cessna four-five Charlie, Mayday, Mayday, Mayday. Midair colli-*

sion with a bloody bird. My petrol tank is leaking, and I'm off the air for now."

She was drowning in gasoline. It was burning her skin, her eyes, her face. "Hoagie!"

"Hang on, luv," he murmured. "Just hang on and we'll see what we can do.

And then they smelled the smoke.

On the *Neptune's Folly,* Mike and Jake had been searching for the great white all morning, triangulating when they heard the boom of his heartbeat, estimating when he faded from their screen, triangulating as he returned within their range.

They had seen no swimmers close to him at any time and had dogged him through the hours just after dawn.

Now they were solidly on his tail. He was doing a steady three knots, due south toward Spanish Galleon Cay, when Mike heard an aircraft engine. He looked up and saw Hoagie's Cessna heading for the airstrip.

He hoped that his mother had enjoyed her evening in Nassau. If Hoagie could only cheer her up!

He was standing at the helm when he heard the sound of gunshots—or an airplane backfiring—from the island's airstrip. It was out of sight behind Masthead Point, and he could not pin it down.

He tried to concentrate on the booming from the speaker. The shark was lazing along. God knew what he was finding to eat below: dorados, perhaps, or skate, or harmless sand sharks.

Then he heard the sound of Hoagie's engine change. Now it throbbed as if pressed. He turned swiftly and searched the northern sky.

Suddenly he froze. A Cessna was dragging a plume of dirty black smoke from the airstrip up, up into the sky. He saw a flicker of flame.

Hoagie? Yes, it had to be.

"Jake!" he screamed. "Get up here!"

The plane would come down in Masthead Sound—if it didn't crash at sea.

Jake was suddenly at his side. He took in the situation instantly. "William! Life jackets, life buoys, anything that floats!"

"Get the dinghy ready!" ordered Mike.

By the time he had the boat heading for the airstrip, Hoagie was well in sight. Mike stared.

He was smoking badly, engine coughing, and he was going to put it on the beach.

Mike dashed into the deckhouse, grabbed his binoculars, and sprinted out again.

He had an awful feeling that Thea was playing in the sand.

Hands shaking, he leveled the glasses.

She was building her sand castle, all alone.

Chapter 7

The aging Cessna fought for altitude in the clear Bahamian sky. Smoke was gushing from the engine nacelle, filling the cabin. Hoagie had a handkerchief jammed to his face, coughing as he wrestled with the controls.

Ellen cringed in her seat, taut with fear, skin stinging from the gasoline, eyes blurring.

"Steady, luv," Hoagie called above the engine's throb. "We'll get this kite down somehow, don't you fear. . . ."

He reached across and squeezed her hand. She dabbed at her eyes with the hem of her skirt. She was soaked in gasoline, choking with it, stinging with its caustic bite. She had an impulse to open the window for air and began to fumble with the latch.

He grabbed her arm and shouted, "No! Leave it closed!" He began to cough. In a strangled voice he added, "Exhaust manifold fire . . . can't . . . risk . . . letting the flames in here."

He was banking, and steeply. She felt a lightness in the pit of her stomach, a queasy, vacant sense of disembodiment. She was thrown against her seat belt toward the ceiling of the plane.

The world was suddenly all askew; the blazing sun was below them, the glittering turquoise sound gyrating above. She heard him curse.

A Klaxon began to croak endlessly. It was the stall-warning horn he had told her of the previous day, the first signal of a spin.

They were spinning, then, and it must be the end.

He eased the yoke forward and fought the rudder pedals. "He hit a control cable . . . knocked it off its pulley, I should think . . . steady, steady, steady . . ." He murmured to the airplane as a rider gentles a horse. "Steady, poor old thing. . . ."

The island, the sea, the point, all swung swiftly around them, again and again and again. The engine slowed, and Ellen could hear the whisper of the slipstream past the wings, and it increased in pitch, rising to a shriek.

"Easy, old girl," he muttered, still speaking to the plane. "Easy does it, dear old kite, we haven't bought it yet. . . ."

Slowly the plane straightened out. The pressure on her seat belt eased. Soaked in gasoline, she peered out of the windshield.

Somehow, miraculously, he had brought sense to a world gone insane. They were over Masthead Sound but very low. Down to her right she could see *Neptune's Folly,* even spot the men aboard. She saw Jake's big frame drop into the rubber dinghy, then pause, riveted, as they passed overhead.

On the stern, Mike was waving frantically. Ellen's heart went out to him. He must feel more helpless watching the burning, crippled plane than she did in the cabin herself.

Sitting erect, impassive, Hoagie was serene but attentive, listening to voices from his stricken plane that only he could hear. In some way she caught his tranquillity.

The smoke was filling the cabin. She could barely see out. She heard him coughing. "Going to try a deadstick landing. Daren't use the engine with that fire."

He cut the engine, and it was suddenly deathly silent in the cockpit. They were very, very low. Once again she could hear him murmuring his checklist.

"Flaps down." She heard the grinding of the flaps

again, and the nose of the plane dropped sickeningly. All at once, beyond waving palms that seemed as high as they were, she saw Michael's home through the smoke in the cabin. A narrow strand of alabaster beach showed that the tide was out. The hard sand gleamed like ivory in the sun.

Hoagie growled into his microphone: "Nassau Center, Cessna four-aught-five-three Charlie, on final, for a go at Masthead Beach. Good day, old man, cheerio, and out."

"The trees!" she said with a gasp.

"Sure, the trees . . ." He banked gently, heading for the shortest of the grove. Through the smoke she saw him smiling. "Poems are made by fools like me . . ."

She stared. He was *enjoying* this!

The palm fronds were suddenly reaching up at them, grasping at their wheels. "Hoagie!"

She heard the whisk of their passage, felt a jarring, and they were free.

"But only God," Hoagie continued, "only God can make a tree."

They were only a few feet above the ground now, and the nose was coming up. It seemed incredible that he thought he could land before they hit the hill on Masthead Point.

She peered ahead. Through the smoke and the oily windshield she glimpsed a tiny tanned form in the distance, where Thea and she had started their castle. "Hoagie!" she screamed. "Thea's there!"

He switched his magneto on and jammed the throttle forward, but the engine only belched and flamed. She saw Thea turn, throw up her hands protectively, and then the propeller, tossing shards of sunlight, cut off her view as the nose came up.

"Oh, my God!" Hoagie grunted. "Oh, my God!"

* * *

Carlos Flores stood gripping the stainless-steel handrail as they bounced around Masthead Point. He kept his Panama hat on his head with his other hand. The M14 was safely back in the locker, in its bag. He sagged with relief. The Cessna was twisting and writhing, and he knew that it must fall.

The Englishman obviously had spotted him before he'd fired, and Carlos was proud that he had hit it, despite the pilot's desperate moves.

"Ay!" he exulted, wiping his glasses as he saw the smoke begin. "I am not too old to be a *contra, no es verdad?"*

"Viejo, who could have missed?" said Alejandro, scoffing, his strong young teeth flashing in the sun. "My baby brother could have downed it with his slingshot!" He glanced at the plane and added, "Besides, it is not down yet."

"No hay problema." The big man shrugged. "He is dead."

Some of the joy of the kill had fled with the young man's stupid jest. It was true that it had been like shooting a pigeon that was coming home to roost, until el Inglés had begun waltzing over the sky like a drunken goose.

Slingshot? No. For then he had needed all his skill, and he had put at least three rounds into the frail and ancient airplane, at under two hundred yards. He relived the jolt of the heavy piece against his shoulder, the smell of smokeless powder in the breeze, the thrill he had felt when he knew the rounds were home. Not bad.

He peered into the blazing sky. Now the plane was spinning. At any moment he expected to see it tumble from the sky.

"Slow down!" he yelled at Alejandro over the rumble of the Chevy's engine as they were hurled across the chop. *"Más despacio, amigo!* I want to see it hit the water! When we bounce, how can I see?"

Alejandro cut his power, and the big man stumbled against the forward panel. *Idiot,* thought Flores. He found the airplane again and focused.

Mierda! Somehow the pilot was recovering from the spin. And now he seemed to be heading for a beach near Prince George Town.

Flores swallowed. He glanced at Alejandro. The youth was watching the plane, openmouthed. "*Ay,* Conejo! He will try to land it on that beach."

"He will never get there."

"I think he will." The boy grinned.

Whose side was he on, anyway? He should throw him to the sharks. "Well, he will not!"

Wallowing in the swell, Flores could not see. He took his glasses off and cleaned them. When he put them back on, he could see too well: The plane was still aloft.

"Madre de Díos," he breathed. "Let him hit those trees!"

Panic began to engulf him. His hands were clammy with sweat. The plane was below the palms, must surely strike them, was smoking worse than ever. All at once it seemed to soar—a burst of flame, thank God—no, it was past the trees.

The big man kept his eyes on the plane, while his mind scurried like a cornered rat. He had a .38 Magnum in a shoulder holster and a derringer strapped to his calf. He could storm ashore and kill the Englishman easily enough, if he survived the landing.

"Go in there," he said. "Go in to that dock."

"No, el Conejo Grande," said the youth. "El Patrón's instructions were quite clear."

All right. He would force Alejandro off the boat at gunpoint, kill him in the water, and somehow drive the craft to Union Dock in Nassau. A taxi to the airport, and by the time Rico discovered that el Inglés lived and Alejandro was dead, he could be aboard a plane to Mexico.

He had money in the Bank of Panama to last him all his life, even though he'd have to spend it on the run.

The hell with Rico, the hell with el Viejo, the hell with the *coquero*'s life. He was as free as a bird.

He turned swiftly, reaching for his gun. He froze. Alejandro, grinning hugely, had a .45 leveled at his chest.

"El Conejo Grande," he said, smiling softly, "I think you have failed again."

"No!"

"Your Magnum, *amigo, por favor?* And the little gun besides."

Flores handed them over, his hand shaking. The young man dropped them delicately in the water.

Now the terror was washing over him like waves in a storm. "Alejandro, we are friends too long for this. . . ."

"We are still friends, el Conejo Grande. Have a seat."

The youth jammed the throttle forward. The boat sprang through the sea, and el Conejo Grande found himself in the stern, flat on his back.

He knew that he would be better off if he dived over the side and let Alejandro put a slug through his head while he was in the water.

But his legs had turned to liquid, and he could not get off the deck of the lurching, bucking speedboat.

As Hoagie pulled the nose up, the plane continued to settle. Ellen heard him curse. Again he jammed the throttle forward, and the engine belched and died. They struck the beach with a jar.

"We've hit her!" she shrieked.

In one motion he cut the ignition, hauled the wheel of the yoke back into his lap, and jammed on the brakes. Jolting and skidding, they came to a stop six feet from the bracken on Masthead Point.

He lunged across her, opened her door, and pushed her out. She landed in a heap, and as she scrambled up, she saw him sprinting back down the beach.

When she got to the castle, he had Thea in his arms. "Jumped clear," he muttered, touching the child's cheek. "There's a good girl, now. It's over, Thea, right?"

Thank God, she thought. Thank God. . . .

Thea pointed at their castle. There were tears in her eyes. A tire had demolished the whole elaborate structure. Turret, drawbridge, the princess's conch-shell balcony, all were scattered far and wide.

Ellen took her from his arms. "We're going to build a better one. With *two* balconies for the princess and a portal for Prince Charming to ride through—"

Her voice caught and she could not go on.

"When?" asked Thea, squirming to get down. "Now?"

"Not now," she said, "but later."

Hoagie looked into her eyes and murmured, "You're a very cool lady, Ellen."

"And you saved our lives," she said. Then she took Thea's hand and led her to the house.

At the house she turned. Hoagie was back at his airplane, shooting foam into the engine with a fire extinguisher. Michael raced up the path from the dock. He took her into his arms.

"What happened?" he murmured. "What happened, Mom?"

She tried to smile. "I don't really know." She looked into his eyes. "It could have been worse, but just more bad luck, I guess."

Mike watched Hoagie sip his gin and tonic on the veranda. Carla was searching for scrap metal from a wreck at the southern end of the island, on Bowsprit

Point. Ellen was showering the smell of gasoline away. Thea, who seemed to care more about her sand castle than her narrow escape, was bent over a coloring book at the other end of the porch.

"What do you mean, you hit a *bird?*" demanded Mike.

"A tern," said Hoagie tersely. "Saw it just before it hit."

"Can a bird put a hole in your wing tank?"

"At eighty knots, Mike, yes." Hoagie nodded at the plane on the beach. "She's not a Harrier fighter, you know, just a beat-up old Cessna with tissue-paper wings." He sipped his drink. "I wonder that it didn't take that aileron off too."

"How bad is it?" Mike asked. The plane seemed to be Calypso's only one, and Hoagie's only livelihood. Or was it, after all?

"She'll be all right. I've called in a Nassau mechanic. I'll have her off your beach tomorrow, if I can clear that hill."

"Just *one* bird?" asked Mike. "My mother says she heard more than one thing hit the wing."

"A *flock* of birds," said Hoagie.

"Sure," said Mike sardonically, "one good tern deserves another." He stood up and walked to the railing. "Mind if I take a look?"

Hoagie stiffened. "What are you getting at?"

Mike swung back. "Look," he said, flaring. "I heard *gunfire* from the deck of the *Folly,* halfway across Masthead Sound. What were these 'birds' armed with? Twenty-millimeter cannon in their wings?"

"You heard backfires," Hoagie said calmly. "A rebuilt Continental engine, don't you see?" He lit a cigarette. "It resents it when I make it work too hard."

"That's bullshit!" Mike slammed down his glass. "Somebody almost killed my mother, and I'm calling the police!"

"Now *that* I wish you wouldn't do."

"Why not?"

Hoagie shrugged. "We all have our reasons for disliking prying eyes." He blew a cloud of smoke into the morning air and watched it drift away. "I don't imagine you heard anything *else* in the middle of the Sound?"

"What do you mean?" Mike asked cautiously.

"Well, flying in this morning, I saw your boat. You were moving quite a bit. Powering about, using up fuel, quite like proper yachtsmen, you and Jake."

"Yes?" Mike said softly. "So what?"

"I presume the conch are migrating? And you follow them from the surface? By sound? Like a destroyer tracking subs?"

Mike swallowed. "That's our job."

"Interesting," Hoagie mused. "One sees a lot from the air, you know, if one spent a war doing antisub patrols off the jolly old Falkland Islands. Especially in clear waters like these. I could have sworn, this morning, coming in . . . I could have *sworn* that you were following a most impressive *shark!* Looked almost like a great white from the air."

Mike's heart sank. He said nothing.

Hoagie smiled. "But surely that's impossible. Never this far south! Surely you'd report it to the police."

"It's reported," Mike said dully, "to Government House."

"Which is chartering *Neptune's Folly?* To see that it doesn't gobble some tourist up for lunch?"

Mike nodded. "You got it."

Hoagie rose and joined him at the railing. "I take it you haven't bothered to tell Ellen that you're mucking about with a shark?"

"No," Mike said bitterly. "Should I?"

"No!" Hoagie was vehement. "The last thing she ought to know is that there's another shark on earth!"

He ground out the cigarette on the sole of his shoe and threw it off the porch.

Mike didn't see the point. "What's our shark got to do with somebody trying to kill her this morning?"

Hoagie looked out at the water. "Not her, of course. Me. You're chartered by the government? Well, Calypso's a charter business too."

"So somebody tried to shoot you down for running charters?"

"That's right. We're quite competitive: Sunshine Flights, Out-Island Airways, Turquoise Tours, Calypso's Friendly Charters. It's only that someone wants it *less* competitive, that's all."

It was hard to believe. "Isn't that a little heavy, just to deregulate the local airlines?"

"That's what I thought up to now," said Hoagie. "I reckoned the Kingston Street thing was simply bluff. Obviously I was wrong."

"A little," murmured Mike.

"But I mustn't panic our trade, must I? Right off, we'll have these attacks stopped—"

"How?"

"Surely not by calling the police. On Whiskey Cay they're bought and paid for. No, we suspect one charter company, and my boss may buy them off." Hoagie shrugged. "You handle your shark, I'll handle mine."

Drumming his fingers on the railing, Mike looked out at *Neptune's Folly*. He wondered if Hoagie was leveling. Murder? For an airline shuttle?

"So," continued the Englishman, "shall we keep our bloody mouths shut, tit for tat?"

Mike looked him in the eye. "Not dope?"

"Michael, I warned you about that!" He repeated, "Tit for tat?"

"You *don't* deal in drugs?" Mike smiled. "Just blackmail?"

"Right," Hoagie grinned, then stuck out his hand. Reluctantly Mike shook it. He wasn't sure that he believed him.

"There's one thing, Hoagie. . . . Keep clear of my mother."

Romeo's Cadillac drew up to the porch, and Hoagie glanced at his watch. "Got to get to the airstrip to meet my mechanic. Mike?"

"Yes?"

"I do have to get the plane out, you know." Hoagie's eyes were full of pain. "But afterward, you're right. I shan't be back again."

Mike sat down in a porch chair, brooding over his drink. How he'd tell his mother what he'd done, he was sure he didn't know.

Ellen Brody considered the pancake in her daughter-in-law's frying pan. She could flip it, as she used to at Sunday breakfast for Sean and Mike, or she could take the conservative, safe route and use a spatula.

"Flip it, flip it, flip it," begged Thea, tugging at her skirt. "I want to see it fly."

I want to see it fly. . . .

All the previous day, a mechanic had worked on Hoagie's plane. Hoagie had not come near her. This morning, at dawn, when the air was cool for takeoff and the feeble tide was out, he'd returned in Romeo's Cadillac.

She had run from the porch to wish him luck, then walked to the beach with him. He had been cold and distant to Mike and awkward and stiff with her.

She was hurt. My God, they had been through hell together the day before, and she had not panicked or cried or diverted him. She had been proud, and sure that he appreciated it and that he liked her very much.

She certainly liked him. So why was he so cool?

The wing was patched with a panel of bright aluminum—"al-u-min-ium," Hoagie called it—and the engine sounded fine. He had taxied down the beach under the palms, and swung the craft around.

The rest was out of a newsreel of the first Wright Brothers flight. With Mike and Jake holding the tail down, and herself crouched in the prop blast to pull out his wheel chocks, Hoagie had revved the engine higher and higher until she was certain the propeller would fly off.

He shouted "Now!" She pulled the chocks. Mike and Jake let go. Ever so slowly, over the crunching, stinging sand, the plane began to move. It seemed certain that he would never get to takeoff speed; by the time he reached the ruins of Thea's castle, he seemed to be moving hardly faster than a walk.

But somehow, in the last fifty yards, the Cessna gathered speed. As she stood with her hand to her mouth, begging it to rise, it wobbled into the air. Ticking the bracken on Masthead Hill, it wallowed away, popping and belching smoke.

He circled, passed fifty feet above the sand, and waved them thanks. She was sure, at the very end, that she saw him blow a kiss.

But why the coldness, why the silence, as they'd walked down to the plane?

"Flip it, Grandma, *flip* it!" insisted Thea.

She flipped the pancake, and it landed, half in the pan, half out.

The story of her two-day affair with Hoagie. Half in the pan, half out.

She made Thea a new pancake, and they sat down to eat.

Chapter 8

Carlos Flores—el Conejo Grande—lay on his back in the newest of Rico Lomas's ski boats. His feet and hands were tied.

On his head he wore a bunny hood they had taken from one of Lomas's bar waitresses. From somewhere he heard laughter and mariachi music.

He was staring straight up at a single white cloud. It was pear-shaped and reminded him of the cowled Franciscan priest who had administered el Conejo Grande's childhood church in San Juan de Gracia. Now, out of the past, the padre floated over the turquoise mirror-like water surrounding Spanish Galleon Cay.

It was infernally hot. He was sweating from the heat of the sun, the engine idling only a few feet from his head, and unadulterated fear.

For courage, Flores clung to the cloud drifting high above. It was a divine manifestation, he was certain, of Padre Juan Pedro, dead for forty years. Under the cowl the padre's bulbous nose was running, just as in real life.

Flores, as a clumsy adolescent, had once tried to be an altar boy. The padre had dismissed him the first Sunday: He had burned a hole in the altar cloth trying to light the tapers. The priest above seemed to be scowling, as if he remembered this.

Bless me, Padre, for I have sinned. . . . It has been forty years since my last Confession. . . .

Rico Lomas, in the briefest of orange swimming

trunks, prodded him with a toe. "El Conejo Grande," he said in warning, "don't you die of fear!" He turned. "Alejandro!"

Alejandro moved aft, bent down, grabbed Flores's arms, and hoisted him to a seat.

With glazed eyes el Conejo Grande looked around. To his amazement he found that they were floating fifty feet off a white-sand beach, bordered with swinging palms. A rubber life raft bobbed astern.

The beach was crowded with *coqueros* and *traficantes* he had known for years. When he appeared from below the gunwales, they began to cheer and laugh.

A barbecue was flaming, with *frajitos* on the fire. In a hole filled with ice rested a keg of Carta Blanca beer. The band was playing a folk song he remembered from the *llanos*, of unrequited love between a *campesino* and the daughter of a landowner. Smoke from the *brutos* everyone was smoking drifted on the breeze.

"What is this, *don Señor* Lomas?" Flores demanded shakily. "What are you going to do?"

"We are having a court-martial"—Lomas beamed—"like on a Navy ship." He beckoned, and a half dozen *traficantes* waded to the boat.

As they lined the gunwale, looking in, Lomas cut his bonds. Flores recognized the knife with its jaguar-tooth handle; el Viejo had carried it in long gone, better days.

Lomas spoke to them. "El Conejo Grande cannot shoot straight from a motor scooter. He cannot shoot straight from a boat. He says Alejandro moved the Vespa, he says Alejandro rocked the boat."

"Es verdad!" croaked Flores. "He jerked the scooter, he rocked the boat! Also, it is rough in the ocean, outside of Masthead Cay!"

"Alejandro?" asked Rico pleasantly. "It was rough?"

Alejandro dragged on a *bruto* and exhaled a cloud of

smoke. "Smooth as the cheek of a child, *señor.* Smooth as a virgin's ass."

"So, *compadres?*" Rico asked the *traficantes* gathered around the boat.

Grinning, each in turn extended a hand, and all the thumbs were down.

"You see, old man? I have no choice—"

A rabbit ear fell over his face. Mortified, he tossed his head to remove it, but it flopped limply back. "I have served your grandfather for forty years!" he shouted from behind it. "El Viejo will have you shot for this, I swear on my mother's grave!"

Lomas looked at him sadly. "No," the young man said with a sigh, "el Viejo said to hang you by your bare feet." He faced his men. "I am going to show this rabbit brain how to shoot from a moving boat."

He nodded at Alejandro. Alejandro yanked Flores to his feet, hustled him to the rail, and the *coqueros* lifted him into the rubber raft.

They towed him a hundred yards into the lagoon. As he watched, incredulous, Lomas tossed a ski into the glassy water, slipped in after it, and held up his hand.

Alejandro chambered the first round into an Uzi automatic rifle and handed it to Lomas in the water. Holding it aloft, Lomas swam to the ski, got his foot into it, and signaled. Alejandro gently eased the slack out of the towrope, nodded at Lomas's signal, and put the boat in gear.

With his weapon high above his head, Lomas rose like a monster from the deep, dragging a plume like a knight behind him and whooping like an Indian in a TV cowboy show.

The boat swept across the lagoon until it was almost out of sight, then curved back. The sound of its engine rose. Lomas was swinging in wide, graceful curves across its wake, firing the Uzi into the air at each skidding, breathless turn.

El Conejo Grande could hear cheering from the beach. The whine of the ski boat was growing louder; the *campesinos* clapped and shouted from the shore.

El Conejo Grande looked up. The cloud had drifted to the west.

Ay, Díos Mío, I am heartily sorry for having offended Thee, and I detest all my sins, because . . .

The sound of the engine was deafening. Out of the corner of his eye he saw the boat shoot by, with Alejandro waving.

. . . because I dread the loss of Heaven and the pains of Hell. . . .

He heard three shots, dead behind him. One grazed his shoulder, and another struck his arm. He tore his eyes from the cloud and faced around.

Out of a sheet of spray, ten feet away, the muzzle of the Uzi had a hole like an altar candelabrum's. It licked at him with a tongue of flame, though he never heard the shot.

Slammed backward into the water, he glimpsed the cloud before he died and wondered if he saw a smile on the padre's craggy face.

But of course that could not be, he thought, for the padre never smiled.

The point of the harpoon was digging into the flank of the great white shark. It angered him, as if a remora sucker-fish had fastened himself to his jaw.

All day long the vessel that had put it there had dogged him, frightening his prey, until finally he turned south.

He was famished. He found sparse pickings in the southern lee of Masthead Cay. He continued south, and as he swam, the pain of the harpoon increased.

His kind had evolved to adapt to remora, and other parasites as well, and in his lifetime he had outlasted several that had hung to his nose and his tail. This remora enraged him, and he associated it with man.

The harpoon point was festering inside him, and the shortened shaft grew sore, but the transmitter he carried on his flank did not change his life at all.

Somewhere in his tiny brain a memory remained of the boat that had dogged him everywhere the previous day, and which had caused him all his hurt. He noticed its absence and would know it when he met it once again. Something in its look and feel and smell aroused him.

A deep instinct impelled him to regard the living creatures that swarmed on its back, like lice on a whale, as enemies rather than prey. Before the shock of the harpoon, there had been no room in his mind or his belly for anything but food. Now he was consumed with hate for the beings who had put it there.

He cruised the open Atlantic south of Whiskey Cay for half the day and took three skate, a dozen yellowtails, and a score of flashing dolphin fish. He entered Spanish Galleon Cut.

Here was instant action. He was suddenly aware of sharp concussions above the surface, like the six he had heard weeks before off Amity Beach, but in a different, staccato rhythm, and many more.

Pow-pow-pow . . . pow-pow-pow . . . pow-pow . . . pow-pow-pow-pow . . .

The shots triggered his hunting senses, and the beat of his tail increased. He headed for the beach.

Rico Lomas glanced back. He saw el Conejo Grande pitch backward from the rubber boat, thrash convulsively in the water, and sink like a weighted packet of coke.

He heard a triumphant blast from Alejandro's horn and saw his driver turn back with his thumb held high.

A good man, Alejandro; he had made the run just right. Now he was turning into the breadth of the lagoon, assuming that his boss would want a victory pass at the grandstand.

Well, why not? If you had it, as the *norteamericanos* said, then flaunt it. How many water-skiers could ski one-handed? And how many could pick off a man-sized target at forty knots? From what range? Ten feet? Hell, no—twenty, fifty? A *hundred*. Who, back on the *llanos,* would dare to disbelieve? And el Viejo would bask in this new legend of his grandson's vicious skills.

He glanced at his *coqueros* on the beach. They were applauding wildly, and he could hear their drunken cheering way out here.

He fired a victory salute and gave them three more Christies across the bouncing wake, pumping the weapon up and down like a drum major's baton.

As the boat made its final sweeping curve he hurdled the wake. At top speed, with all the momentum from his tail-of-the-whip ride, he released the towline, flung up his arms to show his driver he was free, and began the long, free glide to the beach, cradling the Uzi like a child.

All at once the cheering stopped. Those of his *campesinos* who had waded out to meet him froze, then scrambled to the shore. A monstrous shadow appeared, between himself and the snow-white beach.

When the shark broke the surface, he had el Conejo Grande—all two hundred and thirty pounds of him—in his mouth. Blood was pouring from the great white's jaws. He grew like a gray ghost from the shallows to full height. From Rico's vantage he dwarfed the palm trees waving beyond the strand.

The shark shed a muddy stream of sand as he leapt

into the bright sun. He shook his head, like a terrier worrying a bone. His great black eye was glittering on Lomas. The shark tossed the dead man from his mouth and crashed down in the water once again.

A sheet of spray spread out, muddied with sand. The fin, as tall as Lomas, was heading for him. He screamed in terror and flung the Uzi over his shoulders, flailing for balance as the ski began to stall.

"*Socorro*—help!" he howled. "Help me, *por favor!*"

But his *coqueros* were fleeing as if the shark could come ashore.

Rico teetered for a moment on the ski, panic clutching at his bowels. He abandoned the ski and plunged into the water like a child: head up, dog-paddling, afraid to take his eyes from the fin, terrified, yelping in horror.

The fin was cutting him off. Slogging through hip-deep water, he tripped and went down.

"Help me, one of you," he pleaded. "In the name of the Lord our Savior, help me now!"

Someone fired from the beach. The fin wavered and stopped.

There was another burst of fire, and then another. The water was pocked with the dimples of pistol bullets: .45s, .38s. Rico could hear the rounds whining as they ricocheted away. He thought of John Wayne landing on Iwo Jima's fiery strand.

Suddenly the great white turned and charged the beach. Lomas, eyeballs bulging, stumbled ashore while the fusillade continued. He sank to the sand. John Wayne forgotten, he found himself sobbing, shoulders shaking, tears streaming down his face. He could not stop.

They must never see him crying like a woman. He turned quickly toward the water to hide his face, but he had recovered far too late.

The firing had stopped. There was a deathly silence. He took a deep breath, somehow summoned a frozen smile, and turned.

"Well, *amigos,*" he said, "We scared *that* bastard *tiburón* away."

Someone snickered. Another joined in. Ricardo, his foreman on the island, glared at them, and then, as others joined in, could not keep his own face straight.

In their minds Lomas had soiled himself forever.

If el Viejo heard of this, he'd order him home and stake him on *los llanos* for the ants.

Rico marched toward them, took a deep breath, and began to speak. "If," he said softly, "I hear of this shark again—if *one* of you talks—I will tear out the tongue of each of you and feed *them* to the sharks! *Comprenden ustedes?* Ricardo?"

Ricardo shrugged. "As you wish."

"Chico?"

"*My* lips are sealed." He spread his hands. "These others? *Quién sabe?*"

"Jaime?"

"Oh, don Rico," the man said with a grin. "In the name of the Lord our Savior—never a *word* from me."

When he was through, the smiles were gone but their eyes were alive with mirth.

He could not resist a study of the water. Alejandro idled the engine ten yards away, as close as he could get. The fin was gone. El Conejo Grande's body had disappeared, but everyone knew that the smell of blood drove sharks into a frenzy.

His three-hundred-dollar competition jumping ski was drifting down the strand. The five-hundred-dollar abandoned Uzi rested somewhere in water as clear as glass.

Well, the ski was scratched and worn, and Uzi automatic rifles grew on trees. Let the idiots behind him slog out and get them both.

"You going to make him beach the boat?" Someone from the crowd laughed.

Bastards . . .

He gathered all his courage and what dignity he could, waded out to Alejandro, and hoisted himself aboard.

As they sped away from Galleon Cay he sat watching his drunken *coqueros* grow smaller under the palms.

His family still controlled the island and its *campesinos*. On the distant *llanos* el Viejo reigned supreme.

But for *him* there was only one path back to power and glory.

Parachute jumps and football goals were useless. He would have to kill the Englishman himself.

Chapter 9

Ellen Brody sat at the mirror in her room off Carla's studio. She could see Michael behind her, sitting on her bed.

Carefully she separated a lock of her hair and wrapped it around her curling iron. She counted: one thousand, two thousand, three . . . up to six. She let it go and looked at the result. Not bad for the tropics, not bad at all.

But for what? She hadn't seen Hoagie in three days. She fought the temptation to ask and lost.

"Did you see Hoagie Newcombe today?" she asked casually. "When you went down into town?"

"Maybe he went to Nassau, Mom. Haven't seen him around at all."

Mike regarded her sadly. She had not admitted that she missed Hoagie, but he knew damn well she did.

Carla had seen her on the beach with Thea, rebuilding the sand castle, shading her eyes to look at passing aircraft.

"Like the ladies on the widows' walks in pictures of old Cape Cod," she had said. "It's heartbreaking."

The hell with it. He had to tell her why.

"Mom?"

"Yes, Michael?"

He caught her gentle eyes in the mirror. His heart moved. She had done so much for all of them, and what had they done for her?

"You're thinking about Hoagie."

She lifted her shoulders and let them fall. "Well, I kind of wondered why I hadn't seen him. Has he got a lady friend?" She smiled in the mirror. "I could change my brand of perfume."

"He has plenty of lady friends, but he's a lonely man. And he probably likes your perfume. He likes *you*."

"I'd survive, Michael, if he didn't."

"You'd survive anything, but he does."

"Anyway, I hardly know the guy."

"*I* know him." He got up and went to the window. "Mom, it's my fault he hasn't been around."

She put down her curling iron and turned to face him. "Are you telling me you ran him off *again?*"

"There's somebody out to get him, dammit!"

"We still don't have to treat him like a leper!"

She was even more shaken than he'd expected. "But, Mom, he won't level with me. And he won't tell the cops." He moved to her and touched her cheek with his hand. "And Mom?"

His hand on her cheek felt like Brody's. She swallowed. He really cared. But he was fooling with her life: She wasn't a child, and she wasn't a little old lady to be sheltered, not just yet.

"Yes?"

"Next time somebody takes a shot at him, I don't want you in the way."

"That's very protective, Mike. But I'm your mother, fully grown."

"Mom?"

"Yes?" Her lips were trembling.

"He *agreed* he shouldn't see you anymore," he said softly.

She felt her eyes filling with tears. "I'm sure he did. He doesn't seem like the kind of man you'd scare off if he didn't want to go. The question is, why did he, if he likes me so damn much?"

Mike took a deep breath. "There's cocaine on this island, Mom. There never was before. It's getting to be another Spanish Galleon Cay."

She knew the answer but had to ask. "What's that got to do with Hoagie?"

"I think he's dropping it. So does everybody else."

"So, good riddance?"

"I don't know." He shrugged. "I guess so."

"That's right," she said, flaring. "You *don't* know. So you guess!" She got up angrily. "Your *father* never guessed! Do you remember when I said you bunged the fender on the station wagon?"

He did remember dimly, but it didn't matter now. "Come on, Mom—"

"And you said you hadn't bunged it, and Brody said, 'He's innocent until he's proven guilty. . . .'"

He put his arms around her and patted her. "You made a fair presumption, Mom. I couldn't drive worth a damn."

"And sure enough," she went on, "Tony Catsoulis called up that night, and one of his trucks had hit it, and I felt like such a . . . *turd!*"

"Well," he said, grinning, "I probably dinged it once or twice and you didn't even know."

"I'm sure," she said, dabbing her eyes. "But I did that *once*, to someone I love, and I'm not going to do it again."

They suddenly stared at each other, shocked.

"Well," she said in confusion, "I don't *love* Hoagie, Mike, I just *met* him. What I meant . . ."

Mike shook his head, rubbed his eyes, and murmured, "Oh, my God."

Hoagie Newcombe paused on Kingston Street at Romeo's Cadillac, newly washed and glittering in the sunshine. As usual, it was parked at the curb outside the

Inn of the Happy Whale. A huge cardboard poster sat on its windshield: SEE HISTORIC WHISKEY CAY; Hourly and By the Day. *On Parle Français Ici. Ich Spreche Deutsch. Se Habla Español.*

Hoagie Newcombe squinted from the glare of the street into the palmettos shading the tropical bar outside the inn. Romeo always blended with the shadows.

"'O Romeo,'" he called, "'Romeo, wherefore art thou, Romeo?'"

"Here, mon," the deep voice boomed from the gloom at the end of the bar. "'Alack! There lies more peril in thine eye than in twenty of their swords.'"

"Bad day," explained Hoagie. "Bad week."

He slid to the stool beside him and ordered them both a drink. He looked around. "See anybody bound for Nassau?"

"Nah, mon. Not just now." He sighed. "Business is terrible."

"Surely not the undertaking trade?"

"Everybody gwine to Nassau to die at Princess Margaret Hospital. My hearse. Ah swear I'm gwine use it for festival tours."

When Romeo was depressed, he talked like a stevedore loading sisal on the docks.

Inside the restaurant, a jukebox was throbbing with a deep calypso beat. A white-haired British couple was sitting at an outside table, having tea. At the far end of the bar two Latinos were drinking beer.

There was the scent of jasmine in the air, the sun was shining, the ocean breeze was cool on his brow, but Hoagie was unhappy too. He wanted to see Ellen Brody again but didn't dare.

The charter business was off; people had heard, on the palm-tree network, of his forced landing and damaged wing—though not the details of the shooting, thank God—and were chartering other planes.

Chartering was dead in the British West Indies, anyway. If he didn't move against Lomas shortly, Calypso would be bankrupt before he could.

They talked for a while of the dope trade. "If a man wanted coca paste," asked Hoagie, "could he get it at Spanish Galleon Cay?"

"No," said Romeo, his chubby face gleaming in the sun. "Only pure cocaine."

"I thought they'd be refining the bloody stuff by now."

"You shouldn't fly down there, anyway, mon. It's like an army camp."

"Don't worry! I wouldn't land there if they had a ten-mile airstrip and handed out free petrol from the truck."

Romeo watched a lanky island woman swing by, hips swirling, a bright bandanna and a basket of yams on her head.

"Did you know, mon," he said idly, "down at Spanish Galleon Cay they have a shark?"

"Who? Lomas?"

"Nah, mon, a *man*-eating shark."

Hoagie raised his eyebrows. "A shark?"

"Not so loud," murmured Romeo, with a glance at the English couple. "A great white shark."

If the *Neptune Folly's* shark had moved to Spanish Galleon Cay, thought Hoagie, Mike and Jake might lose their job of tracking it.

"Where'd you hear that, Romeo?" he asked curiously.

Romeo nodded at the far end of the bar. "Couple of Lomas's *coqueros* I brought in from the airstrip," he said softly. "They speak this crazy Spanish, you can hardly understand. That's all I heard that's worth a thing—the shark."

Hoagie glanced at them without much interest. Calypso could never fly them home; it was enemy turf, and he'd probably end up hanging from a palm tree if he dared.

"Tell me about the shark," he said. If the great white took to visiting all the islands, it could hurt his tourist charters.

Romeo grinned and began to speak the King's English. "Lomas was water-skiing, I think they said, in front of his troops, and this bloody shark cuts him off!"

Hoagie sat up on his bar stool. "And how did Lomas handle it?" he asked, trying to keep the excitement from his voice.

"Not very well, Hoagie." Romeo chuckled and toyed with his dripping glass. "Not very well at all."

"Then tell me about it, Romeo. Remember everything you can."

The calypso music stopped. A Vespa snorted by. The clock on the Anglican steeple began to gong.

And Hoagie sat and listened carefully to what Romeo had to say.

Chapter 10

Alejandro put his *tequila con aqua mineral* on the polished bar and stared at el Inglés in astonishment.

"*Quién?* You want to see *who?* Señor Lomas?"

When he had seen the Englishman coming across the dark, deserted cocktail lounge of the Loma Bella Club, he had very nearly gone for the snub-nosed .38 tucked in his belt.

Now Newcombe was looking at him in amusement. "That's right, lad. Your boss. El Patrón. Rico. El Hombre."

"I unnerstan' English," he said angrily. He didn't understand it very well and ordinarily refused to speak it, but the courage el Inglés showed in coming here had shaken him to his soul.

Was it possible that the Englishman didn't know who had almost blown him out of the sky? He began to doubt his senses.

"*Por qué?*" he mumbled, stalling for time. "What do you see him for?"

"I *don't* see him, lad, not yet. I *want* to see him. Go up and tell him I'm here."

If only there were someone down here to give him some advice! If he shot the man now, would Rico be pleased? El Conejo Grande had had the chance and had failed, and look what had happened to him.

He considered a murder, here and now, with care. There was no one else in the club yet but the bartender, a *traficante* himself, and a few of the bunnies; he could easily handle them. On the other hand, he'd get the Englishman's blood all over the rug, and Rico might not like that.

Perhaps Newcombe was here to seek mercy. The English were known throughout *los llanos* as a stupid and cowardly race. If he had come to beg for his life, Rico would enjoy it. His embarrassment the previous day had depressed him. To hear Newcombe pleading for his life before they killed him would cheer the boss. Perhaps he had better not get in the way.

Or should he solve the whole problem, here and now?

It was all too much for a simple *coquero*—and one so young, at that. He shrugged, slid from his stool, and climbed the stairs. At the top he glanced back to make sure that el Inglés had not changed his mind and left.

The idiot was still there. Alejandro knocked on the door. "I am Alejandro, *señor!*"

"Come in."

He found Lomas shirtless at his window, looking down on St. James Road as he pumped his morning iron.

"He is here, Señor Lomas! We have him!"

"Who?" His boss did not turn from the window.

"El Inglés!"

Slowly Lomas put down the weight bar.

"Newcombe?"

"Sí!"

Lomas turned from the window. He did not look well to Alejandro. He had been drinking since the fiasco at Spanish Galleon Cay and had snorted a line or two of pure Santa Clara coke already, although it was not yet ten. He didn't look as if he'd slept well the night before.

Lomas shrugged. "What is so strange? He has been here before. He was here this week, with the woman."

"But at nine o'clock in the morning? The tables are not open. He is not here to gamble. He wants to see *you.*"

"Only nine?" Lomas looked at his watch, surprised. The coke, guessed Alejandro, had distorted his sense of time.

Lomas moved to the mirror above his private bar. He flexed a biceps, studied it, then made his pectorals firm.

"Shall I kill him, Don Rico?" offered Lomas. "I could put him on the boat—"

"No. Me! I will do it."

"Where?"

Lomas thought for a moment. "Before my grandfather's eyes." He shifted el Viejo's photo on the desk. "Remember the English *muchacha* who OD'd here?"

Alejandro's eyes sparkled. "*Ay!* Blue eyes? And . . ." Expressively Alejandro traced her outline in the air with his hands.

Lomas had found her at the roulette wheel a year ago, underage for Nassau gambling, and had let her play. She was a classic Anglo beauty, with clear skin and a mother who was always jetting somewhere else. She had lost, refused to divulge her identity, and tried to pay him in another more traditional way. When he'd tired of her amateurish sex and threatened to go to her parents for her debts, she'd threatened to kill herself.

She had killed herself, all right, on this very spot, with a speedball of brown Mexican smack. It had all been too pure for her purebred blood, which was as blue as the skies above.

Lomas had sat at the desk with el Viejo's picture, taping her moans and her cries, for the office was quite soundproof and no one below could hear. He had watched while she writhed on this very rug and shuddered and finally died, and he'd called for Alejandro.

They had doused her with rum in case Alejandro was seen carrying her out. Then the youth carted her from the back door to the dock, tied her slim and tapered ankle to a twenty-pound anchor, taken her for her last

Cigarette boat ride, and dumped her past Nassau Light.

That story—of a man with *cojones* enough to watch his mistress die before his desk—was well known among the *traficantes*.

Lomas knew that by nightfall Newcombe's death would be known, too, both here and on Spanish Galleon Cay. It was such tales as this that would drive from their feeble minds the memory of their *patrón*, and his ski, and abandoned weapon, and his panic at the shark.

When Alejandro left, Lomas put on his shirt, then took it off again. Why should he dress for the English pig? Let him see what a real man looked like, just once before he died.

He went to the office closet and opened the door. Inside was a gun cabinet he had discovered when he'd had the mafioso murdered. He had given away the weapons and stocked it with his own. Now he selected a silenced .22, built on a .38 frame, with a six-inch barrel.

With so little weight and shocking power, it would give el Inglés a long, unhappy death. He drew a tiny recorder from his desk. He would tape the Englishman's dying words for the amusement of his grandfather; such things showed the old man that he was in control, and it would take el Viejo's mind off rumors he might hear from Spanish Galleon Cay.

He placed the weapon behind el Viejo's picture on his desk. He sat down to wait, wondering why Newcombe had invaded his lair, unprotected and alone.

El Inglés lounged in the leather chair across from Rico Lomas's desk. Lomas watched him, while Alejandro sat at the bar and finished his drink.

Incredible! The Englishman's nonchalance was blowing Lomas's mind away. With a tiny gold coke spoon Lomas shoveled a snort of the Santa Clara coke from a diamond-encrusted box.

"Señor?" he offered politely. "Santa Clara, pure, from *los llanos?"*

"Never use it."

"Only sell it." Lomas nodded. "Some think that is wise. Me? I like it, it likes me, why not?" He regarded the spoon and smiled. "What is it you say? 'Some men are born with a silver spoon in their mouths'? With me it was a golden one."

"In the nose," said Newcombe.

"Sí." Lomas sniffed it up, then sat back, dabbing at his nose. "I have heard, *señor,* that you had engine trouble yesterday, on your final approach to Whiskey Cay?"

Newcombe shrugged. He drew a pack of cigarettes from his shirt and lit one with a battered lighter emblazoned with the drooping wings of the RAF. Lomas suddenly coveted it as a souvenir. That would be easy enough.

"Bit of an engine problem, yes." He blew a cloud of smoke toward Lomas. "Some think I hit a flock of birds."

Birds? El Viejo would love the Englishman's dry wit. "But you, *señor,* know better?"

"I had the impression," mused Newcombe, "that there were *hunters* firing at the birds. Perhaps I flew into the line of their fire."

"Es posible, very possible," Lomas said with a nod. "Have you considered that they might have been firing at *you?"*

The Englishman's blue eyes widened. "At *me?"*

"At you, *señor."*

Newcombe rose. Lomas's hand crept closer to the gun behind el Viejo's photo, and he saw Alejandro's body tense. But the Englishman only moved to the welded figure Lomas had bought from the Rawson Street Gallery. "A piece of Carla Brody's work?"

"Mine now. And I have the hundred-dollar chip I gave her for a deposit too." He beamed. "The rich get richer, and the poor . . ." He shrugged. "Señor Newcombe, it is sad, but I think they were firing at you."

Newcombe turned back. "Now why would anybody want to kill a humble airplane jockey like me?"

"That is a question." Lomas nodded.

"Would *you?*"

"Me?" Lomas said with a laugh. "Kill a man who loses twelve grand at my tables and writes a check that does not bounce? Why would I do that?"

"Why, indeed?"

"Besides, you take me skydiving. So why would I kill you?"

"Because I wouldn't fly your coke?"

"Nah! Plenty others do."

"Perhaps," Newcombe mused, going back to his seat, "because I own Whiskey Cay?"

"You *own* it, *señor*?" Lomas laughed. "I think not."

The high from the coke was passing; the talk was growing thin. Unable to follow the conversation, Alejandro was jiggling his foot impatiently.

To have Newcombe compare his operation with Spanish Galleon Cay incensed Lomas more and more. "Own Whiskey Cay?" he continued. "I fly *mules* into Miami that own more than you."

"I own that island nonetheless."

"You don't own your airplane!" His head throbbed, and he raised his voice. "I know you, el Inglés. You drop your little packages on Whiskey Cay, a kilo on Masthead Point, another kilo near Prince George Town, a half a kilo on Spyglass Hill. Is peanuts. You *own* Whiskey Cay? Is bull!"

"I *do,* you know," said Newcombe mildly. "I've bought its senator here in Nassau, its island commissioner, its police, its BWI narcotics squad. Customs officer, local judge . . . all tied neatly like a package under the tree."

"Then why do you drop dope there?" Lomas said, scoffing. "Why do you not land it on the strip?"

"Bait." Hoagie shrugged. "Purely bait."

"Bait?"

"As one chums the water for sharks."

Lomas looked up quickly. Had Newcombe heard of the shark? If so, Lomas intended to prove his threat to the *campesinos* was real and cut out some *coquero*'s tongue tomorrow.

His head ached. He sighed. He had let Newcombe's ten-peso operation go on too long. El Viejo would never have tolerated another *narcotraficante* for a month, and Newcombe had been dealing for a year. Alejandro was moving restlessly, doubtful of his boss's resolve. Lomas felt that he should draw the gun and kill el Inglés now, but he was curious.

"'Chum' the water? I do not understand."

"I make a drop, perhaps, at Masthead Point. At dusk, but it is seen. My narcs scream up in their bloody jeeps to impress the local citizenry: guns, searchlights, choppers. They search for half the night. If they find it before some jungle bunny does, then it is theirs. But in the meanwhile . . ."

"Yes?" Despite his impatience, Lomas was interested. "In the meanwhile, what?"

Newcombe ground out his cigarette. "No. I'm boring you."

"I will *tell* you when you're boring me!" Lomas took the gun from behind the picture, slapped it onto the desk in front of him, and glared at the Englishman. "Go ahead!"

Newcombe glanced at the weapon. He seemed hurt. "The gun is hardly necessary, you know. I thought that we were friends."

"*Estúpido!*" shouted Lomas. The man was insane!

"Does a friend try to blast you on Kingston Street? Does he shoot your airplane down?"

"No," admitted Newcombe. "Precisely why I'm here."

"*Ay!* You will not be here long, *señor.* Now tell me 'in the meanwhile.' While the narcs are in the bush?"

Newcombe shrugged. "I rendezvous with Bolivian freighters, in speedboats. Or in fishing boats, offshore. While the narcs are busy at Masthead Point, I off-load coca paste at Spyglass Cove or Bowsprit Point. Next week, the other way around. *Es muy simple, señor.*"

Why would anyone bother with paste when pure cocaine was lighter, easier to handle, and brought ten times the price on the street?

"So why"—Lomas smiled—"would you deal in coca *paste?* Why not pure cocaine?"

"Why pay the price? I process it on Whiskey Cay. We fly pure coke to Savannah once a week."

Lomas stared at him. "You have a *cocaine refinery* on Whiskey Cay?"

Newcombe smiled. "Oh, yes. Oh, yes, indeed."

Lomas peered into the bright blue eyes. The Englishman was lying, of course. Even on Spanish Galleon Cay, which was virtually the family's own, he had never dared set up a refinery. The British West Indies were too close to the United States, the investment was too great, and what if the Nassau government changed and invited in the *gringo* Drug Enforcement Agency?

El Viejo would not have condoned it, either. Traditionally cocaine was made and refined safely in the sheds of the *llanos,* near San Juan de Gracia, where fifty-kilo bales of coca leaves were dried on racks.

There, on the family's home grounds, in the hot, dry sun of the southern plains, the leaves were soaked in kerosene, tossed into plastic-lined pits, then stamped into coca paste by barefoot *campesinos.* The paste was mixed with sulfuric acid, lime, and potassium permanganate, which turned it into coca paste.

It only needed to be soaked in ether and acetone, filtered through cloth, and dried in the sun to become pure cocaine.

The problem was that last month, in a surprise move that el Viejo suspected was orchestrated by the U.S. Drug Enforcement Agency, Leopard and SANU agents had dropped from the sky to the *llanos* plain.

Helicopters had descended on the family's refinery. Three agents and two *coqueros* had died in a hail of automatic fire, and el Viejo's biggest refinery was destroyed.

What if his grandson found a replacement? With no investment necessary, because they would inherit it from Newcombe, who would be rotting at the bottom of the sea? As they'd inherited the Loma Bella Club from the mafioso don?

And what if Lomas took the next Bolivian freighter that came to rendezvous with the Englishman, and its cargo of coca paste too?

Then men would forget the shark very quickly, perhaps before el Viejo heard of it at the ranch.

If the Englishman was not lying. Lomas drummed his fingers on the desk. "How do I know this is true?"

"Come and see."

"I never leave Nassau, except for Spanish Galleon Cay." With a glow of pride he added, "I am on the DEA's most-wanted list, *señor*."

"I've heard." El Inglés shrugged. "Well, you had the *cojones* to sky-dive; I thought you'd have the guts for Whiskey Cay."

"Don't worry about *my* guts, *señor*. Worry about spilling your own." His eyes narrowed. "Why is it you tell me all this?"

Newcombe looked into his face. "Because you finally scared me."

Lomas sat back, smiling. "Good. Now we understand each other. I been thinking you were crazy."

"Well, I didn't survive the bloody Falklands to get my brains blown out up here."

Lomas had had enough. "You are *going* to get your brains blown out, *señor*." He slammed his palm on the desk. "One year ago I give you a chance to fly for me! You say, 'No, if I deal, I deal alone.'" He picked up the gun and got to his feet. "You said this to Rico Lomas, *hombre!* Well, you change your mind too late."

"No. I want to be your partner."

"Partner?" Lomas chortled. "Sure. Why not?"

"On Whiskey Cay and in this club. I'm bloody tired of losing, and I'd like to be the house."

"This club?" Rico laughed, shaking his head. The Englishman was crazy, after all. "*Hombre,* I am going to kill you and *take* Whiskey Cay!"

"I don't think so." The Englishman held up his hand. He counted on his fingers. "One, I've got a Bolivian freighter coming in tomorrow. I think you'd like to hijack it, but you don't know where or when."

Lomas checked the gun. He threw a cartridge into the magazine. "Oh, I think you will tell me where and when."

"Two, I've got a quarter of a metric ton of coca paste on Whiskey, and you don't know where it is."

"I will, *señor,* when I make your kneecaps paste."

"And three"—Newcombe smiled—"there's a letter with my solicitor here in Nassau. It's in Spanish, addressed to your grandfather. There's another to La Prensa in San Juan de Gracia. They'll be mailed if I don't phone back from Whiskey Cay by six o'clock tonight."

Lomas's heart began to pound. His eyes were throbbing now. "And what is in this letter to my grandfather?"

Newcombe walked to the one-way window and drew

the curtain. He looked down at the club and then turned.

"A story. Quite a funny story, from the palm-tree telegraph."

Lomas had a premonition of great doom. "About what?"

"A race."

From the office speaker came the throb of the club's steel-drum band warming up for the day.

"Race, *señor?*" Suddenly Lomas wanted a shot of rum.

"Between a water-skier," murmured Newcombe, "and a shark."

Palm tree sway, pretty girl play,
Why I got to go away?

Lomas sighed. There was a time and a place for everything, el Viejo always said. Partners? Why not? For ten minutes or so. The crazy Englishman was as good as dead. He'd simply get him later.

Sun shine bright, money tight,
Gwine to miss that New York flight.

Newcombe was looking down at the bar. "We really should do something about those stupid bunny costumes, don't you think?"

Lomas told Alejandro to mix them drinks. He lifted his glass to Newcombe.

"*Salute*, partner. A quarter of a metric ton, you say?"

Chapter 11

Just past two A.M. on New Year's Eve, Louisa stepped off the motor-launch ferry she used for the nightly commute from Nassau. It had been a raucous night at the twenty-one table, but a lovely trip back over dead-flat inside waters, along a golden path laid by a lopsided three-quarter moon.

But she had grown more disturbed with each passing minute. In the cabin she had spread her cards. They told her nothing.

She longed for her mother, whose wisdom transcended all. But her mother had died the year before in Port-au-Prince, and if her *loa,* thought to be a wide-winged man-of-war bird, was aloft over Bahamian waters, there was no sign.

Louisa felt evil in the night. Papa Jacques was casting a spell. She had felt it leaving Potters Cay dock in downtown Nassau, and more strongly as they passed abeam of Nassau Light.

If only she had listened to her mother more carefully, she would understand more. It had been *une folie* to ignore her teachings, neglecting them for the things that had amused her as a child.

Now she could dance and sing, and had read Proust and Camus, and what good was it all? She couldn't even concoct an avé love potion good enough to trap Jake.

As they approached Whiskey Cay her apprehension grew. The feeling of impending evil was heavy in the air. She stepped to the bow and looked at the island, sleeping like a basking shark in the moonlight.

Where the eye of the shark would be, at Masthead Point, she saw a flash of light. She felt instantly that it was the focus of the evil. Papa Jacques was there. She knew it as certainly as if she were there herself. And Michael Brody's family was at risk.

The fool! To hurl a *houngan*'s *asson* at the sea! It would be better for Michael if he had strangled the witch doctor where he stood; had Papa Jacques's *loa* become a *diab* from hell, and an eater of men, it was hardly more dangerous for Michael and his family than Papa Jacques's mortal, breathing soul, which was consumed with hate.

She stepped off the ferry at the Prince George Town dock and walked to her little VW. She slipped inside and started the engine.

Then she sat drumming on the wheel. She was frightened of Papa Jacques; more than anyone on the Cay, she thought, she realized his power and his evil.

And she was tired, and Jake would be anxious—she hoped—if she was late.

That Michael Brody was in danger was none of her business: Louisa had done what she could for the child. She had a deep and gloomy conviction that Jake's friendship with Mike was dangerous for him and would come to no good end. So why should she risk a spell on herself for a family of fat-cat whites?

But she loved the little girl, liked Ellen, and though she thought Carla's talent overrated, Mike was Jake's best friend. . . .

Mama, Mama . . . what shall I do? Give me a sign.

A sea gull swooped past, cawing in the moonlight. Not a man-of-war bird like mama's *loa,* but a seabird nonetheless.

Reluctantly, and full of dread, she turned toward Masthead Point.

Carla Brody lay staring at a moonlit patch of the bedroom ceiling. Slanting through the plantation shutters between the bedroom and the porch, the shadows made prison bars, and behind them a ghost—the essence of the moving curtains of chintz—paced silently.

She could not sleep. Too much New Year's Eve champagne. Tomorrow Michael and Jake would have to lift the metal sculpture into the four-wheel-drive and take it, shrouded in its canvas, to the speaker's stand in the plaza at the beach in Prince George Town.

There it would be set on its base, a stone block already waiting. In the morning, before the *goombay* dancers assembled for their grand parade and the New Year Junkanoo masquerade began, she would trundle up her oxyacetylene tank and weld base and sculpture together.

Then, as if written in granite for the ages, the name of Carla Paxton Brody, immortal sculptress—or charlatan—of Whiskey Cay, would rest throughout eternity, to be pointed out with pride—or laughter—to tourists.

Unless the Prince George village fathers, in their wisdom and their rage, elected to have it torn down then and there. . . .

Three thousand dollars it was costing the town, to be paid to an artist who did not truly know yet what it was supposed to represent.

Suppose the citizenry rebelled? Suppose the Town Council refused?

There was a tab to pay at the grocer's, and the butcher was growing cool. The milkman had lingered yesterday, shy and diffident but determined, until she'd finally scraped up fourteen dollars to pay the previous month's bill.

And if it were all for nothing? And they laughed her off the stand?

She had neglected Thea and Ellen and Mike, to finish on time. By evening every day, her sandpapered eyes had given her a grinding headache.

She'd been rebuffing Mike for a week in bed, she'd been so tired.

She was suddenly frightened, and she wanted him, his tenderness and strength.

They slept beneath a single sheet in the Bahamian night, warm even in winter. He was breathing deeply, an arm thrown over his eyes, but he was always easily aroused. The line of his jaw was carved in Doric strength by shadows, like a marble by Pheidas, and she began to trace it with her finger.

From somewhere out near Masthead Point a dog was baying. The curtains moved. The ghost behind the bars on the ceiling stirred.

Mike's eyes opened slowly. Astonished, she saw that they were full of fear.

And then the screaming from her studio began.

The great white shark, frustrated at Spanish Galleon Cay by the water-skier's escape, had returned to the fresh corpse he had disgorged and this time swallowed it whole.

His appetite whetted, he headed west, across Tongue of the Ocean deep, toward Andros Island. In Tongue of the Ocean, at fifty fathoms, he found giant squid in great numbers, but something drew him north. He cruised past Guana, Hawksbill, and Ship Channel Cays until he reached the shallow waters of Masthead Sound again.

He arrived by moonlight and cruised under ebony waters splotched with molten gold. As always, night was day to him, for he simply hunted with his sensors now, by instinct, hearing, and smell.

By midnight he was patrolling the waters off Masthead Point, famished and alert. His slim tail, as tall as a man, moved ceaselessly.

The point of the harpoon had worked its way farther into his flesh. Passing a reef, he tried to rub it off. He only drove it deeper. The transmitter on the stub of the shaft was scratched and battered but still operating.

His heart rate had not changed at all: *Boom . . . boom . . . boom.*

On *Neptune's Folly,* tied to the dock, Mike and Jake had left the battery switch and the transducer speaker on, to alert Mike in the main house if the shark returned.

All at once, in the deserted deckhouse, a series of marching peaks appeared on the computer's emerald screen, and a muffled drum began to echo, bow to stern.

Boom . . . boom . . . boom . . .

Neptune's Folly tugged at her lines like a living thing, but it was far past midnight now, and there was no one to hear.

Ellen swam through jet-black waters that grasped at her like liquid lava but were as cold as ice. Ahead, through swells that hid him, lifted him, and dropped him again, struggled Marty. His eyes, when she could see them, entreated her to hurry, but though his mouth was open, as if he were shouting to her, no sound came out.

She swam in total silence, save for a slow, incessant drumbeat growing closer. *Boom . . . boom . . . boom . . .*

Marty's heart? No. *His* heart was weak, and this one was strong.

A shark? Now he was pointing, whenever he was

lifted by a swell, pointing behind her, but she had no time to turn. She must get to him before he drowned; she knew mouth-to-mouth resuscitation, she had tried to give it to him when he died, but if he had died, how could he be drowning? It was not Marty at all but Sean! Not Sean but Mike—no, Thea . . .

She awoke wide-eyed and sweating, panting in the night.

And then she saw it through the studio door, on the wall beyond the statue.

An enormous shark, as black as the night, was rising from the deep. In his jaws he clasped a skeleton, arms hanging limply, and his dorsal fin was moving as he leapt.

She heard screaming, steady screaming, and the sound of voices in the air, and the pounding of bare feet on the studio's wide porch.

She sat up, clasping a hand over her mouth.

It was she who had been screaming!

All at once Michael burst in. He put his arms around her, holding her close. "Mom," he murmured. "Oh, my God. What happened?"

Speechless, she pointed at the door to the studio, but the light went on inside. She glimpsed Carla's statue. The breeze through the window was blowing the jib cover, moving the shadow to and fro. Carla hurried into the bedroom and closed the studio door.

"Ellen, what is it?"

"A dream. A bad, bad dream." She looked into her eyes. No, Carla would never do a statue of a shark, not after Sean.

"You had a nightmare." Carla smiled. "*I* thought it was Thea . . ." She looked around the bedroom. "Where is she?"

In the distance, a pack of dogs were howling at the moon. A cricket was shrilling. She could hear the gentle lap of waves by the dock where the *Folly* lay.

"Where is *who?*" asked Mike softly. His eyes were widening with fright.

Carla leapt to her feet and ran to the window. She looked out and swung around. "Thea! I thought she'd come with you! She wasn't in her room!"

Mike dived for the door, and Carla followed. By the time Ellen was out of bed and flying across the porch, she could see Mike sprinting down the trail to Masthead Point.

Carla was already halfway to the castle on the beach, and Ellen could hear her calling into the night.

Louisa knew from the moment she parked the VW on the dirt path that led to Clarence's home that Papa Jacques was inside.

Shivering, she glanced at her playing cards. The pack had insufficient power to be a *gad*—a charm to protect her against the evil she sensed inside.

One could make a *gad* from an alligator tooth soaked in a *mavangou* bottle full of *migan* broth: gunpowder and Shrove Tuesday ashes soaked in a mixture of the water from a forge or a tannery, the blood of a red herring, and the blood of a virgin mouse. She had seen her mother do it and had worn one as a child, until her English teacher, a Catholic nun, had forbidden her to wear it to school anymore.

A charm fed once a year with such a broth, it was said, was protection even against bullets. Men during the "time of the bayonets" on Haiti, a hundred years ago, had proved it so.

Having no such amulet, she clutched her cards, anyway, and crept close to the shack's single window.

The light from the pane shone on a fallen palm trunk. She climbed up on it to look. Inside, kerosene burned in a stone bowl, throwing shadows on the black faces of a half dozen island women in sparkling white dresses and white bandannas.

They sat on chairs at the side of the room. Four men faced them, sitting on Clarence's communal family bed. One clutched between his legs a painted *hunto* drum. He was tapping it softly, and she could feel, more than hear, the gentle booming of its beat.

Clarence was nowhere to be seen. Neither were his daughters, Cissy or Deenie, or his wife.

A central pole had been erected in the manner of the peristyle shed of a *humfo* voodoo church.

As her eyes grew accustomed to the flickering light within, she saw Papa Jacques emerging from the shadows. He was dancing the *yanvalou* around the central pole. As he passed the women he tapped one with his *asson* on the head. She rose, blank-faced, and the two clasped hands and twirled, in the ancient way.

The woman broke away. In a full trance, she kissed the ground before the *hunto* drummer. He increased the beat. He was calling the woman's *loa,* and she began to writhe. Another woman joined her, and another, and soon the room was swirling with jerking, twisting bodies and minds gone quite adrift.

She remembered her *mambo* mother, presiding with great dignity over dances much like this. But Mama's were for good *loa,* not for evil ones, and these drums spoke of horror and death.

Mama, Mama, protèges-moi . . . Protect me!

All at once Deenie, Clarence's older daughter, appeared from out of the bushes. She grabbed Louisa's hand.

"Louisa!" the child whispered. "We scared, we out in the bush. Papa Jacques make me take Thea's bucket off the beach! He gwine give Thea to his *loa!*"

From the central pole inside hung a child's red bucket, a little doll painted on it. She knew that she must somehow get it, but she was frozen with fear.

Papa Jacques rattled his *asson* at the bucket, and though she did not think he touched it, the bucket began to swing to the beat of the *hunto* drum.

Papa Jacques stooped, and when he straightened he had a live chicken. He held it high, put its neck to his lips, and suddenly ripped its windpipe open with his teeth.

Holding the shuddering bird by the legs, he let its blood pour into the swinging bucket. Paralyzed with terror, Louisa could only watch.

Chapter 12

Ellen regarded Carla and Thea. Carla was kneeling on the sand in the moonlight, staring into her daughter's face. Thea was pouting, patting the sand with her shovel.

"But, darling, why? You've never done this before!"

"Maybe she had another dream," suggested Ellen. "Her grandmother certainly did."

Carla looked helplessly toward Masthead Point. "Your daddy must think you've run away. God knows where he is now!"

Thea looked up and smiled. "Maybe he's gone to Clarence's."

"We'll be lucky if he hasn't called the cops." Carla sighed. She shivered and rubbed her arms. "It's spooky here. Come on, Pumpkin, you're going to bed. And don't do this again."

Thea looked up at her and shook her head. She was smiling, but in the moonlight her eyes seemed empty. "I can't," she said simply. She looked directly into Carla's eyes and added, "I have to find my bucket."

Carla and Ellen glanced around. "It isn't here," said Carla. "You can find it in the morning."

Thea looked at Ellen, the court of last resort. "Grandma?"

Ellen hid a smile. "You heard your mother, Thea, dear. You've sort of scared us all."

"Don't be scared," Thea said wisely. She put up her hand for silence. "Listen."

From *Neptune's Folly* at the dock, a hundred yards away, came a slow, steady drumbeat: *Boom . . . boom . . . boom . . .*

The deckhouse was dark and the boat seemed deserted. "They must have left something on," said Carla. "I'd better take a look."

"Well, *I'm* looking for my bucket," insisted Thea. "It was right here on the beach."

"I'll stay with her while you check the boat," murmured Ellen. There was something strange in Thea's eyes. She thought of the *loa* and shuddered. Surely not again . . .

Carla shrugged and headed for the ketch.

Mike Brody, jogging in the moonlight along the path to Masthead Point, heard the drums long before he reached the clearing where Clarence's house stood.

He cursed under his breath. Whatever had possessed him the last time he had traveled this path had been exorcised by rage this night. Something had made Thea leave her bed again—the sound of drums . . . or singing, perhaps—and Papa Jacques was at the bottom of it. If somebody didn't get him off the island soon, the whole place would go voodoo, and then where would they be?

He saw a dark figure step from out of the bush and block the path. Alert, ready for anything, he stopped. "Who's that?"

"Clarence, mon." The tall, slim black hung his head. "Papa Jacques, he say we mus' get out. Ah don' pay his pittance. We be livin' in the bush. Deenie, chile, come here."

In the moonlight Mike saw Deenie join her father. She was staring at the ground.

"Tell Mr. Brody, Deenie. Tell him what Papa Jacques make you do."

Deenie looked up. Her eyes were white with fear.

"He make me take her bucket. From our castle on the beach!"

"Why?" He grabbed the little girl's arms. Compared to Thea's, they felt like sticks. "Deenie, is Thea in there?"

"No, suh." Deenie gulped. "Jes' her bucket. I don't know where Thea is."

"Clarence, throw out that son of a bitch! Or I'll go in and do it myself!"

"Mon, I cain't! He is *very* angry now. Louisa, she afeared to go in there, and she half-*mambo* herself."

"Louisa?" Mike strode toward the shack in the clearing.

The great white shark, far out on Masthead Sound, swam silently, listening as only his species could: totally, from the tip of his nose to his pointed tail.

His ears were tiny ducts, invisible to man, but inside them lay three chambers. Each was tuned exquisitely by the aeons to the scale of an oceanic symphony that ranged from the deep bass groans of the humpback whales to the chittering of shrimp.

In each chamber was a calcified ear stone, connected to hairlike, sensory cells. Vibrations of a thrashing fish or a lumbering elephant seal would set the stones to oscillating, the sensory cells to resonating, and the shark himself to closing on the source.

His tiny ears were backed up by the lateral canal system just below his skin. They picked up pulsations in the tiniest motions of the slowest prey.

He was unsleepingly alert every second of his life, from birth to death.

Now, as he cruised, tortured by the point of the harpoon, his pygmy ears picked up the reverberations of an incessant booming near the shore.

Once, when he was half his present size, he had

heard a similar pounding: a pile driver on a barge, driving logs into the sand of Boston Harbor.

And only a few weeks back, zeroing in on the ceaseless sound of a drifting pile against a buoy had given him a meal in Amity Bay.

On this night the sound was so faint at first that he ignored it. But when it continued, he stopped swimming.

He glided for a moment. Then he turned toward shore.

The *boom . . . boom . . . boom . . .* ahead of him grew louder in his ears.

Ellen Brody, halfway up the beach, stirred a clump of brush with her foot, looking for Thea's bucket in the moonlight.

A strange hour. The nightmare was still with her. She shivered. What was she doing, past midnight, looking for a child's bucket on a foreign beach?

The slow, alien drumbeat from *Neptune's Folly* was growing louder. She looked at the dock. She could see Carla walking on it, toward the boat.

The moon was flirting with the clouds now. She saw Thea standing by the castle, staring out at Masthead Sound.

Thea was acting oddly, but so was everyone else. The next day's sun would burn it out of them, and the festivities at the plaza would do the rest.

She heard splashing. She stared. Thea was wading out into the water. At night? A cold chill struck her soul.

"Thea!" she called. "Come back!"

Her voice sounded tinny and weak in her ears. Something strange was happening. Her legs began to twitch. Some kind of stroke?

"Thea!" she called again. The little girl turned. Her

distant face, bright in the moonlight, was blank, and her eyes were empty.

Thea pointed to the water. Faintly Ellen could hear her voice. ". . . floating away. I have to get it."

No! Thea swam like a pollywog but not at night! Suddenly dizzy, Ellen tried to call. Not a single word came out.

Was this a nightmare too? Her limbs began to jerk as if on strings. She found herself whirling on the sand, possessed by a hundred impulses she had never known before.

She saw herself as if from a distance, frozen-faced, as stiff as a zombie, spinning and strutting, lurching on the beach.

The child, knee-deep in the water, gazed out at the Sound. Then she squatted, shoved off carefully, and began to dog-paddle away.

Screaming silently, her grandmother danced in the moonlight, all alone.

Carla peered from the wharf down at the darkened ketch. Suddenly she was frightened. She was rape bait out here, in her filmy shorty nightgown, with Mike out God knew where, chasing a wraith.

Ridiculous. There was no rape on Whiskey Cay, or anything else.

Boom . . . boom . . . boom . . .

"Is somebody aboard?" she called, shivering. If anyone answered, she'd flee.

Boom . . . boom . . . boom . . .

Whatever it was, it was getting louder. They would easily hear it from the house. It would keep them up all night.

She stepped aboard. The drumbeat was coming from the deckhouse. She crossed the deck and peered in a porthole.

The lab inside was bathed in a weird, greenish glow, as if existing at the bottom of the sea. The computer screen was lit, and a series of peaks was marching across it, moving from left to right.

My God. All this noise from the heart of a conch no bigger than her foot?

She tried the deckhouse door. It was locked, but she knew where Mike kept the key. She moved to the mizzen, reached under its canvas sail cover, and touched a halyard winch. Hanging from the winch by a lanyard was the key, buoyed with a cork from a bottle of Dago Red in case it dropped into the water.

She opened the deckhouse door. Inside, the noise was deafening and getting louder all the time. She flipped on a light and looked around.

She hated to fool with Jake's equipment; even Mike was leery of his partner's temper. But the drumming, if it kept increasing, would be unbearable.

The computer was easy; she'd had access to an Apple Lisa, herself, in Boston, taking a course in computer-aided design. The switch was invariably behind them so that you wouldn't inadvertently turn them off. She found the switch but didn't have the guts to try it. Suppose she lost data he wanted to save?

She glanced at the other equipment on the chart table. One gray-paneled unit looked promising. It read "Transducer and Sonic Amplifier, Mark I Mod. 2."

She found a rotary switch labeled "Audio Gain: Up. Down. Off."

She hesitated. She'd better not touch that, either.

Boom . . . boom . . . boom . . .

She stepped to the engine panel. She knew, from weekend cruises, that the battery switch overrode every circuit in the boat. Once Mike, leaving the vessel, had told her to turn it off.

Familiarity bred contempt. Let them take her out and

feed her to the conch if she destroyed their data; she needed her sleep tonight. She took a deep breath and turned the switch to "off."

The booming stopped.

Thank God.

She locked the deckhouse and stepped out onto the wharf. She paused for a moment, looking at the beach.

Ellen was whirling in the moonlight, on a dune above the place where she had left them.

Presumably they'd found the stupid bucket and were waiting for her, goofing around on the beach.

The great white was homing in on the deep, throbbing beat that filled his world when suddenly it stopped.

Confused, he drifted. He was perhaps half a mile from the dock where *Neptune's Folly* rested, and his appetite had been whetted by the booming, which to him had sounded like the heartbeat of a nurse shark or a whale.

All at once he sensed another vibration in the water. It was on the surface, but it lacked the smooth pulsations of an amphibian. A seal—even if there had been any in waters as warm as this—would have been slinking with half the noise and disturbance.

A human, perhaps a small one.

The graceful tail began to sweep again.

Mike Brody stood with Louisa in the door of Clarence's house, staring at the writhing dancers. None of them seemed conscious of him. A frozen-faced woman, jerking and lunging across the room, caught herself as she was about to fall, and was suddenly erect, arms up, strutting to the beat of the drum.

"We must get the *wanga*—Thea's bucket," murmured Louisa, "or he will make her sick again!"

He saw Thea's beach bucket hanging on the pole in

the center of the room. Wildly he looked around.

In the far corner, away from the dancing flames that lit the shack, he saw Papa Jacques.

His flat black eyes were glittering. He held his gourd rattle—his *asson*—in both hands with the blunt end pointed at Michael. He was smiling, and his yellow teeth looked like fangs.

He was chanting something under the beat of the drums. His gleaming eyes were merciless, and Michael could not tear his glance away.

All at once Michael felt the jungle rhythm entering his legs, his arms, his heart, his soul.

He fought for control. Louisa squeezed his hand. "*Gardez*," she warned. "Do not give in!"

He pulled away and strode into the room. Papa Jacques approached him through the smoke, and there were only the two of them and the merciless drums.

The witch doctor took the bucket from the pole and offered it, as if it were a glass. Mike took it and lifted it.

"Drink, *mon ami*. It is your daughter's . . ."

Through a haze, Mike looked into the bucket. It was half full of blood. He found himself lifting it to his lips, unable to control his arms.

"*Non!*" called Louisa.

Michael stared into the bucket. The blood was swirling in a vortex, drawing him in.

"*Non!*" Louisa cried again, grabbing his arm. He dashed the blood into Papa Jacques's face, grabbed the *asson*, and smashed it on the pole.

The witch doctor's eyes seemed to grow in size. The drum stopped. The dancers froze. Louisa stared at the smashed *asson* in his hand. Her hand flew to her mouth.

He put his arm around her waist, pulled her to the door and flung bucket and gourd into the bush. They scrambled into her car and bumped down the road toward the beach.

"Ellen! Ellen! What are you doing?"

Carla's voice came from a million miles away, and all at once Ellen was staring into her daughter-in-law's face in the moonlight.

"Ellen, I've been shaking you and screaming! What—"

Release came instantly; why, she did not know.

"I . . . something happened. Oh, my God! Where's Thea!"

She was suddenly racing for the Sound.

"What is it?" Carla yelled after her. "Did she go into the *water?*"

Then there were two of them, dashing for the surf.

The great white, which had been drawn to Masthead Sound by forces few could understand, was suddenly on his own.

But he was not entirely without mental resources. Millennia of species intelligence were packed into his tiny brain, and his synapses were flashing swiftly, stoked by hunger.

He increased the beat of his tail. He centered on the vibrations of the living thing he sensed close to the beach. He suddenly became aware that two more beings had entered the water near the surf line.

His brain could perform any computation necessary to feed his body. In an angular interception of a seal playing in the breakers or a pelican skimming the surf, he could calculate a collision course, like a fighter tracking a bomber, rather than the long, inefficient pursuit curve of a heat-seeking missile zeroing in on its prey.

The targets he tracked now were traveling slowly and presented no mental problem at all, as long as they continued on their courses.

But now the original quarry, closest to him, stopped, turned back, and moved toward the two new sources of vibration.

For an instant he glided, as his brain evaluated this new data. Then his tail began to move again, dragging a vortex along the ebony surface above. He raced for the group as it merged.

Waist-deep in water, Ellen watched Thea dog-paddle into Carla's arms. All at once she wanted them out of the water, all three of them, *right now.*

"Carla, let's get *back!*"

"Okay." Carla's voice was brittle as she held Thea close to her breast. "Thea, what were you *doing!* If Daddy knew you were swimming here at night—"

Ellen turned and looked out at the water. "Hurry, Carla, please!"

They began to swish toward shore. A great black cloud slid in front of the moon. It was suddenly pitch dark, and only the lights from Carla's studio and the main house kept them on their course. Ellen took Carla's hand. If only she would hurry. There was something bad out there; she could feel it in her bones.

"Here, give her to me," she pleaded. Carla was moving too slowly, feeling her way in hip-deep water as black as ink. Ellen wanted to dash for the house lights ahead. She heard Carla stumble. "Carla, let me have her," she begged again.

"No. Do you know, she's gone to sleep?"

"But *hurry*! I want us to get in!" She tried to hide the panic in her voice and failed.

"What's wrong? You sound as if—" Carla's voice

dropped. "Oh, I see! Ellen, I understand, but this isn't Amity, thank God. Now calm down or you'll step on a shell!"

Headlights appeared ashore, on the road past the house, and approached the beach, where they shone on the water. A golden pathway led to safety, if Carla would only *move*. Ellen put her arm around her and urged her on. In the light she could see Thea's slumbering face.

Hurry, hurry, hurry . . . Knee-deep now, then ankle-deep . . .

At the edge of the water, Mike was waiting with Louisa. "What the hell!"

Carla handed him Thea. "Long story, Mike. Don't be mad at her. Right now I'm bushed, and tomorrow's a big day."

They said good night to Louisa, and she climbed into her little car and left. As her headlights swept across the waters Ellen thought she saw something cut across the path of golden light. It was as gray as death, immense, and as swift as flight.

To her it seemed like a fin.

Impossible. Too big. A trick of the dark, dancing water, perhaps. As Carla said, this wasn't Amity, thank God.

She turned and followed her son and his wife toward home and the welcoming light.

Mike had paused for a moment before he started up the sandy slope of the beach. With Thea in his arms he cocked his head toward *Neptune's Folly*.

He listened intently. There was not a sound from the boat.

So the shark had never returned. Jake was right. It was probably half an ocean away by now.

He sighed. Unless the conch study was renewed, he and Jake were out of work. But with the shark gone, at least he could be at the Junkanoo tomorrow—for the festival, and water sports, and speeches on the platform, and Carla's moment of glory when her statue was unveiled.

PART III

Chapter 1

The great white shark first sensed the festive drums at dawn, as he swept in from Masthead Sound to Prince George Town Bay, swimming twelve fathoms below the blue-green surface at a steady hunting pace.

Most of the fish large enough to be his prey had sensed his presence and deserted the sound. Skates, dolphin fish, tarpons, and sand sharks had scattered far and wide.

Ashore, Prince George Town was awakening to its annual island festival. In cabins and shacks in the palm groves and mansions on the hill, scissors were snipping, and men, women, and children were pulling on crepe-paper costumes for the Junkanoo Parade.

Tourists were arriving from Nassau on the early ferry and by plane; Romeo, who had an appointment at nine-thirty to meet Hoagie Newcombe at the Inn of the Happy Whale, on a matter far more important than the tourist trade, had grown so busy shuttling between the town and the airstrip that he feared he'd be late.

By nine A.M. the bell on the Anglican steeple was tolling continually. Family street stalls—assigned when America was a colony hardly more valuable to the British Crown than this lonely island chain—were set up on Kingston Street and on the beach.

By nine-thirty, artists—American, British, and native—had their paintings set up along Old Town Plaza. Shell engravers and woodcarvers were hawking their wares on the steps of Town Hall.

Village boys were selling Goombay Punch, pineapple-flavored soda, from boxes strapped around their necks, and natives from the bush had set up stalls to peddle fruit.

Speedboats, which would offer parachute rides along the beach, were arriving from across Tongue of the Ocean. Owners of fishing boats for the Prince George Cup Race were hoisting their ragged sails to air them in the sun.

The Aquatic Club of Prince George Town was setting its buoys off the beach for the swimming race. A long yellow inflatable sled, shaped like a banana and meant to be straddled like a horse by a half dozen riders clinging to handholds, arrived from Nassau. Towed by a waterskiing boat, it offered two-dollar rides.

Over it all, the jungle rhythms of Africa's Gold Coast boomed from the shore. The *goombay* drums of steel or wooden kegs, covered with goatskin and kept heated and taut by tiny fires inside, talked to each other from one end of the island to the other. The rhythms of the songs throbbed of their Bantu past.

On Princess Square by New Town Dock, the masqueraders were assembling. Cowbells clanged, tin whistles shrieked, poinciana-pod rattles whirred, and lignum vitae sticks clicked like castanets.

But it was the drums, pulsing with the rhythm torn from African roots two hundred years before, that pulsed through palm groves, over beaches, and in the gentle turquoise waters on the island's festive day.

They excited the great white shark and made his hunger grow.

Hoagie Newcombe sat with his back to the bar at the Inn of the Happy Whale, watching the masked islanders, with their crazy musical instruments, hurry past.

He looked at his watch. Ten o'clock? Where was Romeo?

He felt naked and defenseless. Thanks to his own efforts, Rico Lomas was on the island somewhere for the first time, using the festival crowds as cover from possible informants from the U.S. Drug Enforcement Agency. Hoagie assumed that Alejandro was here, too, and God knew how many other *traficante* thugs. A very dicey business but drawing to the end.

"Señor?" The voice startled him. He was unarmed, certain that he would be frisked by someone before Lomas showed up.

He swung around. Alejandro was staring at him coldly. *"Buenos dias,"* offered Hoagie. *"Y Señor Lomas. Dónde está su patrón?"*

"No! We speak English," muttered the *coquero*. "That Spanish of Castile, it is for womans. Make me sick."

"As you wish, old chap."

"Good. Where is your factory?"

Hoagie smiled. "Where's Lomas?"

Alejandro shrugged. "He does not come."

He was lying. Lomas would never trust a goon like Alejandro to evaluate a site. Somewhere, in the crowds on the street, or in some Cigarette boat offshore, the boss was waiting for a signal from his hooligan to move.

But he had better play it straight. "I have a quarter of a ton of paste in there. I shan't deal with gorillas. Deal is off."

"Okay. Is off." Alejandro smiled broadly. "He says, 'If he does not show you where it is, you kill him.' For me, *es mejor:* better. He say, 'One English *traficante* in Bahamas is too much.'"

Hoagie raised his eyebrows. "Did he mention a couple of letters—*cartas*—at my lawyer's? About a shark that panicked him at Spanish Galleon Cay?"

Alejandro nodded slowly. "He says, 'Tell him if his lawyer send a letter to el Viejo, you will find him and kill the lawyer.'" His grin grew wider. "'Also you will kill Newcombe's friend, Ellen Brody, and the child. Also, you must kill Brody and his wife the artist, *sí?* Also, if they have a cat or dog or parakeet, then you will kill them too.'" He lit a cigarette. *"Comprendes?"*

"And you'd love all that?"

Alejandro shrugged. "Is my job."

"Some bloody job."

Alejandro's eyes were suddenly blazing. "I tell you about 'jobs', el Inglés. Last year I am nineteen years old. I am a 'treader' on the *llanos*. You know what 'treader' is?"

"No," said Hoagie. "No, I don't."

All at once the *coquero* was speaking in Spanish, angrily and swiftly, so that Hoagie could hardly follow him.

"Without 'treaders', el Inglés, you have no dope. El Patrón pays off the comandante of the Leopard anti-drug squad in town. A pit is dug. In the pit is plastic lining. They put in there a hundred pounds of coca leaves. It costs, how much, those leaves, from the *campesinos* what grow them?"

Alejandro was testing him. "Fifty dollars"— Hoagie shrugged—"more or less. On the *llanos*."

"Sí, fifty dollars to the *campesino* who grows them and carries them on his back." Alejandro lit a cigarette. "So, in the pit is the coca leaves. They put in kerosene, sulfuric acid, lime. Then they put you in, to tramp on the leaves."

"What's this got to do with—"

"Silencio, el Inglés! You ask me why I like my job, why I kill for el Patrón? So, I am telling you, okay?"

He puffed furiously at the cigarette and went on. "In

that pit you got no shoes; who has shoes? You tramp those leaves in the hot, hot sun. You steal a leaf and you chew it, your feet sting so bad. You ever bathe your feet in hot sulfuric acid? By dark, that hundred pounds of coca leaves is ten pounds of coca paste. What *you* pay for ten pounds of paste?"

"Off the freighter here? Perhaps five hundred dollars."

"*Sí*. You know what *I* got? Me, who made that paste?"

"A dollar an hour?"

"A dollar a *day*, el Inglés—if I don't get shot by a Leopard drug policeman from a U.S. Army helicopter. If my skin stays on my feet so I can climb out of the pit. If the sun don't bake the brains from out of my head. One dollar every day, el Inglés, whether I and my poor old *mamacita* need it or not." He spat on the sidewalk. "All so some *norteamericano* kid can suck it up his nose." He regarded his cigarette, glanced at his Rolex, and grinned. "Yes, I like my new job, *es verdad*."

"I see," said Hoagie softly.

"And I *will* gladly kill you and your friends." He flicked the cigarette toward the street. It spun in an arc in the bright sunlight. "So where is your 'factory,' and how do we get there?"

Romeo's Cadillac slid to the curb. Hoagie got up and paid his bar bill.

"Just come with us, my friend."

Ellen Brody and Thea checked the equipment spread out on her bed off Carla's studio: a beach towel to sit on while they watched the swimming races; a Styrofoam ice chest for Cokes and Goombay Punch; dark glasses for herself; camera and film; Thea's sand shovel for when the child got bored with the festivities and wanted to dig a hole to China.

Coppertone. Sun block. Beach bag. Straw hat for herself and a baseball cap for Thea, which would certainly be lost.

Umbrella; folding chair for the unveiling in case nobody had reserved one for her in the stands. Binoculars from *Neptune's Folly* to watch the Windsurfer races and the Aquatic Parade. What else?

"What have we forgotten?" Ellen asked, brushing the hair from her eyes.

"We don't have a bucket!" Thea announced.

Oh, God, not that again . . .

Mike had said quietly at breakfast that he'd found her bucket at Clarence's house, full of muck, and thrown it away, but it was all very mysterious and he wouldn't talk of it because today was Festival and they had to get the statue to the plaza, and nobody had seemed to have the time to talk about the night before—or anything else.

Anyway, he assured Ellen, there'd be a dozen Bahamians selling buckets on Township Beach.

"Grandma will get you a bucket at the beach," promised Ellen.

"With Rainbow Bright on it?" challenged Thea.

"We'll see what we can do."

The child ran off to help her daddy with whatever he was doing. The sounds around the house were becoming frantic and strangely sinister: hammering from the porch outside the studio as Jake and William constructed a crate for the statue; the crash and clank of Mike's jeep as he mated it with a trailer to trundle the statue off to town; the screech of Carla's grindstone as she made some last-minute change.

The unveiling was scheduled for one P.M., and the statue was still here!

The grindstone stopped behind the door. In the sudden silence Ellen was certain that she heard Carla sobbing.

No one was supposed to enter the studio, in case the statue was unclothed. She knocked.

"Yes?" There were tears in Carla's voice. Ellen heard the rustle of the sheet as she covered the piece. "Okay, come in."

The figure was covered, still an enigma beneath the great white sail. Carla was sprawled on a chair in her leather apron, tearing off her gloves. She was crying.

Ellen went to her and kneeled by the chair. She took her hand, as hard and callused as Mike's. "Carla, what *is* it?"

"I'm going to destroy it!"

"You will if you keep this up," she promised quietly. "You have to *stop*, Carla. You're having labor pains!"

"Oh, Ellen," Carla said fiercely, "that's talk-show artist crap!"

"I'm no artist, but we're mothers." Ellen got up and moved to the window. "Before Mike was born, I was so happy pregnant, and *he* was so safe, and it's a cold, cold world . . . and at times I didn't want it to end for me, or him."

"You don't understand!"

"Your work is ready to be born, Carla." She looked at the robed form. "Bear down hard and let them cut the cord."

Carla rose suddenly. She moved to her welding torch. "No. I'm going to scrap it."

"What?"

Carla's eyes blazed. "Why do you think I wouldn't let anybody see it? Not you, not Thea, not Mike?"

"Because it wasn't ready!"

"No." Carla unscrewed the head of her welding torch, moved to her workbench, selected another, and screwed it on. "Something happened after we came back from the funeral."

"Carla, what do you mean?"

Carla gave her a piece of rusted steel from her scrap pile. "The damn metal," she whispered. "Look at it. It's from the sea. It *knows*."

Ellen shivered. "Knows what?" she murmured.

Carla shrugged. "You heat steel . . . you fire it to lay a bead, and it's red, you know, blood-red. . . . Usually it's friendly and wants to help . . ."

"Yes?"

Carla glared at the piece. "But this batch, when I'd torch it, it would stare back, glowing, angry, and *dare* me . . . and I'd hammer it one way, and it wouldn't go. And the flame marks . . . sometimes I'd see things in the flame marks . . . and it fought and tried to hurt me, Ellen. Look at this!"

She sat down, jerked off one of her ugly men's working boots, and pulled a sock from over one of her leather trouser legs, where she tucked them to protect her ankles from sparks. She rolled down the thick wool.

Below her calf was a glowing scar, livid and obscene.

"Molten copper! Look, if Mike is made of mild steel, and Jake's pig iron, and you're spring steel, then *copper* is as soft as Thea and wouldn't hurt a thing. I was bit by the sweetest, most innocent metal in the world." She rolled up her jacket's leather sleeve. There was another burn on her forearm. "A drop of red-hot steel! How'd it get under a leather sleeve, tell me that?"

"Carla, please—"

Carla went on fiercely. "Flame marks on the metal make patterns! Good! You want them. A patina every metal sculptor tries for. But you can't control them. A crapshoot! They've been very good to me. Angels, cherubs, cloud forms. *This* time there are gargoyles, dragons . . . Angry metal, Ellen. Why is it *angry* at me?"

"Carla, you've been working too hard!"

Carla pulled away. Her voice was tight with tears. "It isn't that. And we need the money!" She tossed the scrap back on the pile. "It's what that damn stuff made me do!"

"*Made* you do?"

Carla lit her torch. "I couldn't force it," she said fiercely, "but it *could* force me, and it did what it wanted."

"And what was that?"

"Jesus," Carla said, sobbing, "*you* know! You saw it on the wall last night!"

"But covered. And I'd been dreaming!"

"When you told me, then I knew! With Mike, if you thought you had a *monster* in your womb, then what? Ellen, tell me that!"

She tore the sail from the figure. Ellen stared.

It towered above them, vibrant with motion. It was smooth and sleek and curved gently from its base, tapering at the top. Two great fins spread from the torso, as if flailing for balance in the air. At the top a lacy member crossed at right angles, delicately, and seemed to drip down the creature's flanks.

It was frozen energy, form without detail, mood without substance, vigor without body, energy without mass, a dream welded into being, inscrutable and aloof.

It burst from its base on sweeping tubes, like streams of water cascading as they leapt. Its sides were of sheet metal, shimmering in the sunlight with a hundred changing patterns. Near the top was a wide, staring circle of ebony.

Papa Jacques's eye? Seen in this light, perhaps.

"Oh, Carla," she breathed. "Oh, my God."

Carla turned a valve and lit her çutting torch. The gas began to roar. She approached the figure. Ellen grabbed her arm. It felt like the steel of the figure she attacked.

"Carla, you can't! I don't care what *we* think it is. It's alive, you made it live!"

"I want it *dead,*" said Carla. "Ellen, get out of my way."

Thea burst in from the porch. "Daddy says if we don't haul our butts—" She broke off, staring at the form. "Mommy! There it is!"

"*Was,*" muttered Carla. She adjusted the flame.

Thea did not hear her above the torch's roar. She ran to the figure. On tiptoes, she ran her hand down the sleek metal body.

"It's *Peeper*. You made Peeper!"

"Get out of the way, Thea," Carla said gently. She paused and looked into her daughter's face. "'Peeper'?"

"The doctor bird! This is his tail." The tiny hand caressed the tubes from which the figure rose. She pointed at the lacy cross member far above. "And he's taking that thing to Jamaica to build his nest!"

Carla stepped away from the figure and studied it, running her finger along her lips. Slowly she reached down and turned off the flame. She pulled off her leather gloves, tossed them onto her workbench. She bent swiftly and kissed Thea on the top of her golden head.

"Mommy, let's not show Daddy! Until they have the undressing?"

"Unveiling," Carla said. "Okay."

She threw the sail over the work and went to the door. Her face was troubled.

"Mike," she called, "it's ready! Let's get it on the road!"

Mike Brody inspected the caravan. The shrouded form was in the padded crate they had constructed for it; the crate was lashed securely to the sides of the jeep-trailer; the trailer hitch was checked. The road to Prince

George Town would be full of potholes, even after it turned from dirt to macadam, and the whole enchilada seemed precarious.

He still had not been allowed to look at the figure, although Ellen and Thea had.

Women . . .

He started the jeep. Jake was taking William to the Festival in the project's old Ford station wagon, and Ellen and Thea too.

Mike glanced toward the water. Jake was standing on the dock, listening for the last time to make sure that the shark had not returned.

When he came back, he said, "Gone forever. I told you he'd leave."

Mike sighed. So much for his learned paper, *Great White Shark in Warm Waters: Aberration, Trend, or Migration?*

"Well"—Mike shrugged—"one swallow never makes a summer. Back to conch?"

"Yah, mon, I just hope the Ministry doesn't run out of funds."

With the shark gone back to wherever he came from, at least they could go to the Festival and ogle the pretty girls.

Chapter 2

The great white shark had cruised from Masthead Point south to Pretty Sally Bay, sensing the activity in Prince George Town and excited by the drums. He was ravenously hungry now, and the wound in his flank enraged him.

In Pretty Sally Bay, bordered by the whitewashed cottages north of the village, he hit a diving cormorant the instant the bird struck the water, swallowing it whole and hardly knowing what he did.

All at once he sensed cooler water ahead. A flood tide was sweeping through Bowsprit Cut, south of Whiskey Cay, and the idle shallows he lazed through now were heating from the morning sun.

He hesitated. The drums of Prince George Town were even louder, arousing his curiosity. But cold water meant bigger prey, and he was famished.

He turned away from the drums and swam south.

Suddenly he heard, as the drumbeats faded behind him, the booming of the Outer Passage surf. Something massive was punctuating its rhythm; a slapping jolt, a half dozen breakers, then the jolt again.

He picked up speed and swam out Bowsprit Cut.

The blond, lithe young man on the Windsurfer skimmed along the surf line past the cut at the southern end of Whiskey Cay.

He was a pre-law sophomore at Yale, with a minor in the classics, Skull and Bones, squash team, vice-president of his class. He had launched his twelve-foot Mistral board, made in France and bought in Nassau for twelve hundred U.S. dollars, as the morning breeze ruffled the waters off his family's winter estate on Harbor Island Beach.

He was bound this morning for the Windsurfer championships at Prince George Town. He had won in the semis at Nassau the previous week and had placed second in the Third Annual Water Junkanoo at the Matthews Town Regatta.

He was hot on the island circuit this vacation, lean and hungry for silver cups to join the others in New Haven in his dormitory room. His father was a Wall Street lawyer whose demands on his only son were simple: always win.

He was flying a sixty-five-square-foot, full-battened, high-aspect rig from a mast that towered seventeen feet above the board.

He was halfway to Prince George Town when he heard the surf in the outer passage. He was making a good twelve knots on a starboard reach, spewing a swirl of water through the chop, mated to his board with foot straps. Occasionally, out of sheer good spirits, he would lay back against the wind, gripping his boom. He would hike the thrumming sail so far past the vertical that he could let his head fall back and dip his hair in the water.

The sound of the surf distracted him. He glanced at his two-hundred-dollar sixty-fathom watch. Nine-fifteen—the races would not start until ten, and he was only fifteen minutes from Prince George Town right now. Across Masthead Sound he could already see the houses by Pretty Sally Bay.

He eased off, bounced through the incoming tide, and within three minutes was paralleling the beach outside the surf line, waiting for the Wave of the Day.

When he found it, it was a grandfather. He caught its

curve perfectly, skimmed diagonally down its face, hit thirty knots in the curl, and, just before it broke, swung up to its crest.

The world fell away below him, and he was airborne, flying, the board strapped to his feet, his stomach in his bowels, the Bahamian sun tossing golden droplets from his mast.

He howled in ecstasy, caught another set, and flew again. God, he could do this all day long; it was better than sex, more fun than racing. He had enough cups . . .

"So, son, did you win at Whiskey Cay?"

"Didn't get there, Pops. . . . There was this set coming in at Bowsprit Cut. . . ."

No way. Not with twelve hundred dollars of the old man's money invested in the board.

Regretfully he jibed at the end of the surf line and started back. He sped on a starboard tack, staying just ahead of the curl. Suddenly he caught a glimpse of something white through the plastic eye-level window in his sail. It was matching his speed on the outside of the surf.

Triangular, high-aspect ratio, port tack, just like him. And really hauling ass too. . . .

Another Windsurfer come to race? The image through the window smeared with foam. He let go of the boom with one hand and wiped the plastic.

Not a Windsurfer. A sailboat? No, too small.

A fin? A shark fin?

He had been brought to the Bahamas every year since the age of six. He had never heard of a man-eating shark anywhere near here.

But it *was* a shark, and if that was its fin, only God knew how big its body was.

His knees began to tremble, and he almost capsized. His hands grew slippery on the boom. If he fell off now, he was doomed. . . .

His salvation lay in speed and in his gear: the full-batten sail, the waxed-glass bottom, the tapered skeg, the computer-designed centerboard, the camber inducers. He could make twenty knots in the chute.

He strained for the last knot he had. As long as his equipment did not fail him, he could outdistance any shark with the speeding tunnel of the rushing surf to help him.

"In the chute," he whispered to his board. "Stay in the chute. . . ."

The breeze stiffened. He was tearing through the water now, sail thrumming above, sucking a long, slim wake, he was losing him, if only the surf stayed up . . .

His heart sank. A thousand yards ahead—eight hundred now, then six—the water was as calm as glass. Fat Molly Hill, the only southern rise on Whiskey Cay, was going to cut off all his wind.

He had only once choice, and no time to make it. He leaned back, back, back, trailing his blond hair in the water, hearing the swish of his wake, feeling the board alive beneath his feet. . . .

Gripping his boom, he shifted his weight and slammed the board up the face of the wave, rising, rising, rising toward the morning sun.

At the crest he leapt as a ski jumper leaps, with calf and thigh and gut. He left the water and flew in the last of the wind, climbing like Icarus toward the sun.

He glimpsed the fin, far astern, and felt wind, blessed wind, ruffling the waters below. He had timed it perfectly and was out of Fat Molly's grasp. Once back on the wind-skimmed surface, nothing in the ocean could catch him—this he knew.

He whooped in triumph.

Then his left foot strap broke and he was suddenly tumbling, flailing in the air. His boom, released, swung out of his reach. The sail filled, took the boom, and slammed it into his stomach.

He hit the water on his back, arms and legs askew. For an instant he lay in shock.

By the time he righted himself and struck out for shore, he knew that he was finished.

The great white hit him once, at fifteen knots, shearing him as a scissors cuts a paper doll. The torso it ingested while it glided on toward shore; the lower half of the body, trailing guts, it took when it turned back to the sound.

It swam north again, toward Prince George Town. The drums were beating louder.

Romeo's Cadillac nosed along a street already jammed with revelers. He inched through the Royal Bahamas Police Force Band. Flown in from Nassau, they were assembling in Whitechapel Square in their white jackets and red sashes. From the tops of their white tropical helmets rose shining spikes of gold. They parted for the Cadillac, ebony cheeks gleaming in the hot morning sun, and closed in after the limousine had passed.

From the sidewalk a Junkanoo dancer, masked and hidden behind cones and ruffles of pink, purple, yellow, and orange crepe paper, waved a garlanded staff at the car; at its end glared a long-billed duck that must have taken weeks to fashion from papier-mâché.

Romeo turned off Kingston and drove along a quiet street. He stopped by a white picket fence.

His funeral parlor lay shaded by palms on the shores of Pretty Sally Bay, with a dock reaching out to the water. Alongside the dock was a Cigarette boat, as ominous and black as the one that Lomas used.

A gleaming sign above the fence read, ROMEO JOHNSTON, LICENCED UNDERTAKER, Your One-stop Funeral

Home: Embalming, Caskets, Mourners, Burial Plots, Memorial Stones, Service Arrangements, Off-Island Shipment of Remains. Also: Car Rentals, Guided Tours, Insurance.

In the shade of the palm grove sat Romeo's hearse, an ancient, beautifully polished black Chrysler with purple curtains in the rear windows.

Hoagie got out. He glanced back toward Kingston Street. As he had known from watching Romeo's eyes in the rearview mirror, they had been tailed by a taxi. Three blocks back, it was rounding the corner, slowing, parking.

The street was quiet; only the faintest rumble of the *goombay* drums reached here. Alejandro, glancing quickly around, got out behind him. His linen jacket bulged ominously. It would be useful to know his firepower, before they learned it the hard way, but Hoagie saw no prospect of finding out.

"Qué pasa?" Alejandro asked suspiciously, jerking a thumb toward the sign. He shot a glance at Hoagie. "El Inglés, what is it goes on in there?"

"Our clients," Hoagie told him, "are dying to find out."

Alejandro did not smile. "No games. Is this your factory? A house of *death?"*

"Por qué no?" Hoagie nodded, gesturing toward the home. "Why not? We have the dock there for deliveries, and the islanders don't like to get too close to stiffs."

Alejandro was suddenly sniffing the air for ether and acetone. Good, thought Hoagie; the smell of both was heavy on the breeze. Romeo explained their odor to his neighbors as a constituent of embalming fluid, like formaldehyde. No one knew the difference, anyway; happy with the money Romeo spewed around, no one cared.

They passed into the funeral home. In the reception

room a pretty black girl sat reading a paperback. "My daughter, *señor,*" Romeo told Alejandro in Spanish. They moved through a casket showroom and the tiny chapel behind it. Romeo unlocked a door behind the altar marked EMBALMING.

Alejandro studied the embalming room as if he were an artist about to paint it. He moved to a closet, swung it open quickly, hand close to the bulge in his jacket. He went to the rear entrance, unlocked it, surveyed the back. He pulled aside a blind and peered down at the dock. Then he eyed the back of the room, past a cadaver on which a scrawny young white woman was applying makeup.

Two black men, stripped to the waist, were siphoning a mixture of ether, alcohol, and cream-colored coca paste from a stainless-steel keg through a transparent plastic tube. It was dripping into a GI can through a tightly woven cloth stretched across a wooden frame.

On top of the cloth was a slurry of white powder, still damp. A horizontal rack of cloth filters was drying by the side of the table.

Alejandro moved to the rack, took up a pinch, tasted it, smelled it, and finally snorted it into a nostril.

"Where is the quarter of a metric ton, el Inglés?"

Hoagie grinned. "Not for you, Alejandro. That's for Lomas. He's on this island somewhere."

"Perhaps. Perhaps not."

"He's here on Whiskey Cay, Alejandro. I think he's parked in that taxi that followed us. Get him."

Alejandro regarded him for a moment through his glittering snake eyes. Finally he shrugged. "Take me outside again."

Hoagie followed him back through the funeral parlor. Two blocks away, the taxi sat. Alejandro took out a cigarette, elaborately tamped it on his wrist, and asked

Hoagie for a light. Hoagie snapped open his RAF lighter and lit it for him.

It was their signal that all was well. The taxi drove up and parked behind Romeo's Cadillac. Rico Lomas stepped from the rear seat. He was dressed as a tourist, wearing mirrored sunglasses and a straw hat with a band of cowrie shells. He walked swiftly under the funeral parlor's sign and joined them on the porch. He glanced around, grim-faced and taut, obviously unhappy at being there.

"You have seen the stuff?" he asked Alejandro in his rapid Spanish.

"Only that which they are processing now."

"And?"

"Grade *B*, *señor*." Alejandro shrugged. "Perhaps *B+*."

"*A*," said Hoagie evenly. "And he knows it."

Lomas faced him. "Where's the quarter of a ton?"

"Here, definitely here. Are we partners?"

"Bring me to it, then we talk."

Hoagie stood for a moment, gazing thoughtfully into the distance. Out of the corner of his eye he caught a movement of the curtains across the hearse's window, but neither Lomas nor Alejandro noticed, and he relaxed.

I've got you, you murdering bastard, he thought. *I've bloody got you now.*

"Talk? Absolutely, *compadre mío*. Come on in."

Chapter 3

Mike Brody sat with Carla at a table in front of the Inn of the Happy Whale. In the shade of its umbrella her face was tense with worry.

"Relax, honey," he said, taking her hand. She managed a smile, watching the crane across the street back away from her veiled statue. Two stonemasons began to trowel smooth the holes in the granite foundation where its underpinning was set.

The stand facing the figure was filling with spectators. Jake and Louisa were in the front row. They were saving Mike a seat, and two more for Ellen and Thea, who were watching the swimming races from the beach.

Mike saw a gray government limousine creep through the masked Junkanoo dancers shuffling on the street; it beeped its horn. A black Bahamian senator from Nassau mounted the speaker's platform.

"Curtain time?" Carla asked.

He glanced at his watch. "You've got five minutes. Finish your drink."

He had dragged her there to calm her nerves. He hadn't been successful, but at least she'd given him a smile, the first in a week. He touched her cheek. "Come on, Carla. They'll love it."

She pressed his hand to her face. "Thanks, Michael." Her eyes filled with tears. "Mike, I've been such a bitch! All the time Ellen's been here, I've been neglecting her and Thea and not letting anybody see the damn thing. . . ."

"You're an artist, Carla—different. You give good statue, baby."

"Thank you," she murmured.

"And we'd be dead if you didn't." He studied his Yellow Bird cocktail and looked up. "Everybody knows I'd rather play tag with fish than do an honest day's work—"

"Stop it," she said softly. "Stop it, Mike!"

"An artist"—he shrugged—"is entitled to a mood or two."

A masked dancer shuffled up, small enough to be a child. He was "rushin'," in the strange, sliding, distorted Junkanoo style, to the beat of a companion's goatskin drum. Between them he thrust a staff with a snake head atop it and shook it. It rattled.

Absently Mike brushed it aside. A strange chill came over him as he touched it. The dancer tapped him on the head, chortled, and sidled away.

"Besides," Mike said with a grin, "you're pretty. And a wonder in the sack." He swirled his drink, tasted it, and added, "As I remember."

Her eyes flared, and all at once he would have given the world to have swallowed the words. *Why now, you idiot?* It was too late.

"Meaning?" she asked evenly.

What in the world had gotten into him? "Meaning nothing. You've been busy."

"Last night," she said, protesting, "I *wanted* you, and I was trying to wake you up, and then the screaming started. . . ."

He felt his temper rise. "Let's not blame our sex life on my mom, okay?"

"Nobody *blames* her. But her shark thing rubbed off on Thea so bad, it made her sick!"

"While you were in Nassau playing roulette?"

"I went to buy a welding head!" she said, furious.

"Remember *that* next time I'm trying to pay the milkman."

"Well, whatever Thea had, it wasn't Mom's fault," he said angrily. "Of *course* Mom's got a 'shark thing.' She isn't over Sean!"

"And neither are you, my friend."

"No," he said, agreeing. "Why should I be? I loved that guy."

"I loved him too." Her eyes blazed. "But when you remember him, the rest of your life, do you think of a shark or *him?*"

"It isn't that easy," he said morosely. "For Mom. Or me."

"But she's obsessed! She even got to me!"

"Meaning?" he asked coldly.

She swallowed and looked across the street. "I think I sculpted one in steel."

He felt a shiver run up his arm. "A *shark?*"

She shrugged. "It turned *into* a shark."

"I don't believe it!" he said. "You wouldn't do that to us!"

"Not on purpose!" She tried to calm him down. "It's like all my things. *You* may see Christ on a cross, or yourself on a cross, who knows?"

"Well, it damn well better not look like a shark to the Commissioner of Tourism." He took a deep breath. "Because Carla . . .?"

"Yes?"

Quietly Mike said, "There *was* one."

She looked shocked. *"Here?"*

He nodded. "It left two days ago, heading south toward Spanish Galleon Cay."

Her eyes widened. "How do you know that?"

"We tagged it. It's transmitting its own heartbeat. We followed it for a day."

"I thought they didn't like warm water."

"This one did. You noticed a pink submarine around lately?"

"The *Whine Bottle?*" She gasped. "No!"

"Well, you've been busy," he said bitterly. "He damn near ate it up."

Her eyes widened. "Was anybody in it?"

"Me, but not for long."

"And you tagged it and shut up?"

"Seventy percent of this island's income comes in the next twenty-four hours." He waved his hand at the carnival stands, the fruit stalls, the vendors. "These people would starve in their shacks. So they chartered us instead."

"You bastards!"

"Look, we knew we could stay on him; he didn't travel fast! Anyway, he's gone. We saved the island, Carla!"

She stared at her glass. "I see why you didn't tell Ellen, Mike. . . ."

"Good."

"But," she said, flaring, getting up, "you sure as hell could have told *me!*"

"Why?" He jerked his thumb at the figure across the street. "You didn't tell me about yours! You've hardly said a word to me since you married that goddamn thing!"

A whistle shrilled, and the Royal Bahamas Police Force Band, white jackets and pith helmets glaring in the sun, was suddenly marching. In the easy British Army stride, they moved from the Government House down Kingston Street toward the bandstand by the statue.

The drum major raised his staff, with its glittering silver sphere. Ponderously he brought it down, and the band boomed out, "Hail Britannia, Britannia rules the waves . . ."

Carla, white-faced, glared at Mike, turned on her heel, and ran across the street.

* * *

The slight, masked Junkanoo dancer and the *goombay* drummer who always stayed close at his side slipped from the crowds on Kingston Street. The dancer carried a staff with a crepe-paper snake at its end. They moved down an alley of rickety houses, each with its hex sign above the door, leading to Pretty Sally Bay.

The dancer's shuffling, jerky gait changed, and now he moved with a sense of purpose. They paused at a palm tree surrounded with tin cans and rusted gasoline drums. From behind a drum the masked dancer picked up a paper bag.

Ignoring a little black boy squatting in the shade of an abandoned sugar warehouse, they walked to the end of the alley. They moved along a twisted dock, projecting like a beckoning finger over scummy tidal waters.

Below them, swarms of tiny "no-see-'em" gnats circled a wooden fishing boat, half sunken at the dock.

The dancer took from the paper sack a child's beach bucket and a smashed gourd, a silver bell dangling from it.

The drummer ripped off a crepe-paper mask of violet and orange. She was a woman, wearing a white bandanna and earrings of hammered brass.

With half-closed eyes she sank cross-legged to the dock and began to drum softly. She increased the beat and the rhythm until the distant brass band faded.

In her high, clear voice, the *houngenikon* called for her ancient *loa:*

Maître Agwe, where are you?
Don't you see I'm on the reef?
I've a rudder in my hand . . .

Only then did Papa Jacques unmask. Black eyes glittering, he unfastened his shark's-tooth necklace. He dangled it high.

His eyelids dropped. He entered a trance. He chanted, in a high, wailing monotone:

Mâitre shark, where are you?
Don't you see I'm on the reef?
I've a two-legged goat for you,
I've your teeth in my hand,
Use them and dine well.

He hurled the bucket and gourd into the water. They floated gently, moving slowly in the current toward the beach around the point.

He touched the necklace to his lips and flung it after the bucket.

Then he turned swiftly, and, followed by his *houngenikon,* walked back to Kingston Street.

When they were gone, the little black boy ran from the warehouse and picked up his mask. He held it to his face.

The distant pulse of the Royal Bahamas Police Force Band made the dock planking shiver:

Oh, Britannia, Britannia rules the waves,
Britons never, never, never shall be slaves.

The little boy began to shuffle to its beat.

Chapter 4

Hoagie Newcombe's fingers were damp with sweat. He was trying to open the vault in a storage room off Romeo's embalming lab.

He had gambled a year of his life on this sting, and today he was gambling the rest of it. But now that they were on the verge of success, he had forgotten the combination to the safe.

Behind him, he could feel Lomas's eyes drilling into his back. "Ten . . ." Hoagie chanted, "eight . . . six . . ."

The last three numbers were his daughter's birthday, but what *was* it? March 12, 19— what? March was three, then right past zero to twelve . . . but 1968, 1969, 1970?

If only he had his flying log. He'd been flying from a carrier in the Persian Gulf when he'd gotten the dispatch from his wife in Nassau: "A girl, Prudence Amelia Newcombe, seven pounds three . . . your eyes, my hair . . . wish you'd been here instead of me."

Nineteen sixty-eight or 1969? He tried 1968. The vault wouldn't open.

All right, work backward. How old was she when she disappeared? Seventeen? Or eighteen? The man behind him would know, but he couldn't ask him.

Not yet . . .

He dried his fingers on his shirt. He could hear Alejandro muttering to his boss in Spanish but could not make out the words. He felt supremely exposed.

He took a deep breath to settle his nerves. He must

not fail now. He had worked too long on the scam, against too many odds.

He and the U.S. Drug Enforcement Agency were on their own; he had not dared to trust Government House or even Scotland Yard. Lomas already owned half the cops on New Providence Island, and God knew how many here. If the kidnapping failed, he and Romeo and the agents could end the day in a Nassau jail.

It had taken a year for Hoagie to get Rico Lomas off his island, onto Whiskey Cay. Now a private twin-engine Beechcraft Baron was waiting to kidnap him at the Whiskey Cay airstrip, chartered by the DEA out of Miami.

Hoagie had been deputized a year ago, and Romeo just last month. The two blacks working the refining vats were U.S. agents out of the Savannah office, and one held a black belt in karate.

The woman touching up the corpse was a forensic scientist from the DEA's Washington, D.C., headquarters; sent, Hoagie suspected, to the Bahamas for the sting as a reward for long and faithful service.

She was ready with two syringes, a hundred milligrams of Nembutal each, powerful enough to put Lomas and his gorilla to sleep for half the day. When they awoke, Hoagie hoped, they'd be in a Miami cell.

In the hearse outside were two more agents, ready for the trip to the airstrip.

If he could open the blasted safe . . .

He worked the combination again, with seventy. It failed.

"El Inglés," hissed Lomas, *"qué pasa?* What are you trying to do?"

"Steady, lad," muttered Hoagie. "Steady as you go."

He tried seventy-one, and the vault opened.

She'd been just sixteen years old . . .

He took out the plastic-wrapped package on top.

He'd bought the coke as bait in Nassau three nights before, wanting to make sure it was what Lomas would bite on best; since the chances were that Lomas had been its importer, it should pass any test he had.

He moved aside to show Lomas the vault. It was stacked with plastic bags like the one in his hand, but all the rest held sugar.

He carried the sample to the lab desk. Romeo stood by the entrance to the embalming room. On the makeup table by the corpse, under some towels, lay a .38 Magnum for Romeo and .25-.20 for the forensic chemist.

The black agent, sucking on a siphon, smiled into Hoagie's eyes. Hoagie had seen him swipe with the side of his hand at a two-by-four and break it; that one needed no weapons but his fists.

Lomas nodded at Alejandro. Alejandro opened the package and tested it as before. He nodded and indicated the powder to Lomas. Lomas wet his finger, touched the coke, tasted his finger. He sniffed it delicately and nodded.

"Okay," he said affably. Hoagie took a deep breath. He was sure that Lomas planned to kill them all, today, for the quarter of a ton, and timing must be precise.

He let his gaze wander around the room. Everything was set. The scientist was powdering the corpse's nose, Romeo was leafing through an account book, the black with the tube in his mouth had spit it out and was straightening, ready for action.

Hoagie took a deep breath and stuck out his hand to Lomas. It was the signal.

"Partners!" he said.

The corpse sneezed.

It was a Vesuvius sneeze, an eruption, a cataclysm. The makeup table fell over with a crash.

Alejandro was magnificent. In a swift, invisible motion his gun was out, and he slammed Lomas behind him, toward the back door.

The *coquero* was firing before a single agent got to his gun. His first slug caught the black belt in the belly and knocked him across the room. His second missed Hoagie, who was diving for the vault. His third nicked Romeo's shoulder, before Romeo could move.

"*Vamos!*" he yelled at Lomas, but Lomas was already gone.

The corpse rolled, fired once, and caught Alejandro in the head.

Hoagie, splattered with his blood, stood up behind the lab table and yelled to the forensic scientist. She tossed him her weapon, and he burst from the back door.

Lomas stood in the alley. In one arm he clasped a little black boy, who was wearing a Junkanoo mask. In his other hand he held a .45 automatic. To Hoagie its muzzle looked like a five-inch gun he'd seen on an Argentine cruiser.

He dived behind a clump of grass as the .45 roared out.

He hugged the sand, waiting an eternity for death, eyes closed, drained and sick at heart. When finally he found the courage to raise his head, the alley was empty.

Cautiously he got up. He saw a spot of purple and orange crepe paper near a garbage can.

Pulse pounding, he moved closer.

Crumpled into the can was the little black boy, an arm flung over the rim. His eyes were staring upward, and his leg was shuddering still.

Distantly Hoagie heard the Royal Police Band and voices singing proudly:

God save our gracious Queen
Long live our noble Queen
God save the Queen.

Tenderly he lifted the child out and laid him on the sand. Someone spoke above him, and his voice was deep and awed. It was Romeo, holding his left arm in a blood-soaked bandage.

"My God, mon! He broke his bloody neck!"

"You call the police?" demanded Hoagie.

"What are they going to do but put us in jail?"

"But surely we'll have to report *this.*"

"I'll find his kin. We'll bury him."

"Are the DEA agents clear?" Hoagie asked distantly.

"On the way to the airstrip in the hearse. Carrying their dead. They'll be in Miami in an hour."

"And Alejandro?"

Hoagie said with a growl, "'You kill a snake, you mus' bury he 'fore dark, mon, he come bite you once agin.' Old Creole saying."

Hoagie glanced at the arm. "You okay, mate?"

Romeo shrugged. "'He jests at scars, that never felt a wound.' I needed that slug to cool me down."

"I'm sorry we blew it, old chap."

"Well, I'm out of Drug Enforcement, as of now. And Hoagie . . . ?"

"Yes?"

"I recommend the same for you."

Hoagie shook his head and looked down at the little boy. "First I'm going to find the bloody bastard who did *this!*"

Romeo didn't know the whole story, and there wasn't time to tell him now. Hoagie started down the alley at a fast clip, toward the sound of the big brass band.

Send her victorious,
Happy and glorious,
Long to reign over us
God save the Queen!

He had unleashed a monster on the island. There was no way on God's green earth that he could quit.

Carla sat on the speaker's platform. Her stomach churned with anger. Below her, the Royal Bahamas Police Force Band, in their bandstand gazebo, made ready to do her and the statue homage. The Prince George Town Village Choir, sweating in blue blazers, sat behind her.

And in her hour of need and triumph Mike hadn't even crossed the street.

The black senator reminded his constituents that he had paved the road from Prince George Town to the Whiskey Cay Airstrip.

"Yah, mon," someone called from the rear. "That de *tourist* side de town. You buyin' us pretty statue, ay? When you be pavin' roun' Pretty Sally Cay, where de black folk live?"

The senator, not in the least disturbed and speaking in Oxford English, concluded on a note of welcome, begging his American friends to spread the fame of Whiskey Cay far and wide. The mayor, Jason Witherspoon, rose.

And still no Mike. She could see him across the street, sitting at the table, drinking all alone.

He was not himself. Something had been wrong ever since they'd returned from Amity. And it wasn't all her fault. . . .

Thea was fidgeting in the first row, below, and tugging at Ellen's arm, craning back to see the beach, where her friends were playing.

"Shall I take her?" Ellen mouthed.

Carla could see, over the heads of the people below, a dozen children from Thea's preschool class, herded by Margaret de Lacey, the local dentist's wife.

Carla nodded at Ellen. "Sure"—she pantomimed it—"go ahead." Thea was gone like a shot. Ellen excused herself to Jake and Louisa and followed her granddaughter to the beach.

Still no Mike. . . .

"And so the moment of truth has arrived," boomed Witherspoon. "And our community will be graced by something we shall look at every day, something we shall think beautiful, like the famous sculptress herself. . . ."

He turned and beamed at Carla, the sunshine gleaming off his jet-black skin.

Politicians were all the same: Witherspoon, Kennedy, Reagan, Aquino . . . black, white, or brown . . . oblivious to their listeners' boredom once they got the floor.

"Something that makes us stop and ponder . . ."

The statue had made *them* stop and ponder, all right, she and Mike, and she hoped their marriage would survive the pondering. . . .

"Something that makes us question the wonder of life becomes unique when it falls to the artist's eye. . . ."

This artist's eye was on her husband's vacant seat. How could he? Her throat was tight.

"Art transforms the ordinary into the unique." He took a breath. God, he was putting Jake to sleep.

"*We* see a sunset in all its glory, yet the artist, perhaps because she comes from another land, sees something that isn't there for the rest of us. . . ."

This artist sees a shark and hopes that no one else does.

It stood with its sailcloth cover flapping, an enigma to them all, including her.

Suppose it *was* a shark to the rest of them, and not a bird, or a free form, or just a shape, to be cherished and admired?

Her heart began to beat harder. And then suppose Mike's shark came back and ruined the tourist trade and there's a statue in the town square to commemorate him . . .

Did they still burn witches at the stake in the Bahamas?

The great white had returned to Pretty Sally Bay from Bowsprit Cut. Now he lolled offshore, digesting the blond on the Windsurfer and parts of his board as well.

A steel-drum band was pounding reggae somewhere on the water, to a beat stolen from Bob Marley and the Wailers. The thumping interested the shark. He cruised from the quiet of Pretty Sally around Harbor Point. Here he swam into a cacophony of sound.

He did not know where to head, but he was back where the action was.

Carla was growing more uncomfortable on the stand with every word of the mayor's praise.

From the government barge that would review the Aquatic Parade she heard the steel-drum band.

Closer yet, on Kingston Street, a *goombay* drummer began a deep, slow jungle pounding.

Boom . . . boom . . . boom . . .

Something tugged at her memory. Mike said they'd tagged the shark. How? With one of their little transmitters, like a conch?

Would the heartbeat sound like a conch's? Or deeper, slower . . .

Boom . . . boom . . . boom . . .

An awful thought plucked at the back of her mind. Something forgotten, some error she had made?

The drums were making her head ache. The mayor droned on. She flashed on Ellen, dancing out of her head on the moonlit beach . . .

Boom . . . boom . . . boom . . .

Witherspoon's voice rose. "Today we are privileged to dedicate a work of art that I am sure will reflect the true tone of our community."

Last night, on the beach, she had done something just as weird as Ellen. What was it?

Witherspoon dithered on. "A work of art that none of us has yet seen but which we know reflects the true spirit, the free expression of life here in the Bahamas."

From the platform she could see over the Royal Police Band, past the seated spectators, to the beach. The Windsurfer races were over, the swimming tournament done.

Sailboats flying pennants and burgees from half the yacht clubs in the Bahamas were circling offshore, waiting for the grand finale, the Annual Whiskey Cay Aquatic Parade.

Powerboats manned by masked Junkanoo revelers, canoes and kayaks, graceful, island-built wooden fishing boats with their tattered working sails, ski boats and jet skis, dugouts and dinghies, racing sculls and paddleboats, all were gathering for the climax.

King Neptune—a smiling, jet-black bartender at the Inn of the Happy Whale—was seated on his throne on the anchored government barge. He wore a golden crown. His men-at-arms, armored in cardboard, stood behind him. Beside him sat his queen, a lovely Nassau

TV newswoman, dressed in a shimmering mermaid costume.

A ragtag steel-drum band thumped from the barge's bow. A huge British West Indies flag—of green, black, red, and gold—flapped at her stern.

The inflated banana boat was loading on the beach. The last ride was always free. Carla saw Thea tugging at her grandmother's arm, begging to be allowed to go.

"Carla Brody," Witherspoon said, beaming, "a grand addition to our community, an American artist of growing reputation, who was commissioned to express our way of life in permanent form . . ."

Hardly listening, Carla kept her eyes on Thea.

She glanced at the bar across the street. Mike, weaving a little, was shouldering his way through the crowds.

"Carla"—Witherspoon smiled—"would you care to say a few words?"

The jib from *Neptune's Folly* shivered on the statue in the breeze, as if the figure beneath it was moving, straining to be born.

Neptune's Folly, at the dock!

Boom . . . boom . . . boom . . .

Tied there to act as a monitor, with the loudspeaker turned up high?

In case the shark returned? Mike and Jake did that often with conch, so that they could sense their movements while sitting on the porch drinking beer and without staying on the boat.

And the night before, she had turned it *off?*

And never bothered to tell Mike?

Suppose the shark had come back?

"Carla?" Witherspoon urged. "Mrs. Brody? Would you say a few words?"

Her eyes were focused past the audience, on the beach.

Down there, Ellen was nodding reluctantly; Thea had won the argument. The child waded out, holding one of Margaret de Lacey's hands; Margaret's daughter held the other. There were three seats left on the banana boat. Margaret hoisted both children into place, with Thea on the stern, and climbed between them where she could hang on to them both.

The banana boat, low in the water and laden with screaming children, headed for the rear of the waterborne parade.

Mike was passing below the stand. He tripped over someone's feet, bowed elaborately, and stumbled into his seat. He patted Louisa on the knee, gave Jake a high-five handshake, and defiantly frowned up at Carla.

She hadn't seen him drunk in years, but she was too frightened to care.

Boom . . . boom . . . boom . . .

Suppose what she had heard the previous night on the beach was the heartbeat of the shark?

"Mrs. Brody?" Witherspoon said, prodding her and indicating the microphone.

She ignored him. "Mike," she called, "I turned off that loudspeaker last night!"

He sobered instantly. Jake came awake and half rose from his chair.

"What?"

"Mrs. Brody!" protested Witherspoon. A buzz ran through the audience. The mayor gave up, shrugged, stepped to the statue, and yanked off the cover, as the conductor of the Royal Bahamas Police Force Band rapped on his music stand.

She heard gasps as the sail fell away. Mike vaulted to the stand.

"Why?" he demanded.

"We had to sleep!"

"Oh, my God!" Mike moaned. For an instant he

stared into her eyes. Then he yanked the microphone from the mayor.

But the Royal Police Band had been restrained too long. The bandleader tapped his music stand and raised his baton. He brought it down. The cymbals clashed, the clarinets blared, the tubas throbbed.

"Clear the water!" shouted Mike. "Get them out!"

In the blast of brass and the rumble of snares, hardly anyone on the stand, and no one on the beach, could hear.

The parade of vessels began to flow by King Neptune on the barge.

Chapter 5

Ellen Brody watched the banana boat pull away from the beach, fighting the dread that grabbed her whenever she saw a Brody in the water.

First she had said no. But the shattered look in Thea's eyes when she learned that she could not go with the others had brought Ellen back to Amity after the time of the first shark.

Brody had passed an edict: No more swimming for the boys off Amity Beach.

Sean had been easy to convince; he remembered the first shark and wouldn't go near the water, anyway.

But with Mike, it had been different; he'd begun a hunger strike. It had started because of a printed application form for a scuba-diving course. His friend Andy had picked up two copies at the Amity Sport Diving Center and given one to Mike. Andy's father had signed Andy's, and Brody refused to sign.

So Mike went without two meals in a row. Ellen told Brody. Brody found him lying on his bed in his room, reading *Skin Diver* magazine.

The magazine was the top issue on a pile a foot high. Brody, trying to bring up the subject of the missed breakfast and lunch, leafed through one of them. He stopped at a full-page ad from U.S. Divers.

A macho diver, who wore a husky mustache, dripped with seawater and gleaming new equipment. A model, who looked as if her wet suit had been sprayed on her, gazed at him, wet-eyed with lust.

"What are you going to do, burn them?" complained Mike, addressing the ceiling. "It's not *porn.*"

"No, Mike. I almost wish they *were*. Porn won't kill you."

"You want porn? Okay, I can take care of *that.*" His voice was strangled. "Magazine rack at Starbuck's, okay? Jackie won't even open them, they're so raunchy." Jackie was Mike's first love. "I saved the money for the scuba course; I can buy the *porn* instead."

"Take it easy, Mike."

Mike rolled over, facing him. "Then see, Dad, while Andy and Chip and Larry, you know, and everybody else in the crummy town is diving, I can, you know, lie up here with *Gallery* and—"

"Cool it!" Brody barked. "Look, if you want to swim, use the town pool. Your baby brother's got more sense than you!" They'd both been near victims of a shark attack a year before, in the time of the first Trouble. "And *he* was on the beach. *You* were in the ocean."

"In the ocean," squeaked Mike. "For the last time. I can swim like an eel! I live on an island! And I'm not allowed to—"

"I let you sail."

"And *that* took an Act of Congress! I'm tired of the dumb sailboat—"

"You're the best sailor in town!"

"But I want to be the best scuba diver instead, okay? It's *my* life!"

"You aren't living it right. You've got to eat. You look awful." He crossed the room to feel his forehead and found it hot.

"You think I'm *sick?*" Mike's voice quavered. "Maybe I am sick. Sick of your hang-up. Sick of Spitz."

"Who's Spitz?"

"Mark Spitz." Mike was crying now. "Great Olympic . . . swimmer. 'Hey, Spitz, come on down to the beach, you won't get wet. . . .' 'Gimme a swimming lesson, Spitz. . . .' 'Spitz, hey, move your beach towel, man, tide's coming in.'" He drew in a great, shuddering sigh. *"I'm* frigging Spitz."

"Mike—" Brody began helplessly.

"I wish we lived in Omaha," blurted Mike, "so *nobody* could dive!"

"But we live here."

"Dad?"

Brody brushed his son's hair from his eyes. "Yeah?"

"The shark is dead."

"Yes," Brody admitted, "the shark is dead." He finally talked Mike into going down to let Ellen make him a sandwich. Then he sat, flipping the magazine pages, until he realized that he was not really looking at them.

He knew suddenly that he was wrong. He was trying to plant cowardice in his son, who was trying to overcome a fear.

So he had signed the form and bought Mike a wet suit. "Ellen, we mustn't hang our own panic on those kids."

Here on the beach, Ellen felt Brody very close. To keep Thea from her playmates in the safest waters in the world was to taint her with useless dread. Ellen had looked into the hurt blue eyes.

"Okay, Thea," she said, lifting her up. "You can go."

The child nuzzled her neck. "Thank you, Grandma."

"Thank *Grandaddy,"* she murmured. "He told me to let you go on the banana boat, before you were even born."

"You're being silly again, Grandma." Thea giggled, but she threw back her head and piped at the sky, "Thank you, Grandpa Brody. Thanks a bunch."

She squirmed loose and ran to grab the hand of her friend's mother before the last seat on the banana boat was taken.

Now they were catching up to the parade, towed by a ski boat, and Thea was waving at her. The band at the speaker's stand suddenly thundered forth, and she heard a burst of song:

Columbia, the gem of the ocean,
Home of the brave and the free . . .

She'd apparently missed the unveiling. Too bad, but Carla understood. She could see the statue looming, glittering darkly in the sun, bare of its cover at last.

Something odd was happening around it. She saw Mike on the platform, yelling into the microphone, and wondered why.

Shrine of each patriot's devotion
A world offers homage to thee . . .

Then Mike and Carla were racing through the crowds on the beach, and Jake and Louisa were fighting their way to the water, screaming and signaling the boats. In a moment, all those near them were waving at them too.

Puzzled, Ellen swung around to see what they were motioning at. Everything seemed fine; the people on the boats were waving cheerfully back.

And then she saw the fin, chasing the parade and closing fast.

Hoagie Newcombe stopped at a phone booth next to the Inn of the Happy Whale's outdoor bar. There he could watch the passing crowd for Lomas, who might try to lose himself in it until he found a way to get off the island.

Scanning the faces of those passing on the sidewalk and the autos crawling up Kingston Street, he made a call to the tumbledown operations shack at Whiskey Cay airstrip.

He asked for the on-duty narcotics control officer. When he got him on the line, he described those of Lomas's aircraft small enough to get into Whiskey Cay: a split-tail Beach, a Cessna Centurian, and a Piper Twin Comanche.

None had landed that morning. Both Lomas's Learjets were too hot to land on the strip.

Unless the narc had been paid off, Lomas must have come by boat.

The *coquero* leader had two Chrysler-powered Cigarettes, the black one that had tried to shoot him down, and one of green. Hoagie called the harbormaster.

"Trevor, how many Cigarettes came in today?"

"'Bout a half dozen, from Nassau, ay. Couple from Gregory Town. Yah, mon, and one from Tarpum Bay."

"All at the Town Dock?"

"I'se lookin' at 'em out de window now."

"Black one?"

"Nah, mon."

"Green?"

A pause. "Don't see none green."

"None of them left yet?"

"Hoagie, you is messin' up my head wit' questions! I busy, mon! Aquatic Parade still goin' on!" There was a sharp gasp. "Oh, my God *A'mighty!*"

The telephone clicked off.

Hoagie tried to remember the number of docks on Whiskey Cay. The wharf on Mike's beach, a few half-ruined landings like the one behind Romeo's funeral home, where they'd tied a DEA Cigarette to make the scam look more legitimate—that was all.

And the landing at old Salt Hole, on the ocean side

of the cay, where Lomas had launched the hit men who'd made a sieve out of his wing.

He stepped out of the booth and joined the crowd on Kingston Street.

Something was happening on the beach. On the bandstand, the Royal Bahamas Police Force Band was ending "Columbia, the Gem of the Ocean" in a reluctant, discordant sigh, as if nobody knew when to stop. Behind Carla's statue, which he saw as a frozen waterspout hurling a dugout aloft, the municipal choir was deserting the stand.

Whatever the problem on the beach, he had no time to be curious. He must find Lomas before Lomas escaped, regrouped, and had him killed.

The great white shark was excited. The reggae music thumped above, magnified by the steel hull of the municipal barge. The rhythm struck a chord in his brain; it seemed to match the heartbeat of an albacore being pursued.

The snarl of the outboard engine towing the banana boat infuriated him. Dimly he associated it with the growl of the diesel on *Neptune's Folly* and the harpoon point working its way deeper and deeper into his flesh.

He would have gone for the towboat had it not been for the high-pitched voices he heard laughing and screaming above. He diverted his course and made a pass below the banana boat.

From below, it looked like a swimming centipede. Ten legs dangled, tugging myriad bubbles as they moved swiftly through the water.

He banked like a cruising airliner, circling his prey. When he attacked, he came at the banana boat from the rear.

Margaret de Lacey, with a hand on Thea's leg, glanced ashore. Everyone was lining the beach, waving.

She could not remember such enthusiasm in prior years, but every year the parade grew more elaborate. They were probably cheering the TV queen from Nassau, who was popular in these outlying islands, which felt themselves to be cut off.

Suddenly the banana boat hit the wake of the big Egg Harbor cruiser ahead. She could hear Thea squealing as they hobby-horsed through the waves. She turned to see that the child was hanging on.

Behind Thea, she saw a fin. From her low vantage point it looked like the Rock of Gibraltar, awash in a streaming tide. It was rushing up their wake.

Instinctively she turned her body, yanked Thea from her place, and body-slammed her athwartship between her daughter and herself.

Her last thought, as she braced to take the impact, was that she'd sprained her back.

For an instant she was in shadow, as the great white's jaws sprung open.

Then she and the last five feet of the rubber boat were crushed into a jumble of flesh and neoprene rubber as the swords of glittering ivory met and pressed.

The banana boat lay limp in the wake of the cruiser. No one ahead noticed. The children, screaming, flailed and thrashed in their life jackets.

Mike and Carla Brody hit the water like racing divers. So did Jake, two black lifeguards, and a retired American insurance salesman who hadn't swum in years. But before they reached the spot, the harbormaster's workboat had picked up the survivors.

The children, most of whom could swim almost before they had walked, hardly realized what had happened, but two of them were in shock. One was the heroine's daughter and the other was Thea.

Ellen was knee-deep in the water when she was intercepted by the first clarinet of the Royal Bahamas Police Force Band, in full uniform. She had fought the musician all the way back to the shore.

In Dr. Stanford's little clinic, as Mike and Carla sat by Thea's bedside, Mike noticed that his mother seemed detached, quite calm, and absolutely mute.

He was near shock himself, at what had happened to Margaret de Lacey and had almost happened to Thea. He blamed himself and Jake. When Ellen left the clinic without telling him, she had been gone an hour before he noticed it.

Chapter 6

Hoagie Newcombe could not find a taxi in the crowds on Kingston Street, so he jogged along the deserted residential ways to his digs on Devon Square to get his jeep.

He raced up the stairs and opened his bedside table drawer. He left the Drug Enforcement Agency's .25-.20 automatic there and took out the old .455 Wembley he had carried on his carrier strikes.

He was a poor shot with a handgun and disliked them, but he had an old, old score to settle. If he found Lomas, he would need the most powerful and familiar weapon he could get.

His jeep was parked under a satinwood tree. As he had for the past year, he checked quickly under its hood and body for a bomb before he started it.

Then he headed for the airstrip and Salt Hole.

Ellen Brody moved in a daze down the dock. In her hand was the police revolver that had been her husband's—and her son's. She had loaded it carefully. Brody had taught her to handle it during the time of the first Trouble, when feelings against them had run so high in Amity that someone had strangled their cat.

Neptune's Folly groaned at her lines, as if she knew what she was going to be asked to do. Too bad. Ellen, in her strange, dead-eyed anger, felt older than the vessel and as tired, but the shark had challenged her to the death, and one of them would go.

She remembered the fin, and the poor woman lifting Thea from her place, and the awful snout growing from the water, and the blood streaming from its jaws.

But after that she had only the dimmest recollections: a tiny clinic in the doctor's home; Carla massaging Thea; hushed voices; a doctor; a syringe that looked far too big for such a little child.

She stepped into the deckhouse. The boat-smell of varnish and damp canvas brought her back to the days when her father had chartered ketches much like this and they had cruised the coast of Maine. Her mother hated boats and had stayed at home.

Ellen had loved the ocean then, but she'd loved her father more, and the ocean was a place where she could have him to herself.

"First-rate first mate," he'd called her, his crinkling eyes all soft. Anchored on a summer evening off some granite Block Island cove, he would toast her with his first drink of the night: "Sun's over the yardarm! To the best little seaman a father ever had!"

Long, long ago . . . and how had she used to start the diesel?

She looked at the instrument panel by the inside helm. "Battery switch: #1, #2, Off, Both." She remembered and switched to "Both." The computer screen lit up, and a faint, rhythmical thudding sounded from the sonic speaker. She must be listening to conch, along the bottom.

She found the engine shift. "Neutral." Starter switch: "On."

There was a grinding from the engine room, a reluctant cough, and then the deep rumble of the diesel. So far, so good.

In a queer, muddled fog she cast off her lines, pushed her bow out with a boat hook, and let the ketch float clear of the dock on the offshore breeze. She stepped to the wheel in the cockpit, aft, threw the boat in "Forward," and was smoothly underway.

She had a rendezvous with a great white shark that was trying to kill her family off. She knew somehow that he awaited her in deep ocean waters; not here, in Masthead Sound, but at sea, beyond the point.

She brought the helm to starboard, lined the bowsprit up with Masthead Light, and eased the throttle forward.

She was going to kill the shark before it destroyed her and her family.

Kill him or die herself.

Papa Jacques had followed the beach line alone all the way from Pretty Sally Bay to Masthead Point. He passed through the hysterical crowds on Harbor Beach at the height of the excitement, when the children were pulled out of the water, and hardly spared a glance.

He knew that his *loa* had failed in its attack on the Brody child, somehow felt it deep inside. Perhaps the child's bucket had not been a proper *wanga*, or perhaps Damballah, the African serpent god, had simply decided to spare the little girl and instead take her elders one by one.

When he reached the beach in front of Masthead Point, he saw *Neptune's Folly* underway, heading to sea. At the wheel, all alone, was the accursed American's mother.

He was not surprised, for he had foreseen it. He knew that the shark had gone to sea, felt the cold depths on his own skin and the beat of an alien heart.

And he felt a searing pain in his side, deep and festering, that had begun just the previous day.

"Papa Jacques?" piped a voice. "Where Thea's grandma goin', all by hersef?"

The pain eased. He looked down at Clarence's daughter Deenie, his patient's older sister.

"To find my *loa, mon chéri.*" Papa Jacques smiled softly. "He has tol' me he will kill her in the ocean." He jerked a thumb toward Prince George Town. "Back there, he almost kill your lil' white friend."

The child stared up at him in shock, turned, and fled toward the main house.

Mike Brody was halfway home along Aerodrome Road—dotted with potholes and gravel fill—when he saw Hoagie's yellow jeep approaching in his rearview mirror.

The Englishman was making a good seventy miles an hour. Mike hugged the left, English side of the road. Hoagie swung around him to the right and passed, with a beep and barely a wave, intent on the curves ahead. Mike caught a glimpse of CALYPSO'S FRIENDLY CHARTERS on the door, and then the pilot was over the next rise in a shower of roadside gravel.

On a day when half the drivers on the island would be drunk, the Englishman was insane. But Mike had no time to puzzle over Hoagie. His own mind was on the shark and how best to track him down and kill him.

As he crested Spyglass Hill he saw that the dock in front of his home was empty. He cursed under his breath. Jake must have gone without him, taking *Neptune's Folly* out to search for the shark alone.

Then he saw him talking to Deenie on the porch of the main house. Jesus, where was the ketch?

He slammed the jeep to a stop below them, in a cloud of sand and dust. "Where the hell is *Folly?*"

Jake glared at him. "Ask Deenie!"

Mike looked at the girl. Her eyes were wide with fear. "I seen it passin' Mas'head Point, suh. 'Bout an hour ago. Thea's grandma take it."

He stared up at the porch. "Who?"

"Thea's *grandma!*"

He couldn't believe it. "My mother? And who else?"

"Jes' her! My daddy seen her too. She be headin' out the cut."

He leapt out of the jeep. "Jake, call the Royal Bahamas Police!"

"I did," said Jake. "They said, 'You reporting a stolen boat?' so I hung up."

His heart began to pound. "Jake, she's flipped! She's after the shark!"

"What'll she do if she finds him?" demanded Jake. "And why does she think he's gone to sea?"

"God knows!"

"Papa Jacques," said Deenie suddenly, "he know too."

Mike studied her. "What did you say?"

"Papa Jacques, he say shark waitin' outer waters. Waitin' to kill her."

"We'll borrow a speedboat," decided Mike. "Deenie, when she cleared the cut, which way'd she turn? North or south?"

Deenie shrugged and pointed east. "To sea. Cain't even see her now from Masthead Light."

"The hell with a boat," decided Jake. "Let's charter a plane. When we spot her, we'll call for a boat."

Mike nodded. The two of them jumped into the jeep, rocketed up Mike's private road, hit Aerodrome Road, and headed for the airstrip.

At least Mike knew where Hoagie was.

Hoagie Newcombe approached Salt Hole cautiously, parking his yellow jeep below the crest of the hill that overlooked it and moving quietly up to the ridge to reconnoiter.

He peered down onto the old quay. There was no boat there, and none at sea. But Lomas would be heading the other way, back to Nassau, or south to Spanish Galleon Cay.

He turned and inspected the airstrip, a half mile away. The runway shimmered in the late-afternoon sun.

The field was full of parked aircraft here for the Festival, but there was not a sign of life around. Everyone was in Prince George Town, getting drunk. The beacon on the battered operations building was not even turning; it cost too much to keep it on in the daytime, and the field closed nowadays at dusk.

Along one side of the runway stood a line of chartered planes, waiting to take tourists back to Nassau when the annual Junkanoo was over. There was no pilots' lounge at Whiskey Cay, so the pilots had gone into town too.

There were a dozen cars and jeeps parked by the operations shack: private pilots who had left for Miami for New Year's and had not yet returned. The Shell Aviation gas truck, battered and rusted with the ocean breeze, sat at the tiny shack.

He was running out of hope, but there was a slim chance that he might intercept Lomas yet. If he took off and searched the route to Spanish Galleon Cay and then to Nassau, he might spot one of Lomas's vessels—speedboat, powerboat, or cruiser—from the air.

He climbed into his jeep and headed for the airstrip. He parked in a spot marked with a shabby sign: PILOT, CALYPSO FRIENDLY CHARTERS.

Tiredly he walked into the hangar he shared with three other charter operations. He moved past private planes: an ancient Luscombe that seldom saw the light of day and a gleaming vintage Bellanca kept up by a retired engineer.

He paused at the love of his life, the ancient yellow Stearman open-cockpit biplane. He had bought it the previous year and restored it for aerobatics and for old times' sake. Sometimes he used it to tow advertising banners over Nassau and Paradise Island. Someday he would fly it to Jamaica and retire.

He looked at his watch. There was no time to waste; by speedboat, Lomas could be halfway to Nassau by now. Hoagie went to the office he rented in the darkest recesses of the hangar.

He unlocked the door, picked up his leather flight bag, and called the gas-shack to see if the Stearman had been gassed.

"Cedric? Hoagie here. Did you fill me up with petrol?"

There was a hesitation. "Nah, mon . . ."

Strange! He'd left the prop turned vertically, as a signal for refueling. Cedric seldom missed. He thought he heard a voice in the background, over the broadcast of a football game from the States. He wondered if Cedric was celebrating Junkanoo all by himself or had visitors in the shack.

"You mind getting on it, then?"

Another pause. "Yes, suh . . . jes' go on out."

He looked at his watch. Four-fifteen; not more than two hours of daylight left for searching. Lomas was getting farther from his reach with every moment. He picked up his flight bag.

He had the strange impression that someone had been in his office. He glanced around. Everything seemed okay: typewriter dusty but covered; sectional chart racks full of seldom used U.S. charts, in case anyone chartered for Miami; flight clothing hanging; the 'chutes he kept for sky divers sitting on their repacking table.

He heard quick, frantic footsteps echoing in the hangar. Mike and Jake appeared at the door.

"Hoagie," Mike burst out, "my mom flipped. She's after that shark with *Neptune's Folly* and she's headed out to sea!"

Hoagie stared at him. "Alone?"

"Alone."

So much for the hunt for Lomas.

"Well, then, let's go," he said.

Cedric Farthing, Supervisor of Fueling Operations at the Whiskey Cay Aerodrome, hung up the phone and stared into the muzzle of the gun.

Cedric was a tubby little black man who drove the gas truck and supervised only a black-and-white mouser named Ricardo, provided by Government House for rat control. Ricardo was regarding his employer and the intruder with equal disdain from the shack's windowsill.

The man—South American or Mexican from his accent—had invaded Cedric's private domain in the little shack, arriving like a paratrooper, strapped into a 'chute, almost an hour ago.

He had been sitting in Cedric's chair on Cedric's pillow, 'chute and all, next to the door ever since, listening to American football from Miami. He looked like the soldiers Cedric had seen on TV flying toward France on D-Day in Normandy.

Cedric had been sitting, pillowless, on a carton of aviation oil cans ever since. This angered him greatly. He needed his pillow; he had piles.

The whole thing was a nightmare, and Cedric still could not credit his eyes. "Mon, I done what you said. Now what *you* gwine do?"

Lomas regarded him sleepily. What he was going to do to the fat little black man would only panic him, and when men panicked, they sometimes were more trouble than when they had hope.

"Don't worry, *amigo*. Nobody will harm you."

Lomas got up from the chair, slapped the cat to the floor, and peered out the dusty window. Ricardo, in shock, regarded him from the floor, lifted his tail like a periscope, and paraded out the open door in injured dignity.

Cedric watched him go and felt even more alone than before. There was only one other employee on the field, the operations man. Even the narcotics officer had finally left to go to the Junkanoo.

Run to Operations, he begged Ricardo silently. Or to Calypso Charters. Meow or something, let them know. Why couldn't the government have given him a dog? A German shepherd or a Great Dane?

Past the intruder, Cedric could see Hoagie Newcombe and two other men—the conch experts using government funds to chase conch they never ate—heading toward Newcombe's Stearman.

"I awready gassed Mr. Newcombe's plane," he complained. "Now he goin' out there, thinkin' I ain't worth nothin'!"

The man turned from the window. He took the gas-truck keys from a hook by the door.

"He's right. You ain't."

He closed the door, took the pillow, folded it over the gun, and pressed the muzzle to Cedric's head.

He almost lit fire to the pillow, but the dull report could hardly be heard outside the gas-shack.

He stuffed the weapon under his chest strap, walked outside, and climbed into the gas truck.

By the time Hoagie had preflighted the plane, climbed in next to Mike, flicked his master switch, and noticed that his tanks were, after all, full, it was too late.

The petrol truck had parked to the left of the plane. Lomas was under the port wing at the pilot's open door, and Hoagie was looking down the barrel of his gun. The whole operation was Lomas's show.

"Now give me your gun, el Inglés." Lomas smiled. "And do it very carefully."

Slowly Hoagie pulled the gun from his belt, under his tropical shirt, and handed it to him. Behind him, in the right rear seat, Jake murmured, "Mon, oh, mon . . ."

"Take off the jump panel," demanded Lomas. Hoagie looked into the muzzle, leaned across Mike, and unlatched the wide, modified panel, containing the right door and opening up the entire cabin on the starboard side. He had installed it for dual and triple jumps, and Lomas had dived through it, screaming "Geronimo," in his famous jump to win the soccer game.

"Let it drop," ordered Lomas. The panel clattered to the tarmac. Wherever they were bound, it promised to be a cold and windy ride.

Lomas, holding the gun against his head, climbed clumsily with his backpack 'chute into the left rear seat behind him.

"I trust your flying okay, el Inglés," he said. "But I think I keep my parachute on this flight."

"*What* flight?" asked Hoagie tersely. "Flight to where?"

"A *memorial* flight for my friend Alejandro." Lomas grinned. "We are going to do a four-man jump on Spanish Galleon Cay."

Chapter 7

A stinging lash of cold salt water flew over the canvas cockpit dodger and dashed Ellen in the face. It brought her to her senses. She was out of sight of land, the sinking sun at her back.

She had left Masthead Light far astern. She realized that she had been plowing mindlessly to sea for a full two hours.

Standing at the wheel in the cockpit, dressed in her swimsuit, she found herself shivering, still half damp from her sprint into the water after Thea.

Marching swells were all around her. The boom was creaking against its crutch. The water was sapphire blue. To the north a thunderhead was building; they would have an evening storm.

She had no idea what had possessed her to take the boat, or why she was here. Dimly she remembered being drawn by her rage to Masthead Point. Then she had been impelled to sea, by a crazy conviction that the evil thing was here and would return to kill her family if she did not confront it now.

Insane! What could she have done with a pistol, even if she'd found it?

She glanced at the compass on the pedestal before her. Gimbaled, it was the only horizontal object in a swaying, lurching universe.

Apparently she had been steering due east. If, in her madness, she had not swung off-course, she need only turn 180 degrees to 270 magnetic, power two hours back, and she would be back at Whiskey Cay.

She must have lost her mind.

The ketch was rolling heavily. She looked astern. She did not dare turn into the swells at full power. She eased the throttle back. The drone of the diesel eased, then died.

She pressed the starter button on the compass pedestal. She could hear the starter whining, but the engine would not fire.

Again and again she tried, until she began to fear that she would run the battery dead. She began to tremble, not from cold now, but from fear.

No one knew where she was. It would be dark in an hour.

The boom creaked, and the hull had come alive with a hundred squeals and screeches as the ancient planks protested against the sea.

Faintly she heard another sound: *Boom . . . boom . . . boom . . .*

She stepped to the deckhouse and peered in through the door. The computer screen glared at her greenly, and across it moved a stately procession of peaks.

Boom . . . boom . . . boom . . .

It was the rhythm Carla had turned off on Masthead Beach the night before. But this was not the heartbeat of a conch! It was deeper, slower, heavier, and very, very near.

Boom . . . boom . . . boom . . .

She lurched back to the wheel. Had Mike and Jake tagged the great white shark?

Spanish Galleon Cay, from two thousand feet, was a half-moon of white sand, palm trees, and coral reefs surrounding a turquoise bay. Squarely at the center lay Nevil's Town. Nevil had been dead two centuries; Lomas owned it now. It slept in the afternoon sun.

Hoagie Newcombe decided that finally his string of luck had run out. He was sorry that he was taking Ellen's son with him, and sorry for Jake as well. For the truth was there for all to see; they had not a snowball's chance in hell.

He had once made a night carrier landing in a damaged aircraft in Falkland fog, talked down into a pitch-black void by a clipped, dispassionate radar man's voice that seemed to come from hell.

Now, from the rear seat, above the shriek of the wind past the cabin's open starboard side, he heard the same timbre of death in Lomas's voice.

"Make a pass at Nevil's Town," Lomas shouted. "Fifty feet, el Inglés! Up the *avenida*, past the movie theater, and a wingover at the end. And then back!"

Hoagie had no choice. He pointed the nose at the end of the street and dived. The sound of the slipstream rose. Wind howled through the open side panel. Cockpit dust that had not been disturbed in years flew into Hoagie's eyes and mouth. He sneezed.

At ten feet, above a wide-mouthed *campesino* staring upward, Hoagie leveled off. He could hear Lomas in the rear, leaning across Jake and shouting into the wind, "*Ay! Amigos!* It is Lomas! *Campesinos! Es su patrón!* I am here!"

Hoagie felt the muzzle of the gun behind his right ear. He pulled up at the end of the street, tossed a wing into the brassy sun, and heaved the plane into a wingover.

Pressed into his seat, then flung against his seat belt, he reversed his course. He skimmed down the main street again. Now there were *coqueros* pouring out of the bars, the warehouses, the little houses bordering the town.

"Now we will make the noise," Lomas decided. "Like at the football game!"

Hoagie saw Lomas's hand snake between him and Mike, reaching for the throttle. Before he could push it away, Lomas was jazzing the engine, cutting it, racing it, cutting it again.

The plane rattled in protest, and Hoagie's teeth chattered.

"*Ay!*" shouted Lomas. "Now climb! Ten thousand feet!"

With the attention of the whole island focused on the plane, and the gun against the back of his neck, Hoagie eased the throttle forward. The engine strained and groaned.

"She'll never make ten grand!" yelled Hoagie. "Too much weight!"

"Try, yes?" shouted Lomas. The muzzle tapped Hoagie's head playfully. "Is for your own good, *amigos*."

"Why?" grunted Hoagie.

"You forget, el Inglés. Every thousand feet is five more seconds coming down."

The great white had left the harbor with the woman's blood still warm in his throat.

His swift attack had eased the harpoon point more deeply into his side. He was driven by the festering wound to seek cold water; spurred, too, by currents in an ocean of thought that very few men knew.

He passed the *houngan* standing on the beach at Masthead Light and swam out Masthead Cut. Ten miles east of land he slowed the stroking of his tail. He circled, as if he had a rendezvous.

The harpoon point in his side was working its way into muscle and cartilage and sending waves of pain throughout his body, but it only angered him. It had not weakened him at all.

Of all the creatures of the ocean, he was best adapted

to his environment, molded exquisitely by the aeons for destruction of the slow and the weak.

He was a tool of evolution. Hardly a single species that swam the seas or flew above them had not benefited throughout the ages from his winnowing of the losers.

Without him and other lesser predators, the oceanic chain of feeding would lose its balance; he was an equalizer, a dealer in elemental, primordial justice, without preference or favoritism. If something moved, he struck it. If a pelican dived inexpertly and did not recover quickly, the pelican was finished, and all of its future progeny too.

If a baby seal had not the intelligence, or the timidity, to stay with its mother, it died, before its simple-minded genes diluted the colony further.

The great white was exactly what three hundred million years of selection had distilled him to be: a perfect angel of death.

Now something foreign lay in the ocean a mile ahead. He sensed that it was the boat that had caused him his distress. He had begun to close on it when it was five miles out from Masthead Point. Now, when its engine grew silent, he drifted, listening with his tiny ears, sensing with his lateral canals, smelling, tasting, all without effort or intention.

There were creakings and groanings that man's wooden creatures made when they were thought to be most silent, and for a while he homed in on these. Then, very faintly, he heard, as he had before, the booming of his own heart a mile away.

Its rhythm still excited him, and he swam faster toward the source.

Ellen Brody had tried the radio, and though she could hear distant voices on some of the channels, she got no answer when she broadcast her cry for help.

Finally she gave up. The *boom . . . boom . . . boom* from the speakers seemed louder.

She heard thunder to the north. The seas were growing calm before the storm.

She stepped on deck to check the squall. It was closer.

From the deckhouse the booming seemed louder.

She found herself losing her grip again.

"Leave us alone," she whispered, and suddenly she was screaming, "Leave us alone! Leave us alone! *Leave us—*"

And all at once she saw the fin, knifing through the water a hundred yards away.

She stared at it for a moment, then stumbled into the deckhouse. She took Sean's gun from the chart table where she had left it and lurched back to the rail.

"Leave us alone!" She pointed the gun at the slicing fin and fired. There was a splash, halfway between her and the shark, and a whining ricochet.

All at once the fin was gone, but the *boom . . . boom . . . boom* grew louder.

She could not stand not knowing where the beast had gone. "Come up!" she screamed. "Come up here!"

Boom, boom, boom, boom, boom . . . The drumming grew louder, the rhythm faster, and then, on the starboard side, the great shape loomed against the setting sun, higher and higher, teeth gleaming, and crashed down. . . .

For an instant she was looking into the eye, Papa Jacques's, the shark's—whoever's—but it was as black as the ocean's depths, as black as the River Styx.

She scrambled behind the compass binnacle. The great form crashed onto the deck, half aboard, and slithered back into the ocean.

She stared. The cockpit combing was gone. A single tooth, three inches long, lay rocking on the deck.

From the deckhouse came the relentless beat of the great pale creature's heart.

She crouched, shivering for a moment, staring at the gun.

Its sound did not frighten him off but attracted him —that was easy to see.

She had simply fired too soon.

She had been a fool. She had wasted a bullet.

But she had five more.

One to attract him back?

And the next from Sean, whose gun it was, dead in the gleaming eye.

And if she missed? Then she would have three. . . .

One more to make him attack her.

And another for the eye.

And then, when only one was left?

Before she let him sink the boat and take her, *that* one was for her.

Chapter 8

At nine thousand feet above Spanish Galleon Cay, Mike Brody shivered in a shirt and slacks as the icy wind slammed past his right shoulder.

With the entire right panel of the cabin removed, and eighty knots of airspeed in the climb, the temperature was freezing, but he did not know if he was trembling from cold or from fear.

He glanced at Hoagie. The Englishman's lips were blue. The big automatic still nuzzled the back of his head. He saw his eyes slide sidewise, in his lazy way, and their gazes met, but he could read no hope.

On the sun visor above the windshield was a mirror. In it he could see Jake, in the seat behind him, his beefy, black face tinged with green, his eyes quite bleak with fear.

Mike eyed the altimeter. The little hand pointed at nine and the big hand at three: ninety-three hundred feet and climbing very slowly. The airspeed was down to seventy-five, and the engine seemed to be straining. He wondered if Hoagie was deliberately holding the plane back, to give them more time.

But time for what?

Reluctantly he looked below. Spanish Galleon Cay was tiny in the afternoon sun. He could see cars and jeeps parked in the middle of the street of Nevil's Town, and people running around excitedly, like brightly colored ants.

Lomas yelled suddenly, over the wind, "I think she

will go no higher, *no es verdad?*" He unfastened his seat belt and forced them all to do the same.

Mike could hardly handle his buckle, his hands were trembling so. Lomas reached forward and yanked it off, then tapped him on the shoulder with the barrel of the gun. "You are cold, *señor?* Or frightened?"

"Cold," Mike managed through frigid lips.

Lomas shrugged. "Fifty seconds, sixty, and you're warm. Your friends will follow, have no fear."

Mike twisted and looked into Lomas's eyes.

"Look," he shouted above the howl of the wind, "I got a wife and kid!"

"I will send flowers." Lomas half rose in his seat and craned down at the island. "I think no casket will be necessary."

Mike saw Carla, the year before Thea had come, sun-streaked hair flowing, racing him down the beach; he felt Thea warm in his arms at four months old, smelling of milk, tugging at his ear, the first she'd ever noticed; he saw his mother standing on the beach at Amity, mourning Sean. . . .

"What have I ever done to *you?*" he demanded.

"Nothing, *nada*." Lomas smiled. "But you should pick a better airline." He motioned with the gun and shivered himself. "Now *I* am cold. So, *vamos!* Go!"

Mike turned back and looked down. Why jump? Why not let him blast him here? Maybe Jake could somehow overpower him if he did.

He felt the muzzle pressing at the back of his head, and his muscles turned to water. The gun was forcing him out, pressing harder, jabbing, and Lomas had his left shoulder in a grip of steel, pushing; he seemed powerless to resist, and all at once the icy blast was in his eyes, blurring his vision; below, the island beckoned, in the warmth of the setting sun. . . .

Suddenly the world dropped away, as if the plane had

crested a roller-coaster ride. For a moment the slipstream quieted and he was floating. He grabbed convulsively at the strut outside the cabin, felt back for the side of the plane, hung on, half in, half out, as weightless as air.

He twisted frantically, grabbed the headrest of his seat, and hung on. Lomas was drifting at the top of the cabin, and Jake, pounding him with awkward, sledgehammer blows, was half erect, floating too. Hoagie's left hand was braced on the ceiling, holding him in his seat. His right hand gentled the yoke. He was smiling tersely.

"Don't get off yet, Mike," he called. "Just get his bloody gun!"

Mike, heart thundering in his chest, pulled himself aboard. Hoagie's earphones, a pencil, the radio mike, and a pack of Marlboros were drifting in the air. Lomas's gun was floating past. He grabbed at it and missed. It flew through the open panel, bounced from the strut, and disappeared.

The slipstream had turned from a howl to a scream. They had crested a roller coaster and were diving toward the ground. Slowly, with infinite care, Hoagie eased back on the yoke. Mike felt himself pushed down harder and harder into his seat.

The wings creaked and trembled. Now, as Hoagie eased the nose up, Mike's stomach felt as if it were being forced into his hips. The blood left Hoagie's face, and it turned gray.

In the rear there was silence. Lomas had landed in the right-hand seat. He was bleeding from the cheek and temple. Jake tore open his shirt, yanked Hoagie's gun from the *coquero*'s belt, and checked its cylinder.

"Okay, *'amigo,'*" he said tightly, "we gwine hang you from a palm tree over Kingston Street, upside down. We gwine use your head for steel drum, play the *goombay* music on."

Hoagie leveled the plane and looked around the cabin. "*That* made a proper mess." He hung his earphones on his yoke, placed his cigarettes under the sun visor, and put the pencil back into its clip on the dash. "Seat belt sign's on, no smoking in the cabin." He glanced at Mike. "You decide to stay aboard?"

Mike nodded numbly.

Hoagie squeezed his knee. "Can't afford to lose a passenger, can we?" Hoagie took a chart and studied it, banking toward the north. The howling of the slipstream rose as he added throttle. "Now, let's go out and find your mother if we can."

Rico Lomas slouched in the right-hand corner of the rear seat. He dabbed at the cut on his forehead. With his tongue he felt a loose tooth.

As long as the gun was in the plane, he had a chance. Not one of the three men—except el Inglés, perhaps—looked as if he had the *cojones* to use one on a man.

On the *llanos* there were snakes that feigned death when you beat them, and struck when you walked away. He groaned for effect and slouched lower.

El Inglés turned. He beckoned him close, to hear above the roar of the wind. "You okay, Lomas?"

"You do not hear me crying."

"You like to hear *them* cry? The people you murder?"

"Who do I murder? El Conejo Grande? Yes. I like that. It encourages the others."

The Englishman patted Brody's control yoke and told him to keep the plane straight and level.

Then he twisted in his seat. He grabbed Lomas's harness and pulled him close. When he smiled, a chill ran up Lomas's back. The Englishman's sky-blue eyes were half-lidded, but they were suddenly the eyes of death.

"You listen to me, Lomas," Newcombe said in Spanish. "No lynching in the square, you filthy pig. And no Bahamian jail. You are going to be extradited to the States. You are flying to Miami with me when this is done."

The chill returned. The U.S. Drug Enforcement Agency would throw away the key.

"That is kidnapping, *señor,* not extradition."

"Yes. And I will get you tried for murder too."

Lomas calculated swiftly. "You will go to jail if you return to the Bahamas. It would be wiser for you to take . . ." His mind whirred. How much? El Viejo would spend a good deal to rescue him. And they could always take it back. "What? A million dollars? Two?"

"I think not."

Lomas felt his heart plummet. "No, el Inglés? *Por qué no?"*

"There was a girl, *puerco.*" Newcombe's voice cut like a razor through the slipstream. "She was just sixteen. A *muchacha* of much beauty, blond and sweet . . ."

The English *muchacha?* The Englishman must have been talking to one of his *coqueros;* no one else would know the story of La Inglesa. When he got out of this, he would take the *campesinos* one by one and question them. Then he would know who had the loose tongue, and it would be looser still.

"An English girl?" Lomas shrugged. *"Señor,* she wanted smack. I did not kill her. She killed herself." He moved uncomfortably. He did not like the look in those lazy eyes at all. He swallowed. "What was that one to you?" Suddenly he knew the answer, and where he had seen those eyes. He swallowed. *"Su hija?"*

"Sí, sí, my daughter, *puerco.* This bust was mine, *I* set it up. But it is *her* sting that you feel, you filthy pig!"

The Englishman roughly pushed him back in his

seat. Newcombe turned, nodded at Brody, patted the yoke, and took back control.

Lomas sat back. Somehow he must get his hands on the big English cannon again, or he was dead.

Ellen Brody stood on the starboard quarter of the ketch and fired blindly into the water. The bullet plunged ten feet abeam, and the shot reverberated loudly off the side of the hull.

Through the open door of the deckhouse she heard the heartbeat: *Boom . . . boom . . . boom . . .* She braced herself and moved back, amidships.

Boom, boom . . . boom, boom . . . boom, boom . . . The shark was coming; she could tell by the quickened pace.

This time the fin broke the water five hundred yards away. It was heading for the bow. It broached, far forward, stretching almost full-length from the water, and she could see the ebony eye focused on the bowsprit, as if it expected to find her there.

From here she could never hit it, but she fired, anyway, in blind rage, and saw the slug strike the great creature's flank, near a bleeding wound where someone —Mike or Jake, she imagined—had implanted the transmitting device. A splat of water flew from the side of the shark where the bullet hit, but he seemed not to notice at all.

His enormous mouth opened and clamped the bowsprit, a full six inches in diameter. As the creature slammed back into the water, the bow pitched down and Ellen was thrown to the deck.

She screamed. He was pulling the forty-foot ketch down with him, bow first, as if it were a toy. The stern came up; water washed through the hawse pipes forward and slashed against the anchors on the foredeck.

Then the bowsprit broke with a crack like a limb off a giant elm tree, and the bow came up again.

Shaken, she struggled to her feet and sidled forward.

The end of the shortened bowsprit was jagged. The steel forestay from the top of the mast dangled, swinging in the swell, its shackle and turnbuckle lethal missiles at its end. She dodged them as they crashed against the deckhouse side.

She looked up. The mainmast, without the tension of its forestay, was swaying dangerously with the roll. She knew from her sailing days that she should stay below. The mast was a menace to anything topside, but she could not wait inside for the monster to sink her. She would rather stay topside and fight.

Three rounds left.

She raised the gun and fired at the water once again.

She heard thunder rumbling to the north. From the deckhouse came the steady, ominous drumming, louder with every beat.

To the south she heard the droning of an airplane, but she was so intent upon the water to starboard that she didn't look up.

Or see the fin approaching from the port.

Hoagie was the first to spot the ketch. He saw her from five thousand feet, almost dead ahead, ten miles off Whiskey Cay, slatting in the swells. Her stern was toward the plane.

"I think that's her," he reported tersely. "Dead in the water. Weather coming too."

Behind the ketch hung a cloud formation that reminded him of Longfellow's smithy under the spreading chestnut tree.

The anvil cloud was a black one. There was thunder and trouble in that one, for the airplane and the boat.

He poured on thirty inches of manifold pressure, though it made the old bird shake. And he nosed down, red-lining his airspeed at a hundred and fifty knots, the "never-exceed" airspeed in the book. She had never flown so fast. From the whistling draft through the open barn door and the rattles from her landing gear, he was afraid that he'd tear her wheel pants off.

But he didn't like the look of the storm, and when he identified the ketch for certain, he was going to call the coast guard, the Bahamian Defense Force, and the Prince George Town harbormaster and see who could get there first.

Mike looked better now; his teeth had quit chattering, and he had stopped shivering. Here at fifteen hundred feet the air screaming past his shoulder was warm and tropical.

Hoagie could see that the boat was *Neptune's Folly,* all right. Ellen, in her bright yellow swimsuit and her terry-cloth beach robe, was swaying on the foredeck. She was holding on to the mizzenmast, gazing out to starboard, and had not even noticed them.

Hoagie leveled off at a thousand feet. He picked up the microphone to call for help. And all at once he saw the fin slicing toward the ketch's port bow.

"Oh, my God!" cried Mike. "You see it?"

"I see it, but she doesn't," barked Hoagie. "Hold on!"

He tossed a wing up, pushed his nose down, and rolled into a screaming spiral toward the fin. The slipstream became a maelstrom. His airspeed wavered and climbed: one hundred sixty, one hundred seventy . . . A vibration started somewhere, and the controls grew as hard as steel. One hundred seventy-five . . . one hundred eighty . . .

He pulled out, the wheels clipping the wave tops, and jazzed the engine, once, twice, once again. Then he was past, looking back. He saw Ellen whirl at the sound of his passing. There was a gun in her hand. The great shape rose from the water. The weapon flashed as she fired up at it.

Then everything disappeared below his starboard wheel. He cursed, pulled into a climbing right bank, struggled up to a thousand feet, and headed back for the boat.

The monster was sliding back into the water. Ellen was cowering behind the whipping mast. The boat was at a thirty-degree list to port, from the shark's weight. As it slipped back in, Hoagie saw that it had torn away the varnished rail, from the bow halfway to the stern.

Slowly the ketch righted herself.

What could they do from here?

"These things responsive to noise?" he asked suddenly, twisting around to Jake. "You're the Ph.D."

"Responsive? Attracted! *Fascinated!*" Jake nodded.

Hoagie climbed, reporting a vessel under shark attack to Nassau and Whiskey Cay and giving her position. He searched for the fin, finally spotted it heading for the ketch. He flung up a wing and dived again.

All at once he was back off the Falklands, making runs on an Argentine sub. He went straight for the fin, felt a jolt as he struck it, and buzzed the engine wildly as he passed.

The shark swerved, circled, and seemed to hunt for the source of the sound. By George, they had it, if only he could keep it up!

He climbed again, banking to starboard, and at a thousand feet he lost sight of the fin. "You see it, Mike?" he yelled. "Jake? Can you *see* the bloody thing?"

Jake craned past Lomas, looking. It was a fatal mistake. The *traficante* struck like a snake, with a sharp right cross to the jaw.

The big Wembley revolver crashed to the cabin floor. Mike twisted over his seat back, cursing, trying to scoop it up. Jake, stunned and too big for the space, took a mighty swing at Lomas, missed, and put his fist through the cabin's upholstered skin. Lomas, with a karate chop, knocked Mike's hand away and scrambled for the gun.

He was bringing it up in his hand when Jake braced his back against the left of the cabin, planted a size twelve shoe in his gut, and shoved.

The *traficante* fired once as he flew out the door. The slug whistled past within inches of Hoagie's head and slammed through his side window.

But Lomas was gone with a long, shrill scream; so was the gun. Hoagie horsed back on the yoke, dipped his left wing, and peered back. The figure flailed wildly through the air, a pilot 'chute popped, and after it, the main 'chute bloomed in blue and white and red.

He saw the *traficante* slide the gun into his belt, grab his left steering line, and rotate toward the ketch. He was kicking in the air and trying desperately to land aboard.

But he passed over the stern. He unsnapped his leg straps, freed his chest strap, and plunged into the water from twenty feet. In an instant he was striking madly for the boat.

Shark bait, thought Hoagie grimly. There *was* a God in heaven, after all.

Then he saw Ellen dashing aft. "Oh, no," Hoagie said with a groan. "Good God, no!"

She yanked at a life ring, secured its line to the stern anchor cleat, and hurled it as far as she could.

It fell within two feet of Lomas, who grabbed it. She began to haul him in.

"Cinch up your shoulder straps!" he yelled. "We're going in!"

Chapter 9

Ellen had recognized Hoagie's airplane instantly, from the letters on its fuselage. To her the parachutist he dropped was an angel from on high—but a suicidal one. Hadn't he seen the shark?

When he missed the stern, she panicked for an instant, and then her father's words came back: "If you have to toss a buoy, throw it twice as far as you think you ought to. Secure its line. And don't forget to rig a boarding ladder."

But there was no time to rig a boarding ladder with the monster circling so close. The parachutist—paramedic, policeman, or Bahamas Defense Force officer—was thrashing wildly for the orange life ring in the water.

Ten yards to go, then five . . .

The fin broke the surface a hundred yards beyond.

"Hurry!" she cried. "Hurry, please!"

Three yards, two . . . he had it! She began to haul on the line. Now she could hear his cries of fear: "*Socorro, socorro!* Faster, *señora*, please!"

Spanish, then, or Mexican?

All at once she knew. *Señor* Lomas! The owner of the club! A sky diver! Hoagie had detested him. "Every time his macho needs a polishing, it's two hundred more in the boss's till." But now he was risking his life for her. Her throat tightened.

He was fifty feet from the boat, forty, kicking with all his strength. The fibers of the rope were tearing at her palms. She ignored the pain and pulled faster.

Thirty feet, twenty. . .

Behind her, on the starboard side of the boat, she heard the plane approaching, then heard the engine cut. She could not spare the time to look.

The fin was slicing faster through the water. She could hear the heartbeat from the deckhouse: *Boom . . . boom . . . boom . . .*

Lomas was fifteen feet away. He looked up at her. His eyes were wide with terror. "*Señora!*" he bleated. "Help—"

Boom, boom . . . boom, boom . . . boom, boom . . .

The fin had disappeared. She saw a gray shape in the water behind him and screamed a warning. All at once the swimmer was jerked from below. Then he began to rise, faster and faster. Suddenly he was hurled into the air. The shark grew from the depths, jaws gaping, and snatched him as he fell.

Impaled on the shark's lower jaw, he kicked, writhed, and shrieked. The orange buoy, red with blood, fell away.

The last she heard was a long, shrill wail as the massive jaws closed slowly. The shark sank without a bubble, and the reddened waters closed.

To starboard she heard a Klaxon sounding.

She whirled.

The Stearman was gliding in close to the ketch. Its nose was up, resisting fate; its prop ticked slowly in the golden sunlight; she could hear the stall-warning horn honking from the cabin. Its wheels were only inches from the wave tops.

Like a gull landing, legs outstretched, it groped for the water, crested a swell, and settled with a crash in a sheet of spray.

Its tail rose, higher and higher. For an awful moment she was sure that it would somersault. Then the tail settled, and Mike dived from the cabin. He turned, treading water, and yanked Jake from the rear seat. The side of the cabin was off, and the plane began to fill. Hoagie did not appear.

Boom . . . boom . . . boom . . .

The fin was driving toward them, from the north. "Mike!" she shrieked. "Watch out!"

Mike and Jake were suddenly cleaving through the water. They had fifty feet to go, and the fin was streaking fast.

Not Mike, you've done enough to us, not Mike. . . .

Her eyes met her son's across the water. "Diving ladder!" he shouted, and churned on.

She shoved at the ladder that was hinged to the stern. It unfolded and splashed into the water, hanging three rungs deep.

Boom, boom . . . boom, boom . . . boom, boom . . .

But the fin was ignoring the swimmers. It was heading for the plane. The great shape rose, jaws gaping, and severed the tail from the Stearman in a screech of aluminum plate. Mike scrambled aboard, dragged Jake up the ladder, and stared at his mother.

"Where's Hoagie?" he asked, panting. "He out?"

She shook her head. There was a long, deep silence. Tears filled her eyes.

"You diving chaps should know better," cautioned Hoagie from below the stern. He climbed up the ladder, knocking water from an ear. "One doesn't want to thrash about near sharks."

She flew into his arms. "There, now, there," he murmured. "Haste makes waste, you know."

His lazy eyes swung down to hers. She was basking in their tenderness when, behind him, she saw that the clouds were framing a massive shadow. She pulled him away as the shark hit the ladder astern.

* * *

Papa Jacques clutched his chest. The pain was growing worse. He stood alone on the beach under the ancient Colonial tower of Masthead Light, but he was not there; he was far at sea, torn from the land by his master, the shark.

Thunder grumbled above, and he sensed it through his pain, but he swam three fathoms below, where the light was shafting greenly through the plankton and where a thousand currents of life unknown to surface creatures ebbed and flowed.

The accursed boat was above, its keel barnacled and whiskered with sea growth. The boat had caused the searing wound, which grew worse with every hour.

His master was ruler of the sea, but the vessel defied them. They had attacked her, wrestled off her bowsprit and half her bow, gouged her flank as she had gouged theirs, ripped her stern. And still she floated, her passengers mocking them with their own heartbeats.

Boom . . . boom . . . boom . . .

Men were working aboard her now. They could hear metallic clinking in her bowels and hear them moving about her cabin, which was, of course, her brain.

With a flick of their tail, they soared away from the boat, then circled her, gauging her condition.

They had weakened her ancient planks and frames already. They could already hear water trickling into her hull.

They could sink her and bring her into their own world when they pleased. Of the sixty sawlike teeth—a double phalanx on top, a single row below—they had sacrificed only a dozen today.

They could lose that many feasting on skate. Already the missing teeth were being replaced; sharks lost them continually, all their life. Nature had endowed the species with spares, ready behind each one, and every replacement grew larger than its predecessor; some were four inches long.

The youngest of the men above had destroyed Papa Jacques's *asson*, and speared his flank, and that man must certainly die. Before they sank the vessel, they would tempt him to the shattered bow, bait him into carelessness, and strike.

On Masthead Point, beneath the ancient light, Papa Jacques smiled despite his pain. Damballah, the African serpent god, had gathered the victims as he'd asked. His master, the *loa,* would do the rest.

In the deckhouse, Ellen clung to the helm at the inside steering station. Every time the monster struck the boat, the impact seemed harder. The last time she had been hurled to the deck.

Mike was at the VHF radio, calling the Nassau Coast Guard without success. They had used up most of their battery power trying to start the engine.

At his workbench, Jake was disassembling the camera strobe light; why, he would not say. Hoagie, in the engine room, called up, "Ellen, hit the starter switch!"

She pressed a button by the inside steering station. The starter ground, whined, and the engine coughed but did not fire.

"Bad leak down here," called Hoagie. "Three feet of water in the bilge, and rising. I'm going to bleed your primary filter."

"Okay, Lindberg," called Jake. He was working desperately at whatever he had in mind.

Boom, boom, boom . . . boom, boom, boom . . .

"Here he comes," said Mike. "Hang on!"

There was a mighty crash from forward. The boat heeled to starboard. Water slopped through an open deckhouse porthole, soaking Ellen.

She had two bullets left in the gun. She was damned

if she was going to stand there while the monster sank their boat without using them. She started for the door. Mike grabbed her arm.

"No way, Mom."

"We can't just—"

"No more shooting. It just stirs him up." He took the gun away from her.

"I want it stopped!" she said hysterically. "I want him killed."

He looked into her eyes. "If anybody can do it, it's Jake. So simmer down. . . ."

Jake stood up. "Okay. The strobe's charged. There's enough voltage in this condenser to light him up from nose to tail." Handling it carefully, he laid the waterproof strobe on the chart table. He had stripped it and run wires to copper contacts he had drilled into its shell.

"What do we do with it?" demanded Mike.

"What you *don't* do is touch those contacts. Or you'll fry. What we do now is, we test it." He picked up the slave switch and pulled the trigger. Ellen heard two beeps from somewhere deep in the hull of the boat. Jake stared at the strobe, as if trying to hypnotize it.

"Sonic transmitter's working, anyway," said Mike.

"What the hell good's that?" Jake said, flaring. He glared at Mike. "I told you to keep this thing charged!"

"Somebody turned off the battery power," Mike said simply. "It happens."

Boom, boom, boom, boom . . .

Again the shark struck forward. The bow rose, shivered, and crashed down. Ellen found herself slammed between the chart table and the galley, on the deck.

Jake and Mike picked themselves up. Mike pulled the trigger again. Ellen heard two beeps from below. At the second beep the pilothouse was lit with a flash so strong that for a moment she could not see.

Over the *boom . . . boom . . . boom* of the heartbeat

they heard a feeble whine. It grew louder and higher in tone, like a tiny scream, until the pitch was so high that it disappeared.

"It's recharging!" exulted Jake.

Ellen suddenly understood. The flash unit on her own camera did that when she took pictures of Thea. "But how are you going to get it on him?"

Jake grinned. "Not *on* him. *In* him. With a boat hook."

She stared at him. "From where?"

"The bowsprit. What's left of it. The next time he opens his mouth."

Mike tensed. "That's my job."

Jake looked into his eyes. "No."

"Come on, man. You're too big for tightrope walking. There's no forestay to hang on to. You don't have the balance."

"Better balance than you, harpooner. You almost fell in."

"Well, I speared him, didn't I?"

"So it's my turn now," Jake insisted.

Yes, let him, let him do it! Ellen begged silently. She squeezed Mike's hand. He looked into her eyes.

Whatever he read there, he understood. He sighed and nodded. "Okay."

Louisa was washing Jake's socks in their bathroom sink. It was strange; when she had moved in with him, she found that he wore his socks for a week at a time, then threw them away and bought new ones.

Now, although he wouldn't dream of washing them himself, he seemed to change them twice a day.

She wondered where he was. He had taken off like a scalded cat from the shark attack on the beach, heading for Mike's. He seemed to blame himself, as if the shark were his fault and he somehow thought he could hunt it down with the boat.

He was probably looking for it now.

She looked at the socks. One had a hole. Her mother would have darned it. She didn't even know how. She threw it in the trash and couldn't find its mate.

If one of a pair was gone, what good was the other one?

All at once she was crying. She looked in the mirror. To her the beauty had suddenly fled; she felt old and alone.

Something was dreadfully wrong.

She found herself before the crucifix on their bedroom wall. She crossed herself and found herself praying:

"Holy Mary, Mother of God . . ."

Mama, send your *loa* flying to the sea. . . .

". . . pray for us sinners, now and at the hour of our death—"

She could go no further. She knew with cold certainty that she would never see Jake again.

In *Neptune's Folly*'s cockpit, Ellen watched as Jake bound the strobe to a long wooden boat hook with electrician's tape. He would try to jam it into the massive jaws and run.

The fin was circling. Below, the beat of the heart was steady: *Boom . . . boom . . . boom . . .*

He had abandoned his shoes before the plane was ditched. Now, carefully, he laid down the pole and strobe and drew off his socks. They didn't match, she noticed: brown and beige. Men . . .

He smiled at her and looked to starboard. The fin was cruising, ready for another run. Mike stepped out of the deckhouse with the transmitter to fire the strobe. He looked doubtfully at the squall. "I got through to Nassau. They'll have a boat out from Whiskey Cay in half an hour."

The beat below increased: *Boom, boom, boom . . .*

"He hits us again like the last time," Jake promised, "and we won't be here in half an hour."

The two men's eyes met. "Good luck, partner," said Mike.

Jake nodded, and their palms slapped and flew upward. "Gwine feed our shark, mon," Jake said unsteadily. "Gwine feed our shark a little juice."

With an islander's barefoot grace he moved forward along the lurching deck. Abeam the creaking mainmast, he steadied himself on the ratlines leading aloft. He gazed to starboard, studying the fin. It was coming fast. He gauged the moment, and as the gray shape grew in the water, he ran forward to the stem of the bow.

Knees flexed, riding the swell, he waited, boat hook raised.

The great conical snout rose from the water. Jake crouched low. Slowly the massive jaws opened. Higher and higher the body rose, driving inward over the bow. It dwarfed the man. At the last moment Jake plunged the boat hook into the mouth. Mike fired the strobe.

They heard a *beep-beep*. The cavernous mouth turned blue, and the creature convulsed and jerked into the water.

Folly rolled to starboard. Jake flailed his arms for balance and fell in.

Ellen screamed. Mike ran forward. He saw a swirl of blood in the water. Jake was gone, without a sound.

"No!" screamed Mike. He pressed the trigger: *Beep-beep*.

The shark sprang from the water, shuddering, and crashed down on his flank in a shower of spray. Below, the heartbeat faltered. "Got you, you son of a bitch!" yelled Mike. Below, they heard the whine of the next charge building, building . . .

The engine started suddenly, and Hoagie appeared. "Where's Jake?" he cried, staring toward the bow.

"Gone!" growled Mike. "Mom, take the wheel."

Boom, boom, boom . . .

The shark was still alive! Immortal?

The fin was knifing in from the port, heading for the bow. Mike pressed the switch. The great fish hurtled into the air, fifty yards ahead of them, shuddering in their path. It fell with a crash.

From the deckhouse they heard the condenser recharging with a screech.

Mike hit the switch again: *Beep-beep.*

The sharp leapt again and crashed down, but now the heartbeat was gone. Then the feeblest drumbeat . . . halting, irregular: *Bump, bump . . . bump . . .*

"You're killing him!" Ellen shrieked. "Again!"

Beep-beep.

The monster sprang from the water and directly into their path. It rose higher and higher, until it seemed to be dancing on its tail. From its flank protruded the shaft of the harpoon, a festering, ruddy sore, oozing blood. She gripped the wheel tightly, jammed the throttle lever forward, and aimed for the wound.

When the jagged, broken bowsprit struck, it penetrated to the stem.

Beep-beep.

The shark grew rigid and began to shake in great, rending quakes that shook the craft from stem to stern.

Beep-beep.

The shark, still impaled on the jagged bowsprit, bent double, straightened like a bow released, and convulsed. The ketch trembled as if shaken by a giant, invisible hand.

Down by the bow, stern up, she pitched forward until water was pouring through the anchor hawse. The mainmast cracked, six feet above the deck, with a sound like a redwood falling. Slowly, then faster, the enormous pole fell aft, slamming across the quarter deck three feet from where they stood.

"She's finished!" yelled Mike. He jumped forward, unlashed the inflatable from the deckhouse top, and tossed it over the side.

They climbed in as water poured over the gunwales. They paddled away. Ellen watched the stern, with its gilded letters, slide into the sea.

Thunder growled. To Ellen it sounded like Jake's voice, deep in anger.

"Yes, Mom, but when he smiled . . ."

It was raining, but soon the sun peeked through and tinted the clouds with gold.

In half an hour they were safe on a sixty-foot cutter of the Bahamian Defense Force.

They reported officially that the shark of Whiskey Cay was dead.

The little *houngan* stared out to sea. Great towering cumulus clouds, fat-bellied with rain, were building ruddy spires to the east. He heard the thunder rumbling, and the pain tore at his chest.

The sun was setting above Masthead Point. He could hear the surf on the seaward side of the island booming steadily, the heartbeat of the sea.

But his *loa's* heart had failed. He knew it in his own.

In a high, plaintive voice, he began to chant. Slowly he turned on the sand:

Maître Agwe, where are you . . . ?
Don't you see I'm . . .

He clutched his side. Above him, the light that had guided buccaneers and merchantmen, men-of-war and slavers, began its eternal sweep.

I've a rudder in my hand . . .
Maître shark, I have your teeth . . .

The pain of a thousand harpoons exploded in his chest, and he was one with his *loa*.

He swam east, toward a shadowed coast he had never known, never left.

The light turned blindly above him, and Whiskey Cay turned dark.

Chapter 10

"I never got a proper look at the statue," Louisa said, rising from her chair. *"Excusez-moi?"*

From their table outside the Inn of the Happy Whale, Ellen watched Louisa cross Kingston Street. During the last few days the girl had drawn on some inner toughness. By the time Jake's funeral was over, she had seemed suffused with some firm resolve. The Loma Bella Club was closed, but even if it reopened again, she would never go back to dealing cards; she was going to study nursing and go back to Port-au-Prince.

It was their last meal together: Carla, Mike, Thea, Louisa, and Ellen. Calypso had bought a secondhand airplane and managed to keep its charter franchise to Whiskey Cay. Hoagie was cleaning up the plane now and flying Ellen to Nassau this afternoon, where she would catch an Eastern flight to La Guardia.

Ellen looked around the table. There was a certain sadness in Carla's face—she blamed herself still for Margaret de Lacey's death, but there was plenty of blame to go around: Mike shared it, too, and Hoagie; only Jake had escaped.

Thea squirmed out of the high chair the waiter had brought and ran to her side. "Let's look at Peeper, Grandma?"

Ellen put down her coffee. She wanted to talk to Louisa, anyway, alone, before she left. She took her hand and crossed the deserted street.

The square was deserted. The debris from the Festival had long been cleared away. The statue was a huge success: the senator saw it as the spirit of the Bahamas, rising from slavery to an international Caribbean power; Mayor Witherspoon saw it as a spaceship commemorating the Bahamian down-range role in Cape Canaveral's space shots; Mike saw it as a leaping dolphin; townspeople saw in it everything from a Gold Coast phallic symbol to a representation of the queen.

Only Carla and Ellen had ever seen the shark.

Louisa was gazing up at it.

"What do you see?" Ellen asked her gently.

"Pour moi it is a nun. A Sister of Mercy in Port-au-Prince. She nursed my mother, even when the church said *non,* that Mama must give up her voodoo or go to hell."

Thea said definitely, "No! It's Peeper. He's a doctor bird!"

Louisa squatted and made a ferocious face. *"Non!* Nun!"

"Doctor bird!" Thea giggled and ran back to the table across the street.

"So, then, it is over?" Louisa murmured, rising. She looked into Ellen's eyes. "You have no blame, Ellen."

"I took the boat," said Ellen miserably. "I don't know why."

Louisa smiled. "I do." She glanced across the street. "You are as innocent as Thea, *mon chéri*. All of you."

"You're very kind."

"You were bewitched by Papa Jacques." Louisa shrugged. "There is no blame, for he has gone."

"Perhaps . . ."

"It is not 'perhaps.'" Louisa looked out at the water. "A bird has told me so. And told me you will have a happy life. So this I know."

"And you?" asked Ellen softly. "Will you?"

"Oh, yes." Louisa beamed radiantly. "This bird told me that!"

Louisa squeezed her hand. Ellen felt suddenly freed, buoyant, and full of joy. They hugged and promised to write.

There was something mysterious going on. Ellen sensed it in Romeo's Cadillac, and by the time they were at the airstrip, she was even more certain.

Romeo drove them directly to the tarmac. Hoagie was standing by another high-wing airplane, painted with CALYPSO'S FRIENDLY CHARTERS. It was even shabbier than the Cessna.

Next to it, gleaming in yellow paint, was parked a proud, shining relic of the biplane age. It seemed immense. Romeo parked the Cadillac between them.

Ellen got out while Mike pulled her bags from the trunk. Hoagie was smiling, but there was a question in his eyes.

He kicked the wheel of his cabin plane. "I don't really trust this kite, you know?"

He turned and opened a panel behind the rear cockpit of the biplane. He drew out a leather, fleece-lined jacket emblazoned with RAF wings, a leather helmet, and a pair of flying goggles.

He dangled the helmet and goggles. "You care to be my ballast?"

"To Nassau?" she murmured. "To Nassau, Hoagie, for La Guardia?"

He shrugged. "Or anywhere you'd like."

She pressed his hand. "It's Nassau, Hoagie, I'm afraid."

She kissed Thea and Carla and Mike.

"Mom," he whispered, "he told me what he'd like to do. I think he's too shy to press. The hell with Amity; go south."

"To *Jamaica?* Mike, I can't!"

From the rear cockpit they looked very small below. The engine burst into life, and they were all at once bouncing toward the runway. She peered out of the side of the cockpit. Thea was running alongside, waving. She couldn't hear and lifted one of her earflaps.

". . . hello to Peeper!" she thought she heard but was not sure.

Her heart was pounding. They were suddenly bounding down the runway, as if the ancient airplane could not wait. They roared into the air above Masthead Point, turned back in a graceful bank, and made a run at the field, engine rolling.

Hoagie wagged his wings madly; craning from the cockpit, she could see Romeo's Cadillac, and Mike and Carla waving, Thea dancing between them.

Then they were climbing into the clear, cool air. She could see Hoagie's leather-helmeted head and Whiskey Cay's dazzling beaches below.

How many islands, just like this, was she leaving? And why?

The stick between her legs shook violently. "Take it," he said through her earphones. "Take the stick."

She grabbed it. It seemed alive. "Bank, like you did with the yoke. Press left."

She eased the stick to the left, and the plane responded solidly. "Now . . . a little rudder . . ." She pressed the rudder pedals. "Good."

She flew for a while. "You're heading south," he warned. "Toward Cat Island. Nassau's way to starboard, luv."

She pressed to the right. The stick resisted impassively. She tried again. It seemed as solid as a rock.

"Hoagie! It won't bank!"

"Sometimes she's a mind of her own."

He must have the stick in his hands. "Hoagie, you nut, let go!"

"Can't do a thing with her sometimes. Just like a woman, she is."

"Hoagie," she insisted. "I can't *go* to Jamaica!"

"Then there's nothing more in life for me!" He threw off his safety belt, stood in the slipstream, braced his hands on the side of the cockpit, and turned. "Cheerio, luv . . . ta-ta!"

"Hoagie!" she shrieked. "You get right back in that seat!"

He sat down, and in a moment she felt him take over the controls. His voice came over her earphones, soft and sweet and low.

"Nassau, then? For sure, Ellen? Shouldn't care to press your luck?"

"If we just fly off, you'll lose your job," she warned.

"Best-kept secret in the Bahamas, luv. I *am* Calypso. I'm the boss."

Shocked, she sat back, thinking. Past Nassau lay the cold of Amity; a phone that would never ring; Sean's bed, made up and gaping; and endless nights of mourning.

But past Cat Island? Great Exuma, he'd said, or something like it. Crooked Island, Great Inagua . . .

"Hoagie?"

"Yes, Ellen?"

Jamaica, and those lazy eyes . . .

"You have an ace," she murmured into her mike, "so hit me, one more card."

The world suddenly rolled upside down and righted itself again. Below the yellow lower wing passed stately emerald coves.

She sat back, free at last of fear.

Jamaica, here we come.